To Indigo

To Indigo

Tanith Lee

IMMANION PRESS

Stafford England

To Indigo
By Tanith Lee
© 2011

http://www.tanithlee.com

Cover by John Kaiine
Layout by Storm Constantine

Set in Palatino Linotype

ISBN 978-1-907737-21-3

IP0105

An Immanion Press Edition
8 Rowley Grove
Stafford ST17 9BJ
http://www.immanion– press.com
info@immanion– press.com

Books by Tanith Lee

A Selection from her 93 titles

The Birthgrave Trilogy (The Birthgrave; Vazkor, son of Vazkor,
Quest for the White Witch)
The Vis Trilogy (The Storm Lord; Anackire; The White Serpent)
The Flat Earth Opus (Night's Master; Death's Master; Delusion's
Master; Delirium's Mistress; Night's Sorceries)
Don't Bite the Sun
Drinking Sapphire Wine
The Paradys Quartet (The Book of the Damned; The Book of the
Beast; The Book of the Dead; The Book of the Mad)
The Venus Quartet (Faces Under Water; Saint Fire; A Bed of Earth;
Venus Preserved)
Sung in Shadow
A Heroine of the World
The Scarabae Blood Opera (Dark Dance; Personal Darkness;
Darkness, I)
The Blood of Roses
When the Lights Go Out
Heart-Beast
Elephantasm
Reigning Cats and Dogs
The Unicorn Trilogy (Black Unicorn; Gold Unicorn; Red Unicorn)
The Claidi Journals (Law of the Wolf Tower; Wolf Star Rise, Queen
of the Wolves, Wolf Wing)
The Piratica Novels (Piratica 1; Piratica 2; Piratica 3)
The Silver Metal Lover
Metallic Love
The Gods Are Thirsty

Collections

Nightshades
Dreams of Dark and Light
Red As Blood – Tales From the Sisters Grimmer
Tamastara, or the Indian Nights
The Gorgon
Tempting the Gods
Hunting the Shadows
Sounds and Furies

As when a prowling Wolf,
Whom hunger drives to seek new haunt for prey,
Watching where Shepherds pen their Flocks at Eve
In hurdl'd Cotes amid the field secure,
Leaps ore the fence with ease into the Fold:
Or as a Thief bent to unhoard the cash
Of som rich Burgher, whose substantial dores,
Cross-barred and bolted fast, fear no assault,
In at the window climbs, or ore the tiles;
So clomb this first grand Thief...

Thence up he flew, and on the Tree of Life,
The middle Tree and highest there that grew,
Sat like a Cormorant...

Paradise Lost
Book IV
Milton

1

Breaking in was easy. Although of course, I had been thinking about it, and how to do it, for some time. Really the arrangement was very slipshod. I mean with the flat. And from what I had been told recently by him, it seemed to me anyone could have done something similar, someone with a grudge - or a fear - against or of him. I laid my plans such as they were over the weekend, and made my 'move' on Monday. Which is far too alliterative a phrase, but there, it's a fact. Basically in my own little way, I went in for the kill.

My own little way. And that sounds like Lynda. "You do like to have your own little way," she used to tell me. Not, you notice, my own *way*. My own *little* way. "Go on, then," Lynda used to say. "You just do what you want. It's no good me arguing..." ("*My* arguing" I used mentally to correct her with a sort of dry shiver), "you'll just have to have your own little way."

Did I have my own little way with Lynda? Now and then, I suppose. But that is another story.

When I got to Saracen Road, I stopped a moment and looked over at the park. It was summer. It still is. I wasn't really looking at anything over there, just taking my bearings. He had spoken about the park and the trees. It was as if I had to be quite sure they were all really there. And they were.

So then I checked the parcel.

This was my masterstroke. At least so I thought then.

It comprised a sturdy manila envelope measuring approximately ten inches by twelve and a half - and was far too stout to go through any ordinary letter-box, especially after I'd packed it full with old newspaper cut to size. I had stuck on the anonymous printed label. I had also placed a quantity of stamps on the thing, then lightly rubbed them with an ink-pad - as if they had been smudgily franked. I've had enough such mail in my time.

I didn't think anyone could trace this to me. But then no one, hopefully, would need to see it beyond a cursory glance, if that. After which I intended to remove it, along with myself, from the scene of the crime. On the other hand, if someone insisted on accepting the parcel, no crime could occur. It wouldn't matter. Perhaps not much would.

As for myself, there was my disguise. I'd finally done what he had often told me to do, which was to shave off all my thinning hair. Instead I had grown quite a thick moustache in the space of three days. I'd bought a T-shirt too, black, and put on my tired old jeans that look like every other ageing man's tired old jeans. Oddly, shaven and moustached, I thought I looked two or three years younger than my allotted fifty-fifty-one. There were the smart sunglasses too, somebody else's forgotten pair I'd swiped from the unmanned counter at Smiths those months before. A crime already, we perceive.

Did I look like a thug? No. Five foot ten, skinny, with my hunched shoulders, narrow hands and feet and nose - I wasn't bruiser material.

I crossed the street. It was a quarter to twelve, noon.

Nearly time for *You and Yours*.

That was not what was thumping from the terrace of houses. A selection of rock or pop CD's were mutilating the still just morning air. Which was as he'd told me as well. He had said his particular terrace-house of flats, **66,** Saracen Road, was a noisy place that got on his nerves, or on his 'tits', depending on his mood when remarking.

Not only was it 66, Saracen Road, either. His flat was at the very top. Flat 6 - the Number of the Beast indeed.

I had labelled my parcel carefully. Here was a mistake any flustered, overworked post-person might create.

I looked at the list of names above the bells. Then I pressed his bell. What does that say? My pedantry? My caution? He was not there. I had every reason to *know* he wasn't. Or even if amazingly he was, it might be one more lie, his not answering.

But for whatever reason he *didn't* answer. And I tried the bell annoyingly quite a few times.

About four minutes passed. Now I hesitated and clicked my tongue, perplexed, irritated. After which I started on the next five bells, one after another.

No 5 was in, it was some of their tasteless 'music' I heard hammering on above. They took no notice, perhaps couldn't hear their bell, which augered well. (A *rhyming* phrase now. Normally I would vet and remove it).

It was No 3A which spoke to me. "Yeah?" The voice was male and - shall I say - bored.

"I'm sorry to bother you..."

"*Yeah?*"

"I have a package here..."

"Put it through the door, man."

"I'm afraid it won't fit through the letter-box."

"Shit. I gotta come down?"

"No, no. Excuse me, the package isn't for you."

"Then why the fuck are you...?"

"It's for a Mr Traz..." - carefully I laboured over his name - "*kull*? Flat 6."

Silence.

I said, "It was delivered to me wrongly in Sarandene Road - No 16..." (Such a road did not, obviously, exist).

And "So?" said the other.

"I've come out of my way," I replied sternly. "Mr Trazcool doesn't answer. This is a nuisance. Maybe you could let me in and I'll leave the thing for him in the hall. I'm not coming back with it."

No response save the sudden wasp-like rage of a buzzer as the front door opened.

"Tha..." I tried. Old habits, like war-torn Celtic warriors, die hard.

I doubt the moron in flat 3A heard me.

Then I was inside the hallway, shabby, airy and patchily white from big and grimy opaque windows. A mountain of stairs rose ahead. Evidently I wasn't going to deposit my spurious packet on the dusty table down here. Conscientious citizen as I must be, I was going up the whole bare stairway right to the top, all the way to N.O.T.B. 666. Where, please God, the door was as once he had described it, and the bloody awful racket from unmusical No 5 would continue, so no one would hear me as I smashed the glass panel, slipped my hand across and released the single Yale lock from inside.

ONE

Joseph. This, his name.

He liked to be known as *Sej*. He'd later told me he was dyslectic (normally erroneously spelled 'dyslexic') and possibly that was why he had taken the initial J of his fore-name and fixed it on the end of the se from the middle.

Joseph Traskul: Sej.

It has a sort of Germanic, certainly European ring to it, his full name. It is like that of some mentally tortured poet, probably from a well-to-do mercantile family, dead before forty, circa 1800.

I wondered from the very first if his name was a lie.

I have wondered if all of him was, and is, a lie.

The strangest thing.

But it was all very strange. Or only - very stupid.

I had gone up to London to meet Harris Wybrother. He used to be my agent but had retired a couple of years before. Despite this he still sometimes put publishers my way, or me their way depending on how one looked at it. Harris was only two or three years my senior but I had always found him much *older*.

Maybe he was a sort of authority figure to me. I always remember the first time we met, when I was mid-twenty-ish and he twenty-two-ish going on forty-ish, looming over me from his desk. "This isn't bad, Roy. It has potential shall I say? But you need to do quite a bit of work on it. Don't worry, old boy. We'll knock you into shape. And then - who knows?" Harris had been at Oxbridge. He had connections. I of course had been to the local grammar and then straight into the library service.

I stayed with Harris a handful of times, in the late '80's and '90's, at his father's 'place' in Hampshire. I think the first occasion I expected to step right back into a sort of between-the-wars Wodehouse scenario. It *was* a little like that. But not Wybrother Père. He was a piratical type who acted, and looked if it came to it, very much younger than his son. There was no longer any Mrs Wybrother. Normally a different woman, or once three women, were staying in the house and sharing the pirate's bed, appearing at breakfast in silk dressing-gowns or sporty cotton undies. Harris, though unmarried, had a regular fiancée he seemed always and only to retain in London.

The 'place' itself was big. It was an old vicarage, worth apparently a 'bomb', though the drains and general plumbing were on the sleepy side.

It was surrounded by woods and fields and had gardens. These were maintained by a sort of ghostly ever-grumbling gardener. He would appear suddenly at the windows of the dining-room on summer evenings and stand silent, motionless and glaring horribly in on us all, rather like Peter Quint in *The Turn of the Screw*.

There were a couple of tennis courts as well, and Harris once or twice insisted I play some sets with him. But I'm no good at tennis, or any games, and dislike them all, perhaps only for that reason. That I always went along with his suggestions was less proof of an obedient guest than the fact Harris always somewhat reminded me of one of the more amiable bullies at school.

The house stayed Wodehousian even as late as 1997, by which time the fields had become town, and a new estate had been built practically on the front lawn. But Harris's father had sprung by then what I took for his final surprise. In his sixties he'd been expected hourly to die of drink, or other over-indulgence, but instead he had cut and run to

Spain with a girl of twenty-four. She was rich apparently, too. The last I'd heard he was still there, seventy-one by now and going strong, his child-bride of thirty-something firmly at his side and "Serenely putting up with," Harris had said, "Dad's endless stream of bimboritas from the bars."

No doubt Wybrother Senior's youthful tendencies had moulded Harris's aura of age. (How I dislike the American-ised apostrophe 's *following* an s. But I've given up on that one. Hardly any publisher in the English language would now countenance the old tradition of Harris'. Not that this, as will become obvious, is ever intended for publication).

When I received the most recent summons to lunch with Harris in London, I went. The possible chances of a book contract were usually illusory. So one took what one could get.

Harris came 'down from the country', from the Wodehouse house. We met at a restaurant called Le Grill in Holborn, one of those small quirky venues that can sometimes supply *haute cuisine*, and are a kind of Masonic secret among any that know. Harris had previously ordered me: "Don't tell anyone about this, eh, Roy? Keep it for us. The good and the slightly great."

We ate steak, Scottish, or so it purported to be. There had been starters of something to do with Scandinavian prawns, 'seasonal' asparagus. We drank the appropriate wines, which were very drinkable. Naturally Harris knows exactly what to choose. Frankly I can never be that bothered. If something is palatable, and in my case, affordable, I'll drink it. After the main course there was cheese - actually *very* good. We took coffee.

And now, I thought, having as always been careful and restrained, as my own father would have instructed, Harris might offer a titbit, some man - or more often now, a woman - who might be interested in a book from me. At this point

I'd better add, my *forte* is usually the minor thriller or detective novel. But such basic works may, if wanted, be constructed to incorporate certain preoccupations. Or should I say *themes*.

This time, however my lunch *impresario* did not suggest a single thing. Over the brandy and coffee his eyes grew suddenly like an infant's. And by that I mean through changing colour - to a sort of milky blue; by nature they're grey.

"Fuck it, Roy," he said, gazing out into the vistas of Holborn Viaduct, "Dad's dead."

Such a phrase, *bathetically*, heaven forgive me, alliterative. *Dad's dead*.

But I was shocked too, in my own (little) way. Both at the news and Harris being abruptly so unlike himself.

Stupidly I said, "Your father..." I certainly didn't mean to seem to correct him.

But he snapped, "Dad, yes. My bloody father."

"I'm so sorry, Harris."

"So am I. No, let me be painfully honest, Roy, I don't give a flying - I don't *care*, Roy. Which has to be wrong, yes?"

His milky eyes said something other. Poor bastard, he seemed not to know. Had some hidden unnoted weeping turned his eyes blue?

"When did it happen?"

"Two days ago. Two *days*. Can you believe that bitch Veronica..." he meant the thirty-something child wife, "only called me last night. And do I mean night? It was two minutes to two in the morning."

"Well, from Spain perhaps - And she must have been upset."

"Must she? How would one know? Perhaps. Oh, perhaps. I'll give the cow the benefit of the doubt. I have to go over for the funeral and to sort things out. And there has to be an inquest. Oh *not*," he startlingly nearly bellowed, so our fellow lunchers raised their brows, "like one of *your* bloody yarns. They just do it. Oh God, Roy."

I forbore to ask if Janette, his *glacé fiancée*, was going with him to give support. I'd only met her once.

Possibly she wasn't really as she had seemed to be, not when he and she were alone.

Just then anyhow his mobile phone went off. His ring-tone was a special piece of Brahms.

At once, like Pavlov's dogs, trained to the right response, he was chatting into it in his ordinary Harris manner. His eyes unfilmed, went grey again.

"Sorry, Roy," he said as the call ended. "Emergency over at The Elms." *The Elms* was his name for a well-known publishing house near the Euston Road. "Get me a cab, will you?" he added to the waiter, "and the bill. Really sorry to run out on you. You must email and tell me all your news, what projects you're working on..." Projects meaning books. Projects. "Don't rush off because I have to, stay and have another brandy."

We shook hands and he went away.

I didn't want another brandy, hadn't really wanted the first one. It was quite hot although only April, too hot for excess alcohol.

I walked down from Holborn to the Strand feeling rather flat, although Harris's lunches seldom led to much work nowadays. And I was slightly unnerved. Probably at the touch of what my father had been used to call the Grim Reaper. Harris's father had been just over seventy, but I was fifty. Well over the boundary on the downward path to old age and death.

After all I went into a pub and ordered half a pint of Wincott's Bitter, a funny old brew you see less and less.

Sitting in the dark corner, staring into the beer's murky

depths, I had a bleak look at my life. What was I doing, where heading for? Why? What aims did I have, hopes cherish? It was a sorry and banal *resumé*. I was a plodder, and I did what I was told where I could find anyone - parent, employer, publisher - to tell me. I kept the 'wolf from the door' by hard graft in the softest of professions. I lived slowly and prudently, with little occasional and mundane treats, like the very glass-full on the table in front of me, Wincott's. My life was a glass of bitter.

There was only one thing I *could* cite - even if that too involved my trade. It was the sole manuscript I had never even submitted to an agent or editor. The untitled, unfinished book had begun life in paper form, but had currently lain in the files of my computer for six years. *Untitled* was not a work of suspense or detective fiction. It was a strange thing, perhaps even a sort of fantasy, set in an (also untitled) European country during the eighteenth century. The literary style of the book was also fairly unlike the normally carefully-clipped and controlled prose of everything else I typed in there. And it had a structure that was, perhaps, experimental. It involved no plotting whatsoever, dissimilar to every other novel I'd penned, typed, or ultimately tapped out on the keyboard. And of course, like anything never planned, unplotted, unresolved, meandering and 'free', it frequently stuck. I had begun *Untitled* in 1975, when I was in my twenties. Thereafter, section by section it flowed and stuck, and unglued and went on, until the next inevitable block. Printed up so far, it ran to 318 close pages, but aside from the revisions I sometimes visited on it, it had by now been stalled fairly conclusively since the turn of the century.

Now it came floating up as it were out of the beer glass. *Untitled* was, for all its failings and inertia, the one *interesting* book I had ever attempted. In fact the only book that flew in the face of everything else of any kind I had had to do and done.

Did I say what it was about? If only loosely, it concerned a crazed and murderous young poet, son of a once-wealthy mercantile family, a drug-taker and visionary with black curling hair and wide wild eyes. Aside from his genius, he took anything he wanted, but generally it was given him, and the silver salver his *far* from mundane treats were served on, was often also awash with blood.

Just as I glanced up from the beer, the pub door opened in a sudden sun flash. Two silhouetted figures walked in, two men. One was a suited business type with expensive shoes. The other was the black-haired poet from *Untitled*.

Obviously he wasn't anything of the sort, the young man now leaning against the bar. Actual characters do not, as in one or two peculiar romances they may, leap from the page to take on sentient life.

The resemblance, however, especially as I had just then been thinking of it, was remarkable.

Realistically I've sometimes wondered since, if I *hadn't* been thinking of *Untitled*, would I even have noticed him particularly? Maybe on the train going back I might have thought of it: Oh, that fellow in the pub. He was rather like Vilmos... wasn't he.

Under *these* circumstances I was inevitably intrigued.

I stared a moment, checked myself, and started to scrutinise him more cautiously.

He was definitely quite a handsome specimen. As, naturally, was *Untitled*'s Vilmos. Lynda, with her prissy taste, wouldn't have liked him, I don't think she would. After all she made do with me and my little way for two whole years. Maureen though, I'm fairly sure, *would* have appreciated the man in the pub. She too spent time with me, but I had been a lot younger then, and her husband was also very good-looking in his youth.

This young man was himself about thirty-six or seven. *Not* so young really. And Vilmos - about thirty-five where I'd left him last, wallowing in a brothel on some shadowy cobbled side street of an arched and aching city. Here then, Vilmos abruptly aged by the next unwritten chapter.

He took no notice of anything around him that I could see. He spoke to the Suit-and-Shoes in a muted angry monologue, pausing only to listen to the Suit's own brief comments, here and there inserted, during which Vilmos - I might as well call him that for the moment - seemed both strung-up and contemptuous. The Suit drank a glass of red wine. It was a nice colour, like the bottle Harris had got with the steak. Vilmos drank a double vodka or gin without mixer, knocked it back and stood waiting for a refill. Which was duly purchased.

Already this, his demeanour, seemed aptly reminiscent of what Vilmos's *might* have been in some comparable situation. But what situation was it? Suit-and-Shoes looked composed, almost non-committal. There were a lot of early evening drinkers already in the pub, and more streaming in. I couldn't make out even a single word. Probably twenty years ago I would have. Then other barflies grouped between me and the two men and I couldn't see them well either. Vilmos wore a black shirt and black jeans. They were neither expensive nor tat. He was wearing brown boots that looked as if they had helped him scale the sides of rough chalky buildings.

I took a few more gulps of beer.

It was nearly five-thirty, the middle of what we used to call the Rush Hour. As a rule I avoided travelling this late, or caught the seven-thirty train, which missed the worst of it. I'd dawdled. As if - I was meant to see this man, to be inspired, *Untitled* rejuvenated.

I'd use this scene in the next chapter. Find a good if bizarre explanation for it, the Suit man a creditor or lover, even a sibling. To work on the book tonight could ease the dull feeling of threat that had somehow fastened on me with Harris's words *Dad's dead.*

All at once the crowd round the bar was parting, like clothes in a big wardrobe, as some Narnian-like beast came shouldering forth. It wasn't Aslan.

"Yes?" he said, standing over my table.

My scrutiny, as I've noted here, had been intended to be discreet. Besides he and his companion had been hemmed in. How had he seen the slight low glances I shot at him?

"I beg your pardon?" I asked mildly.

"Well maybe you should."

I kept a blank face. I don't like confrontations, and don't often either invite or get snared in one.

"Well," he said, "you could buy me a drink, then."

His voice was not as I had imagined Vilmos' voice to be. I suppose I heard Vilmos, in my inner ear, speaking a sort of cod Franco-Russian-Hungarian. Something like that.

I thought, *Christ, he thinks I'm after him. Want to shag him. Now what do I do, for God's sake?*

"I'm sorry," I said, "I don't quite..."

He sat down across from me. There was an empty chair there somehow left unfilled. He sprawled out his long legs. "I know you, don't I?" he asked me.

For a queasy second I did think perhaps, despite all common sense, he truly was Vilmos. But I seized the one apparent saving chance.

"I thought I knew *you* a minute too. You're very like my sister's son." I have no sister, and this non-existent She has no son. But would that sweep the problem up?

He said, "Oh really?"

He levelled his black brows. He had good teeth, and a slightly crooked nose. Vilmos? Why not. Perhaps in some fight... I tried to keep my wits.

"I haven't seen him for a year," I elaborated. A writer, or my kind of writer, can do such things *extempore*. "They're in India, he and his girlfriend. So I was a bit surprised..."

"To see me here. Only I'm not, or he's not."

"No. I'm sorry if I stared. That was why."

"It isn't usually," he said.

"Well," I said, "have a good evening." I rose. Thank Christ he stayed in the seat. From the bar, I noticed, his former associate had melted away.

"Cheers," said Vilmos.

He had an actor's accent. His voice seemed trained, expressive, but more lazy now.

He still didn't get up and I wove through the pub crowd and got out on the scorched pavement. I was sweating. God, that had been - never mind. Forward march - my father again. Rise and shine, forward march, the touch of the Grim Reaper, easy come, easy go...

I was walking quickly towards Charing Cross. The best course however would be to go by and on to the Hay Market. I could look at the theatres, I could simply...

"I just thought," said his unmistakable voice behind me. It came from higher in the air. I'm five ten, you may remember, and Vilmos about six three, "you might like to take this."

Trepidatious to the point of agony I turned. He held before me a business card. The very last item I would guess my nerves expected.

I gazed at it. *Joseph Traskul* said the card in plain black Roman on plain dull white. Then an email address and telephone number.

"Er - why would I...?"

Tanith Lee

"Be a sport," he answered with a menacing old-fashioned playfulness.

"Look, I'm really sorry..."

"I'll bet you are, now."

All around the crowd eddied. I knew that if he drew a knife and sliced off my ear, or kicked me in the groin, everybody else would merely fastidiously move round us, not to interrupt.

"All right. Thank you."

"You think," he said, "I'm a gay whore. Or maybe a bi-functional one. Look on the back of the card."

I did so. *Piano Tuner to the Bars* it said.

He laughed then, now not like Vilmos, more gentle, and almost shy. "Had you going there. I thought you looked the type of guy might have a piano, or know someone. Work is scarce this spring. I'll travel, just minimum expenses. The main rates are printed there, too. See you." And he swung himself about, the mane of hair springing up and flopping down on his collar. He strode carelessly away through the splintered westering sun.

TWO

My father used to keep a piano, (I put the word 'keep' advisedly) in the sitting-room. He could play quite well, if rather stiffly, a little Chopin or Schubert, and sometimes Victorian songs. I had piano lessons at the grammar school, which was one of the few still surviving locally in the '60's. Then I too could play a little, if like him without much magic and with less ability. I remember hot summer, cold dark winter evenings, practicing, and my mother putting her head round the door. "That's nice, Roy."

Maureen had a piano too, and she could play very well. She played the kind of thing I liked, unless I only really started to like it because she played it. Rachmaninov and Debussy were a couple of her choices, and Scott Joplin. She'd found him long before his return to the public ear.

Now of course my home premises were pianoless. I had sold it four years after I inherited the house.

It was nothing like Harris's 'place', No 74,Old Church Lane. A long, sloping, winding street with some occasional careering oak trees, and semi-detached villas planted behind short front lawns. I'd grown up there, and later gone away, although only about an hour by train, to a succession of not very salubrious rooms. Gradually the street and the villas changed over the years, the former getting less cloistered and the pavement more worn, the trees being cut down or regularly pruned to stumps. The houses though perked up. They acquired bright red or blue front doors and new roofs, garages where side access had been, and ponds with water-lilies. "People value a house now," my father had remarked. "Because it costs more, it means more." I never really followed that. Houses had often cost a lot more than was affordable. I was more inclined to put the renovations down to the increasing frequency with which everyone else seemed to move out or in, tarting everything up for a quick sale or to please a mortgage company.

I assayed little improvement when I went back. My father had died, having a heart attack at the local, where he'd gone for an unusual drink with some friends. My mother had been dead for years. Breast cancer. There wasn't much they could do for it then. But the house was useful. It was paid for, and once all the legal business was solved I was installed, only half an hour out of London's Charing Cross. I managed to find a gardener too. He was young, quite efficient. He scalped the lawn and hauled the worst of the weeds from the flowerbeds, where a scatter of flowers then bloomed by themselves for several seasons before, finally, untended and never watered except by God, they gave up. In the end the gardener too simply vanished without a word. Perhaps someone had killed him, as happened to gardeners and many others in quite a lot of my books. I got the back and front lawns paved over then, and left the rest to itself. I sold the piano about the same time. I had never been tempted to play it.

That evening I got home around eight. I had just missed a train, then travelled standing on another, amid herds of commuters in the same case, reading papers, chatting on their mobiles, swaying there like bats the wrong way up.

Indoors I made some tea and took a biscuit from the jar, my mother's biscuit barrel that had a fat bear on it. As a child I had loved it, the bear.

I really had altered the house very little. Only neglected it. The agency cleaning girl came once a fortnight.

She was currently a German student, who seemingly spoke only five words of English: *Hello. Yes. No. Done.* And

Ifbee. (Perhaps six words?) That last meant *If I can against all odds*, i.e.: Could you clean the cooker? *Ifbee.*

The sun was at last going down in the fir tree at the end of the garden, not mine, but that of an adjoining plot. Beyond my back fence ran the alleyway, but the fir tree mostly hid it from me. I'd used this tree in swift descriptions here and there, a handy example of nature, its needles against this sky or that. Now a fractured golden sunset sky that had been prefigured in London's radiance.

Mug in hand, I stared into the last light.

Sunset and dusk have a mystic significance in the East, I forget quite what. In France of course, with dusk comes *l'heure bleu*, when phantoms and hallucinations are seen.

The sun went. The fir grew darker and the sky like bronze. Then the twilight blueness. A bright star stood out over the roof of the Catholic church.

Vaguely heard around me the ordinary noise of a radio, some male clearing nasal passages careless of open window or listening ears, a Hoover; a night flight starting off for Europe.

And then, the phantom.

It emerged palely from the umbra of the fir tree and the gathering dark, and gazed in over the fence. Bisected by the fence at the approximate level of his jaw, Joseph Traskul's disembodied head. Vilmos would have liked that.

I didn't drop the mug. Maybe I clutched it far too tightly.

And he? He watched me. He was smiling.

We said nothing, either of us.

And then the owl - there was an owl, it sometimes flew across the gardens in the spring and summer, although where it came from I'd never been sure - the owl sailed by overhead.

And both he and I looked up.

Both he and I - Vilmos - Joseph - and I, looked up at the

passing of the owl.

When I looked down again, the phantom was gone.

2

On the third flight I met one of the neighbours. He came out of a door above and clattered down the stair towards me.

I got ready to show him the forged packet, with its address of Saracen Road and the apparently franked postage. But, thickset and indifferent, he shouldered past me, brushing me over with a leather jacket very unsuitable for the summer weather, not saying a word.

No doubt few of them took any notice of each other in this block. Inner London is like that, even more so than the suburbs where I exist.

I went up the further three flights and reached flat No 6. *His* flat.

It was as he had described it. A door painted a dull white like all the others I had already seen, but this one with a panel of crinkled glass. The door had only one Yale lock. Yet it did not have a number on it, unlike those below. Nevertheless it had to be 6. The stair ended here. There was nowhere else to go.

One flight down, flat 5 was still crashing out its horrible music, tuneless, with only the deadly beat and mostly indecipherable Neanderthal lyrics, to class it as any kind of 'song'. When I had walked by on my way up, not only was I deafened, I felt the racket through the soles of my feet, base of my spine, and punching me in the gut.

Up here, no one else was about. Through a narrow, unwashed window I could see the rear of the other buildings, and not a flicker of life. Beyond those, the London skyline.

I was scarcely furtive. I took the heavy-duty gardening glove out of my back pocket, put it on and made a fist. I smashed the glass with one smack, as if I'd been doing things of this sort all my life. Watching TV I suppose teaches one the worst skills; the morality brigade are right.

Most of the panel fell in. It must have been very inferior stuff.

I reached through and undid the door.

As it swung inward, I thought he would spring at me, out of nowhere, out of thin air.

But he didn't. The narrow hallway was empty. In fact very empty, no carpet down, the paper even scoured from the unpainted walls. There were two internal doors, each closed.

THREE

I went back into the house, through the kitchen door, which I shut, locked and bolted behind me. Then I switched on the external light. Its beam cut hard into the gathering dark, revealing nothing beyond what was normally present, the paved lawn and dead flowerbeds, the fir tree over the fence, the top of the Catholic church. The light dimmed the diamond star that had appeared there.

What had happened? Had I *imagined* him, Joseph Traskul the piano tuner, his floating head swimming by the fence and smiling at me, before the owl somehow diverted both our attentions to the sky?

I didn't think it had been imagination.

Well then, was I going mad?

Putting down the mug I went through into the front room and poured myself a finger of whisky.

Standing motionless, I peered out at the street. The curtains were still undrawn. My mother used to have 'nets' up, to stop anyone looking in at our nondescript activities. But I had taken them down in the end. I had nothing fascinating to hide, did nothing in that room, nor in any of the living-rooms, to merit such strict concealment.

Out in the street a couple of surviving oaks caught the ugly glare of the street lamps. The fifteen-year-old from three doors up was bicycling by, and the man who always walked his Alsatian dog was doing just that. Nor was anyone on the garden path that ran beside the house. The side gate was securely shut.

The clock on the church chimed. 9 p.m.

Nothing else was evident.

Soon I drew the curtains. I put on the hall light and went

upstairs and put on the light in my study, which had once been my parents' bedroom.

Turning on the computer I checked for emails. There was only one, from Peakes about some stationery.

All this time I was thinking, *What did I see? Was it real?*

I didn't feel deranged. Nor did I think I had *not* seen what I had.

The frivolous idea that after all, and truly, the man from the pub in The Strand might be my character come to life failed to resurface. I don't believe such things can happen. And if perhaps they ever could, I would never reckon they could happen to a man like myself.

So it was a mystery. Or perhaps something in the prawns had not been quite right, or the cheese; something as silly as that. I'd heard of such incidents, a mild hallucinatory food-poisoning. But I felt cool and quite steady, not sick, and not sweating now.

Better let the episode go. Perhaps it would prove useful, if not in revitalizing *Untitled*, then in my next commercial work. For honestly, now, I had no desire at all to uncork my unpublished novel from the files.

I did some small chores round the house, had a slice of supermarket cheddar on toast, and watched the news. The world as always was in unremitting chaos, and apparently the temperature in Britain had been an unseasonal twenty – roughly seventy degrees, we would have said in my youth.

I ran a bath, and afterwards went to bed.

Like many of my age I don't sleep as well as I did.

What an unappreciated pleasure, the sleepful nights of my teens and twenties had been, the odd sleepless one an occasion for fretful wonder. Now they're a matter of course, and on a 'good' night I average five or six non-consecutive hours if I'm lucky.

But I lay back and watched the darkness and the faint

municipal lamplight through the curtains. I put on my bed-side radio, Radio 3. They were playing Handel, I thought.

I considered my next commission, which was a small thriller, one in a series devised by someone else and something for which I had no enthusiasm, but it would help pay bills. I often do a bit of work in my insomniac hours, even get up sometimes at three or four in the morning to push some notes into the computer.

My brain however kept going back to the pub, and, nastier, the fence.

At midnight I switched to the news as I habitually do, and listened once more to the rehash of hell on earth.

What was it all for? What was to be done?

I used to get angry and have *opinions*. Now I take it in like a sort of slop. The bloody awful thing is, this rehearsal of horrors usually helps me drift asleep.

Which was what happened. We were on to the World Service by then, a report on some far off disaster beyond human belief, and I was asleep.

I dreamed he and I were sitting on a torn-out palm tree drifting on a salt-dark sea, and he said to me, "The thing is, Phippsy, it was written, us meeting as we did."

To this hour, this piece of dream-dialogue frightens me. Because he speaks in the dream as he *would* speak. Not as I would have him speak, at least partly grammatically. Us meeting, not our. And his use of my name, like the bullies at Chaults Grammar School. My father's, therefore my name is Phipps. Although my professional name is R.P. Phillips. Harris suggested that, while he was dismantling my first book and sending me home to reinvent it. "Phipps - no, old son. Doesn't have a ring to it. *Phelps*, I wonder...? No. No - *Phillips*."

In the dream Joseph Traskul was not in his black clothes and bashed boots from the pub. He wore Vilmos's garments,

Vilmos's loose shirt and broken coat.

The radio must have said it, three hundred people were dead. Both the dream-Joseph and the dream-I heard this.

Joseph said to me, "And I only am escaped alone to tell thee," quoting the *Book of Job*, and also, naturally, Melville's *Moby Dick*.

One gets used to rising early. My almost ten years in the library service had marked this indelibly on my mental clock. Even when I sleep especially badly I rarely get up later than eight.

I used to have a paper delivered, my father's habit. I stopped that too a couple of years back. I seem to listen to enough news. The post, which used to arrive at eight or before, seldom now appears much before 11 a.m.

But today there was an envelope on the mat.

In the brilliant light of too-early-summer morning I bent to see.

No 74, said the hand printing on its surface. The writing was erratic, but I still took it for some circular, a charity appeal, Jehova's Witness threat, or one of those *Householder* issues that suggest to us we can sell our house and then rent it back, must be aware of this or that road-widening, pipe-renewing or other potentially destructive plan, or that our government loves us, and we should be *en garde*.

I didn't bother to open it, only carried it through to the kitchen and put on the kettle for coffee.

Outside sparrows, blue tits and pigeons were flying over in squadrons to the bird-tables and baths of No 72, my attached neighbour, and unattached 76 the other side of the wall.

I have nothing against birds, or any creature come to that. My mother used to have a bird-bath also, but I never remembered to fill it. It was drily down there somewhere by the end fence, among the weeds and ivy. And beyond, stood the fir.

Gradually I glanced out at the fir.

Which was how I saw the thing sitting there on the paving.

It was a large black plastic dustbin. Not, I hasten to add, a *dirty* one. This was spic and span. It looked brand new. There was even a red and white sticker left on the lid.

I switched off the kettle.

Nothing else out there was disturbed. Certainly the airforce of birds wasn't nervous.

Perhaps ridiculously I picked up the bread knife. I undid the kitchen door and emerged.

The air was lit, and peaceable with noisy morning sounds.

I walked over the paving and inspected the dustbin.

It was definitely new, pristine in fact. I don't know why, possibly force of habit for this is what one does with dustbins, I reached out and pulled off the lid.

As I did this, complete terror gripped me. I had an instant mental picture of Joseph Traskul, like some handsome, hideous jack-in-the-box, leaping out of the interior – *Surprise! Surprise!*

But there was nothing like that. There was *something* in the vault of the bin. I could see at once what it was but its incongruity made it incomprehensible to me. I stood there staring. In the end I dropped the lid on, walked back into the kitchen, shut and locked the door. And saw again the letter that had been on the mat.

Now I grabbed hold of it. Dropping the knife I ripped the envelope open.

A leaf of plain white paper was inside with strong, erratic writing in black biro, not astonishingly the very same writing as was on the outside.

I removed it. It could be read clearly enough: *Back garden. See bin. Open to find 1 x bottle of Wincott's Special.*

Which was of course exactly what I had done, and found.

"Hello. I wonder if I could speak to Harris?"

"Arriz," said an unfamiliar and not very kindly female voice. "Mr Why Bother do you men?"

"That's right. I..."

"He's off."

"He's not there?"

"Noah. He's gone to Spine."

"Already."

"Yez. Abuts dad."

"I see. Do you know when he'll..."

"No I don't. I'm hellip for Miss Lornce."

"Oh, I see. I suppose Miss Lawrence isn't..."

"Mss Lornces owd."

"Could you tell her Roy called."

"Ray."

"Roy. Roy Phipps."

"Roy Fibs. Yez, I'll tell."

The phone went down quite forcefully before I could ask if Janette Lawrence, Harris's *fiancée*, would call me back, or when I could call again.

Once more a dead end, then. I'd already tried a couple of other publishing semi-friends, ostensibly to check on business matters, a contract, a payment. I had wanted to try them out, see what they thought it was best for me to do. There is a strange chap who seems to have followed me from central London. No, I haven't a clue why. He latched on to me in a pub, and now he's left a dustbin in my garden.

A difficult speech. No doubt they'd only assume I was trying out on them a new plot-line for some sinister tale.

Actually I could imagine Lewis Rybourne at Gates saying, "Oh come on, Roy. That's drivel. Why would someone do something so - well frankly *soppy*. Is there a *body* in the fucking bin or what?"

Should I therefore call the police? I could imagine *that* too. All the world reeling with terror threats, rapes, murders and burglary with violence, and myself phoning them about *my* problem. "Well, some people, sir, might be very grateful for a nice clean bin. Not to mention a free jar."

It got to noon, and I couldn't settle to anything, or decide what to do. I'd placed the note and envelope in a plastic sandwich bag and put them in a drawer, to protect DNA. The bin and beer I left where they were. A pair of pigeons subsequently flew over and landed there momentarily, and one had relieved itself on the purity of the lid. I went upstairs and belatedly shaved and dressed. I shut and locked every window, even the narrow one in the lavatory. Downstairs, all bolted and barred, I poured the cold coffee I had made and not drunk into the sink. Outside the bin was still there, undisturbed except by me and the pigeon.

The house has a burglar alarm. I didn't very often activate it, as it had a handy knack of going off for no apparent reason. Now I did. Next both sides had people in all day, 72 an elderly but spry couple, 76 a house-husband with a child that went to school and came back for lunch.

I walked out of the house and double-locked the door.

Despite the sun it was cooler today. I scanned carefully up and down the street as I had already done with the path and the back alley from my upper rooms, my bedroom, the lavatory and adjacent bathroom.

All this was very silly. But I write such stories. I *know* how appallingly worrying these tiny incidents may seem. Anything that doesn't fit the everyday, even an everyday established menace - like a thug with a gun or a warning from a gang.

At the end of Old Church Lane I turned into Bulivante Crescent. Round the curve of detached houses, meshed in their hedges and trees, lay the roaring high street. But even as I took in the vista, I saw him, seated on a low wall, drinking from a can of cola.

He wore white today, a white shirt and whitish jeans. Over his shoulder was that kind of male handbag that is so useful, and this too was in a sort of bleached denim. He had already seen me. He got up, smiling, and raised his friendly hand in greeting. No recrimination was obvious at his having had to wait for me so long.

FOUR

No one ever told me anything about the sexual act. As for love, it was something you saw in films. By the time I was seventeen, you could see quite a bit of the sexual act in them, too, particularly in foreign cinemas in the West End. I had also been handed certain educational books by my father when I was about fourteen. He suggested I read them; I was now 'old enough' to 'understand'. Needless to say I *already* understood. One's body tends to inform one. Despite all this however, I wasn't a quick learner, I wasn't ready to equate what I felt with any chance of sharing it. It was a solitary pleasure, as they were wont to say. I needn't, I think, go into details. My own writing is scanty in this respect. I will open the bedroom door and let my protagonists through. But what goes on thereafter the reader may deduce for himself.

Repressed? Of course I was, and am, and very wisely. I was an unattractive thin spotty youth, who grew into a short, thin and nondescript male adult. My hair was already going at twenty, despite all the preparations I tried on it. My height had never materialised. I wasn't a 'Tich', like Mark Brighton, the poor sucker in my last year at school, who was still under five foot. Men go on growing, they say, until they are twenty-one. Maybe he suddenly dashed a final thirteen inches and put them all to shame. But there are short men with plenty of charisma. Not me.

By seventeen I had liked girls, *fancied* girls. (*Fantasised* girls). But I'd never been to bed with one. Naturally I lied about this. Did anyone believe me? Doubtful.

Then I left Chaults Grammar and started to work in the central library. One night when I was eighteen I went to the

Tanith Lee

Feathers for a drink with some partial friends, and there in a corner I saw Maureen Parner.

Truthfully, I barely gave her a second glance.

She was well over thirty, and this was in the early 1970s. She was just a woman with done-up blondish hair, sipping spirits with a fat man who kept laughing. There were girls elsewhere in the bar with swinging hair and off-the-shoulder tops and blue nails. My three male companions ogled them, as did I. "Look at her. What ya think?" "I like her friend best." "Her skirt's too short." "Well, that's OK." "Yeah but the legs aren't good enough."

The evening rambled on, getting smokier and darker. It was just October, and outside the then-white streetlamps lit a scene of rainy murk. In the Feathers rings formed about the yellow lamps, and over there Maureen Parner, barely seen by me, sat on with her fat escort, crossing and uncrossing her plump, shapely, stockinged legs.

Everyone smoked then. About ten-thirty, only half an hour from closing time, the air was tindery stale and brown. Mick and Steve had got off with a 'couple of birds'. Danny, who was a non-starter as was I, decided he needed to get home. "Promised I'd mow the lawn tomorrow. My dad always wants it done, right up till November. Mad. It's my last Saturday off and all."

Left alone in the Bacchanalia, I had another half, I'd already swallowed five or six - abruptly it felt like a whole barrel.

And that was when I *did* see her. Maureen.

A lot of people did.

She got up, slung the contents of a full glass of gin and lime in the fat man's face and said, quite loudly and in a very beautiful voice that had a cockney accent, "You rotten bleeder! Well damn you, then. Get lost."

(Maureen's voice was lovely. When I heard her sing to

38

her piano, the songs of Ivor Novello, Cole Porter, The Beatles, she had no trace of any accent. Hers was a clear rich soprano, silvery on the higher notes and plum-lush in the lower register. She'd sung professionally in her early youth. There'd been talk of light opera, the stage. But her husband happened instead. Back then, the late fifties, women's careers often finished at the altar.)

The fat man rose. He wiped his face, swore, and left her. He stalked past my table.

Even then I used to be careful who I stared at, or at whom I stared, mitigating my glances into something more clandestine, so I hoped.

But Maureen Parner merely got to her feet and went into the Ladies.

As for me, my head was now ringing like a bell. I too hoisted my thin frame upright, left most of my drink, and wavered out into the misty night.

I was sitting on the bench by the bus-stop in the main road when she emerged from the Feathers. She wasn't drunk. She had spruced up her pale pink lipstick and relacquered her hair - not that I could have worked that out then, she just looked fresh, almost new. She came straight along the pavement and sat down beside me, about a foot away.

"Has it gone?"

"I beg your..."

"The bus. The 176."

"Er, no."

That was my bus, too.

"Thank God," she said. "My watch's stopped. Thought I'd missed it. Then it's only the other one and all round the houses. Get home at midnight."

"Yes."

She faced front. After a minute she opened her bag and

took out a packet of cigarettes. She lit one then turned to me. "Sorry, do you smoke?"

"Not - yes."

"Like one?"

I didn't often smoke, it had never got a hold on me, try to let it as I had. And I didn't want one now, I felt saddled enough by booze. But I said, "Thank you."

She let me choose the cigarette, then let me light it from hers. This was very thrilling, strange, disturbing. I could smell her powder and scent. She said, "Don't you speak nicely."

"Er..."

"I suppose everybody bloody saw all that in there."

I said nothing.

She said, "He's an absolute bastard. Don't know why I put up with him so long. And now he's seen someone he likes more than me. Some twenty-one-year-old bloody tart no doubt, miniskirt up her arse and thinks *he's* got some money. Which he hasn't, I could tell her. Worse than my Graham," she added. She had turned again and looked on out into the damp smoke of the night. Across the road cars, the odd last bus, sparkled by; vehicles were scarce now because it was well after eleven, and on such roads, in those days, much of the traffic had eased by then.

She had a face that made me look. It wasn't pretty particularly, not beautiful or even very original. But it was a real face, flesh and blood, and with make-up tastefully applied, and she had such a nice smell. And her mouth was... I kept looking at her mouth.

Finally she said in a brisk sensible tone, "This damned bus isn't coming, is it? Cancelled it, the buggers." I had never, then, heard a woman of Maureen's age, (which was actually about thirty-three) swear such a lot. It had a kind of daring to it, a *finesse*. She said, "D'you fancy some fish and chips? There's a place down College Road. Just make it. Come on, you look like you could do with a good meal."

I scrambled up and went after her, frantically going over in my mind how much money I had left in my brand new wallet. Her high heels clipped along the pavement, and when I got level, she reached across with a weightless gesture and took my arm, as though we had been doing this for months. Only then was I quite sure that I, though so short and she in her heels, was still a good four inches the taller. And that was the moment I felt the rush of desire, the enchantment of relief.

There were a few students from the art college outside the chippy, eating. They were just closing up. But when the man saw Maureen he grinned and said, "Got a bit of rock left, darling. Will that do?"

"What about my friend here?" she said. "He's starved."

"I can see he is. What would you like, sir?"

I said, stammering slightly, "Just chips are fine."

"Oh go on, have a bit of fish, Charlie," said she, inventing a name for me. She leaned across then and kissed me on the cheek, taking my breath away, and in that second she whispered, "I'll pay, darling. Go on. Spoil yourself."

If I had been sober I'd have lighted the shop with my embarrassed blush. But I wasn't sober, although my head had cleared out on the street. I felt ready for much, of which fish was only a minor challenge.

On my cheekbone, her kiss seemed to have been marked in hot and cold.

She and I both had rock salmon, huss as it's now identified, and bags of chips, all this in newspaper, as then it was, thickly dusted with salt and sloshed with vinegar.

Outside, as we ambled along eating, she said, "Didn't mind me calling you Charlie, did you?"

"No. But my name's Roy."

"Hello, Roy. I'm Maureen. Pleased to meet you."

"Thank you for the fish."

"Don't mention it. Well, I expect we'd better walk. If we hadn't missed the blasted bus, we have now. I cut down by the cemetery. Know the one?"

"Yes."

"Not that that's my place of residence. I leave that to the vampires. I've got a flat over the Co-op."

Knowing approximately where she meant I knew this overshot my own turn-off by about a mile. It didn't trouble me.

"I'll see you home," I said.

"What a gallant feller you are."

It was only when we reached the cemetery, running grey, dim, silent and ominous by the road, that doubt began to creep in on me. What would she expect? Despite all the fantasies and those unencouraging books - did I know - *understand* - enough to be capable?

I needn't have worried.

We reached the side street and the glass-fronted shops, bleak and dark, and an alley and a stone stair that led up to the flats, an L-shaped block two storeys high.

"It's been nice meeting you, Roy."

Was she putting me off?

In terror I leant forward and went to kiss her mouth. And she, adept as a dancer, met me with a peerless grace. We leaned there quite some while, kissing in the shadow of the alley. Then she murmured, "D'you want to come up for a coffee?"

Naturally I did want to. Up we went.

About ten minutes later we were through the bedroom door.

"Where shall we go?" he asked.

It reminded me of a politely eager child, not *too* interested, but *rather* interested. There might, on this boring grown-up excursion, be inclusions of toys and other treats.

I stood and - less confronted - then waited before him. I didn't have any idea what I should do. This in a man of nearly fifty-one is perhaps reprehensible, or contemptible.

Eventually I said, "I think you've made a mistake, Mr Traskul."

"Do you?" He sounded surprised, innocent.

"I don't have a piano," I said.

"No," he replied instantly with his smile, "but you do have a new dustbin."

Beyond the Crescent, traffic whooshed. It would be better to get to the high street. People were more involved with each other round here, not like the milling herds of inner London. Witnesses, even help, might be forthcoming.

I started to walk on and as I'd anticipated, he fell at once into step with me.

"I had a fascinating journey down," he said.

I said nothing.

He went on airily, striding, the bag swinging on his shoulder full of God knew what. "The train broke down near Lewisham. We sat there for about half an hour. Then crawled. Or I'd have been here much sooner."

I couldn't contain it. I said, "But you were here last night."

"Was I?" He turned the charming smile on me again, I felt it beamed against the side of my face. "Are you sure?" I hadn't been. Now I was. "Of course, despite the slow train, I was here quite early. *Did* you like the dustbin, by the way?'

"I have a dustbin." I thought, *Shut up, don't respond.*

"Well I reckoned you did. But I needed something to put the beer in."

No, I had to speak. I sounded flat and level. "How did

you know where I lived?"

He laughed. It was a spontaneous, melodious laugh. "How'd you think?"

And how *did* I think?

For a moment I considered the Web. After all I had a website, Harris had arranged it. And you can find the address of almost anyone now, seemingly, by a strategic search in hyperspace. But he didn't know my name. Or *did* he?

"I haven't any idea."

"Well, try to guess. I shouldn't make it *too* easy for you. I don't think I should."

We passed the last house in the Crescent. Here was the wide road with its cars and bikes, and people on the pavements by the frontages of shops. The crossing twenty feet further on was making its fretful hurry-up beeping, and women with children and shopping crossed both ways at once, in an unwieldy dance.

I halted again. "Mr Traskul..."

Predictably: "Joseph. Not Joe, if possible. We'll come to nicknames later, maybe."

"Mr Traskul, why have you followed me here? Why are you here? What do you want?"

Making my stand in the busy street reminded me immediately of my father meeting me unexpectedly from Chaults, of suddenly extricating myself from the attentions of the bullies with a "Leave me alone!" and hurrying to the shelter of a parent. Later when I explained to him the bullying, he said, regarding me with kindly seriousness, "Now, Roy, I can't always be there. You must learn to stand up for yourself. If they think you're afraid, it won't stop." I was twelve.

He faced me, seeming slightly puzzled.

"I followed you because I got on the train. I'm here to see

you. What do I want? Same as former answer: To see you. "

"*Why*?"

"It's a surprise when someone wants to see you, then?"

"A complete stranger. Yes."

"Haven't you *ever* met a complete stranger who wanted to see you again? That's a shame. But there's always a first time."

A police car drove by. I wondered if I should hail it. I didn't. It was gone. No doubt they'd have ignored me in any case.

"I'm not gay," I said. I detest this label, although not the fact of homosexuality.

"Well nor am I, if you're asking. At least I don't think so. You can always get a surprise," he said, (that word *surprise* again). "Mate of mine, couple of years ago, plenty of women, and then one day he finds himself going mad about a guy in the Stock Exchange. I think they're in the South of France, now."

I tried to keep my bearings.

I said quietly and firmly, "I think you should go back to town, Mr Traskul. Thank you for the dustbin and the beer. If I owe you any money for them..."

Now he burst out laughing. "*That'll* look good. You slipping me twenty pound notes."

"I'm not rich. This really won't be worth your efforts to..."

"Well I didn't think you were rich. I'm sorry but you don't *look* rich. I'm not rich either. So, right. Where are we going?"

A woman barging past with a pushchair jarred into me. Joseph Traskul looked at her mildly.

I said, "I can give you the contents of my wallet. And my mobile phone. But it isn't new and probably not your kind of thing."

"But I like all *kinds* of things," he reassuringly told me. I therefore reached into my jacket and he said, "No, I *don't* want your phone. I *have* a phone - *regardez-la!*" And he flipped out of his shoulder bag a steel-blue mobile that might have come on the market that morning. "Tell you what, let's go into that cafe over there. I'm bloody starving. I'll buy you a coffee. We can discuss this. Will that do?"

Something in me gave way. He must have seen it. I said, "If that means we get this sorted out."

"Course we will."

Together we crossed at the shrilly belligerent crossing.

The cafe, which is situated in the bakers and serves fresh-baked bread and every type of English breakfast, welcomed me with the normal cheery "Good morning!" They seemed pleased I was with this nice young man, be he nephew, long-lost son, or rent-boy.

We sat down at the far end beyond the coffee-maker.

The girl came over at once.

"Two coffees," he said. He smiled one of his endless variety of smiles, charming her, or playing he charmed her while she, perhaps used to it all, played at being charmed. "And can I have the full English, with wholemeal toast, no butter, and extra fries."

I thought sullenly, *I'll be paying for that, whatever he has said.*

Through my mind, influenced by so many of my plots, flitted the idea I might poison, or at least drug him. But I had nothing suitable on me, the aspirin were at home.

We sat in silence, his companionable, until she put the coffees before us.

"Well," he said then, "what do I call you? If you're nervous just make up a name. But you do know mine."

Is it only that I had been in some ways so rigorously brought up? I remember Lynda once telling me she had often given invented names to unwanted men who pursued her, though how many *had* pursued her was debatable. But my given name is common, and anyway he might know it. How else had he located the house?

"Roy."

"Roy." He rolled it round his tongue. "That means King, doesn't it?"

Did it? Maybe. *Roi*, Roy...

I tried the coffee. It tasted like nothing; usually the coffee was good here. Even so I hoped it could steady me. "Mr..."

"Joseph."

"If you prefer. No one does anything for no reason at all."

"Perhaps they should."

"Are you saying you've come after me like this simply because you thought you *should*?"

He smiled.

I thought, *He is mad. Possibly he's escaped from some lunatic establishment.*

Given that premise, I could only humour him.

But what was I to *do* with him?

If he refused to leave me alone, I would have to give him the slip somehow, and then run to the nearest police station. I wracked my brains. Harris might have helped but Janette wouldn't. There was nobody else. I heard again the voice of my helpful father, *If they think you're afraid.*

"All right, then," I said, and smiled at him in turn. "The breakfast here is good. You'll enjoy it."

"Will I?" At once, that ironic edge of danger, of challenge in his voice.

"Well, I hope you will. Why don't you tell me something about you?"

"You first."

A knot of sheer anger was forming in my gut. I ignored

it. "Very little to tell, I'm afraid. My wife and I..."

"You're not married," he interjected instantly. It was not a question but a statement.

Jovially I answered, "I'm sorry, Joseph, if you somehow didn't discover that one important item about me. I *am* married. "

"Then where is she?"

"She's out this morning. She'll be back for lunch."

"And what's her name?"

"Lynda."

"Right. But she wasn't there last night, was she?"

"How can you possibly know she wasn't, if you weren't here yourself last night? I believe you said you arrived only this morning."

"Actually I don't think I did say that. Sorry, Roy. I haven't lied. But *you* have, haven't you, saying you have a Lynda."

"Lynda was away last night, staying with her elderly mother. She will be back home later this morning."

"Well I look forward to meeting her."

"No, Joseph, that isn't a good idea. Lynda's mother hasn't been well, and anyway..." inspiration - "my son and his girlfriend will be coming back with her."

Joseph Traskul widened his black glowing eyes and said, "If I didn't know you better, I might *just* believe you."

"But, Joseph, you *don't* know me better."

"Want a bet?"

The girl came up then with the large oval plate piled with breakfast. She laid it all out in front of him, and with the extra chips and toast the table became crowded. I moved my coffee back to make room.

This time he didn't thank her. He had eyes only for the food.

He did seem genuinely extremely hungry. I wondered if

he was.

He plunged in knife and fork and began to eat, quite couthly but fast.

"I'll just go and pay. Get it out of the way."

The rhyme now was lost on me.

He murmured, an assent.

I took my chance. I got up, went to the counter and paid the bill, and all the while he never once looked up that I saw.

That done, I turned smartly and went straight out of the door.

Outside a boiling panic filled me. I didn't even look back to see if he was already up too and on my track. Pure luck - the crossing was already working. I ran across. I ran back along the road and into the Crescent.

I am not especially fit, certainly not athletic, but being thin gives me some advantage. I made it all the way through into Old Church Lane and, gasping, along to my gate. Only there did I look behind me. No one now was on my track.

Through the front door I rushed, locked and bolted it.

I checked every window, and the back door. The day was warm again but nothing could be unsealed.

I stood in the hall and picked up the phone. This time I did call 999.

IX
('Untitled': Page 124)

THE clock on the ancient tower above the Artisans' Quarter was striking leadenly for midnight, and not a creature, asleep or waking in the great City, did not hear it. Its deadly voice entered dreams, entered reveries and fevers, and bats circling the ruined cathedral on the Hill of Kolosian, combered in a cheeping wave away into the dark. The moon had set. The end of its light had a sombre finality.

Vilmos had left the bed of the whore Shosa. She was quite dead, he had taken care to see to it. Despite the fact he knew she had had little choice, he permitted no woman to betray him.

Her blood had dripped down upon the floor, but by now, an hour after the act of murder, its movement had ceased.

Vilmos washed his hands and face in the basin. The night was very hot and now, as the clanging of the clock came to an end, its ominous weight seemed to increase, heavy as a stone lid upon the City.

No one met him as he descended the stair. From the door the old toothless portress had gone off about some affair of her own.

Outside in the alley no lamps were visible, only the thinnest starlight. Beyond opened the Street of the Silver Workers, and even there only occasionally the narrowest of illuminations was revealed between ill-closed shutters.

Vilmos bent and drew up an empty bottle from the cobbles. With a sudden unpredicted motion he flung it violently against the darkened window of the tailor, Mirk, who had cheated him.

Thereafter Vilmos did not break into a run. He sauntered

50

on along the thoroughfare, and indeed no one appeared to detain or upbraid him.

It was not until he had got on to the Flavel Bridge that Vilmos once again paused. Here he stayed some while, staring over at the blackness of the wide river, which poured on the northern side down to the City from the far mountains, and westerly swam away towards the port and the sea. There was little traffic on the water at this hour. A solitary boat had anchored about a quarter mile downstream, and a man's shape could be detected standing up in it, perhaps fishing, or at some more sinister task. The nearer bank was thick with houses and hovels of the meaner sort. Directly across the bridge lay some open land, and there Vilmos thought he glimpsed some things moving skittishly. They reminded him of large pale hunting hounds at play.

Then another came from the alleys and walked out on to the bridge towards him. It was Reiner, with his book under his arm.

"What are you doing here, Vilmos? Go home, for God's love."

"And why are *you* here, eh? To read your book?"

"I'm wanted at the Master's house."

"You are, and *I* am not?" Vilmos was astonished and in his arrogance slapped Reiner across the chest.

Reiner jumped back and the book fell to the bridge with a thud. "There's blood on your shirt, Vilmos! What have you done?"

"Amended something."

"You are *mad* - you are *mad...*"

"No, I am very sane tonight. Come, let's go to the Master's house, and ask him if I am not. Do you see those pale things running about over there? What are they, do you think? I believe they are the ghosts of dogs."

FIVE

The policeman I spoke to was the desk sergeant, and as I had predicted he would be, he was. After a brief recital of my fear that I was being pursued for reasons beyond my knowledge, he asked what exactly the young man had done. He listened. He said, "So this stalker..." his term not mine, although at once the word gained a resonance for me, "has followed you from a pub, come to your house, bought you, you say, a *dustbin*," an emphasis there, "and some beer. And you have bought him breakfast."

A short interval ensued.

I was about to speak when the sergeant went on. "Has he actually threatened you in any way, sir?"

I answered truthfully, "Not as such. But he won't leave me alone."

"Is he there now, sir?"

"No."

"Then perhaps he's got bored, sir. Or he's decided the breakfast was enough. It was a big full English, you said. Sounds very nice."

"But what am I to do if he comes back?"

The policeman sighed. His voice altered and became unpleasantly convivial, demonstrating he had absolutely nothing against my sort. "Well, if I was you, sir, I'd pay him off and tell him to get lost before the wife catches him."

I stood, nonplussed by the inevitable inference he had taken.

He ended, "Thank you, sir. Have a nice day."

After the police I tried Harris's number again. This time a perky P.A. answered. She belonged to Janette, of course.

Janette was staying at the house in Hampshire while Harris sorted out his father's affairs in Spain. However, right now, Janette wasn't available, could the P.A. assist me? Obviously she could not.

After *this*, I went through an inventory of any person who *might* be able to assist, but as I had decided earlier, there was no one. The few non-business friends I now possess are of the acquaintance variety, and the males among them are my age or older, either skeletal or overweight, with diabetes and heart problems, or simply doddery.

I was on my own. The place I have been most often.

Every ten minutes or so I was going round the house, glancing from windows, out at the street, down at the side path and across the garden (where the dustbin still maintained its sentry post) to the alley to the back. I even scanned the frontal oak trees and the fir at the rear. Joseph Traskul, like Vilmos, seemed quite capable of physical feats, such as climbing up into trees. He must have scaled the back fence after all, toting the bin.

Belatedly I wished I had modernised my security. The locks and bolts and the temperamental burglar alarm were all I had. And I had noticed the alarm hadn't gone off when I let myself back in this morning, though I had fumbled in my haste.

At lunch time I checked the fridge and freezer. I don't eat vast amounts, and I had reasonable provinder for a short siege.

I made myself a quick omelette and drank some tap water. I checked my potential armament, which quite impressive, as in most homes it is, if ever analysed. Years of penning my usual kind of book had taught me quite a lot about what can be utilised, and even to some extent how. But I'm not a violent man. To describe a killing and a death

neither excites nor upsets me. But the idea of doing it myself
is still as alien to me as the thought of landing in person on
the moon. Even so, we recall, men have landed there.

I put a couple of meat knives, a screwdriver, hammer,
and a small drill and some other stuff, on the kitchen table,
which by now I'd pushed up against the back door. I'd let
the blind down over the side window of the kitchen, and
stacked up pans in the sink, both to impede an entry and to
make a noise. He would have to break the windows
anyway. That would be enough.

On the credit side, if I ever felt able to sleep again, I never
sleep for long unbrokenly, nor very deeply.

At the other windows on the ground floor I drew other
curtains. The lower storey grew dark and menacing.

How long would this go on?

The telephone still worked. I kept testing it. Even if it
failed - tampered with in some way - I had topped up the
mobile and recharged it only yesterday morning. On the
other hand, if I called them again the police might not
bother. My sergeant had plainly concluded I was an ageing
queer who had had a tiff with his young lover or not
properly recompensed a male prostitute. They had more
important things to see to.

I made some coffee, and having parked the hall table
against the front door and laid various bits and pieces by the
curtained windows to announce entry, I took myself
upstairs.

The computer switched on, I checked for emails. There
were none.

I turned to the notes for the new dry little novel. Sat there
staring at them.

Was I being a complete fool about all this?

The phone in the hall rang at 3.07 p.m. It's handheld, and
when I work upstairs I bring it with me. I wondered if the

police had decided to contact me and quiz me about wasting police time.

"Hello."

"Hello, Roy." he said.

Christ, his voice, so soon, was entirely unmistakable.

What to say? *Who is this*? Or break the connection. Break it, and unplug the phone?

How had he got the number? He could *not* have got the number unless he had found out my second name. And there was no way on earth he could have. Or maybe there was, that thing about searching the Web - every house shown on some sort of map, every name, even the most obscure, locatable somehow...

I hadn't spoken. So he said, gently, "You're asking yourself how I got this number?"

I swallowed. "Yes. I was."

"Shall I tell you? You really ought to work it out for yourself, Roy, shouldn't you? But then, you still don't grasp how I found your house - or have you deduced that?"

Deduce. He knows me. He knows I write detective stories. Is *that* it? But I write as R.P. Phillips...

"I have," I said stolidly, "been in touch with the police."

"Really?" I could hear his smile, all the way along the wire.

"They suggest..."

"If only you knew, Roy, how pointless all this is, on your part. I have become *interested* in you."

Apparently he too understood the police would think this situation irrelevant. But how could he be sure? Perhaps - had he done this sort of thing before?

"Interested in what way?"

"Well, human interest, you know, Roy. No such thing as a dull person. What is that quote from the German – '*scheinst*... *And how the dull shine!*' Bernhardt, isn't it?

Actually a Jewish philosopher, living in Germany. I'm sure you've heard of him."

"No. "

"There, you see, I could introduce you to his work."

"Tell me how you got the number."

"I'm just round the corner. It's taken me until now to digest that amazing breakfast. I'll be with you in..."

"No. You won't be with me in anything. Stop this now. I've told you about the police."

"Oh. That."

I cut the connection.

I sat there. I was imagining him scrambling ably over the fence, tapping out the window with a hammer and brown paper so it made no appreciable sound. I had never had the windows properly double-glazed. A cat could get in if it really wanted.

I went downstairs, carrying the phone, and with the sharpest of the knives I had previously selected.

From the front window I peered out, between my mother's heavy Dralon curtains.

The day had clouded over, adding to the indoor murk. The blonde woman from across the street, No 73, was standing on her front lawn, staring despairingly at her poodle, which was performing the first syllable of its breed name in the grass.

Could I signal to her? It would be useless. She and I anyway had never exchanged more than a polite grunt.

I waited rigidly for the phone to go again, but it didn't. Nor did he appear.

At this juncture I made a resolution. I pulled the phone plug out.

Instead I tried my mobile. Thank God, no sign of unknown calls, no *private numbers*.

I thought of Harris up to his eyes in Dad's Death, and

considered he had, in all the thirty odd years we had known each other, never given me the number of his personal telephone or mobile. Harris too was not a friend. He could, would, do nothing.

I was very angry by now. I was frustrated, jittery, at the end of the proverbial tether.

Probably, I thought, he will get tired of this. And also, if he *has* done this before, perhaps he does have a criminal record. For example, if he had done this to a *woman*, the police would have been far readier to intervene. The name Joseph Traskul - it was much too dramatic. It could well be an invention, and each victim would be offered a different one. I hadn't described him to the police - I don't, in my ordinary fiction, go in for a lot of description, it slows the action down... But I had his letter - handwriting and DNA. I went straight to the kitchen and got that and in that moment the doorbell went.

Naturally I'm not brave. I nearly jumped out of my skin. Which has to be one of the truest analogies ever coined.

The bell went once, then twice, then again and again. And then the letter box flapped up; I could see the slot of light between the table legs of my barricade.

A voice called briskly through to me. "Roy. Are you all right in there? Can you hear me, Roy? Can you answer?"

It wasn't *his* voice.

In the shock of relief I couldn't think for a second *who* the hell it was. Then sense returned and I knew.

"George - yes, hang on." It was my attached neighbour from 72.

"Oh, that's good. You're all right, are you? Only..."

"Hang on, George. *Don't* go away." I got to the door. I was numb with the release of tension.

"But all your front and side windows are blacked out..." George insisted, anxiously harking back to the war years I so wisely missed, "and..."

"I'm fine." I dragged the table away.

George is old, about seventy-nine, eighty maybe. We'd exchanged a few pleasantries, the odd pint of milk or piece of advice on electrics or plumbing. His wife, Vita, once brought me a slice of the delicious cake she'd baked for his seventy-seventh birthday, after I politely cried off the party. But now George, perhaps, was an ally, a character witness. Too old to involve with a stalker, he might still make an impression on the Bill.

As I undid the door I heard him reassuringly murmur something outside to Vita, saying it was all right, no need to be upset.

And I felt very sorry to have worried them both, these sprightly fragile pensioners. Then I opened the door and there they stood. George, and behind him Vita, with both her hands clasped round the right hand of the man beside her, who was a strained, almost tearful Joseph Traskul.

"Oh thank God, Dad," he exclaimed. "I really thought this time you were dead!"

SIX

Having raised the blind, he stood in the kitchen, looking at the pans and bottles erected in the sink to bar his entry.

He seemed to take my precautions quite seriously. He appeared to be considering their value, giving them marks out of ten. As if I'd asked his opinion.

Naturally too he had seen the knives. Not the smallest one, however. I'd slipped this some while ago in my trouser pocket. It had a leather cover on it. God knows what it was for or if my parents had ever used it.

Finally he said, "Should I be flattered?"

"You should be somewhere else."

He smiled. He was, is, always smiling. Yet these smiles do not seem to be gratuitous ever. If I were writing this as an invented manuscript, stylistically I would need to edit some of them out. But then I'm not, this isn't a book.

At the front door he had leapt forward and grabbed my shoulders in a sort of abortive hug.

I tried to say to George round the lean, tall back of him, "Call the police, please, George. This man is insane." But George and Vita were beaming and George now had his arm about his wife. Relief, actual joy at our refinding of each other, his and mine, son and father, had made them both take on that look of sheer youth of which only the ageing or the old are ever capable.

They also looked incredibly and alarmingly frail. One swipe from Joseph's arm might snap all their brittle bones in two.

Besides he was already pushing me, friendly and determined, back into my hall, coming in after me. He called over one shoulder as he went, "Thanks so much. *Thank* you both. It's OK now. Don't worry, I've known about these moods of Dad's since I was fifteen. We'll be fine now."

And George gave me a little kind, rather cautious wave, and Joseph shut the door.

I wanted to punch out his lights, as used to be said.

But I'm no fighter in any area, let alone a physical one. He'd only floor me, and any puny blow of mine might make him worse.

He wasn't holding on to me now. I turned and walked briskly on into the kitchen.

He walked behind me, amiably saying, "It's dark down here."

And then there we were, him letting up the blind, calculating the barricade of the kitchen table and my mother's stainless steel pans in the sink.

"I don't think that would keep anyone out for long."

The verdict. He sounded quite regretful.

"No."

"But then why would they break in?"

I just looked at him.

He turned and sat on the kitchen table. "You haven't got a drink, have you?"

My mind raced. I thought, Yes, ply him with beer from the fridge and then some whisky, get him pissed. It might work. I could powder some aspirin or paracetamol, the ones with codeine, in his later drinks. This might be an answer.

"All right." I said, careful not to seem too eager. "What did you have in mind?"

"Cup of tea?" he winningly asked me.

I saw, or thought I did, he was well aware of any other plans I might have. If he had done all this before, presumably things had been attempted.

I filled the kettle from the tap and switched it on. As I was setting out a mug and so on, he said, "You ought to use a filter."

Try to be normal, if reserved. Treat him like a minor annoyance, nothing too much.

"The water here is all right. They replaced the pipes last year."

"Well, I wouldn't trust it, but there."

I wondered if he would have some problem with the tea bags or milk - but he didn't. He didn't want sugar.

When I handed him the mug he gazed at it, examining it scrupulously. I didn't think he was already checking for attempted drugging. He seemed curious, as one is sometimes about another person's things. This was confirmed.

"I thought you might still use a cup and saucer."

"How do you know I don't?"

"Well I don't know. Maybe you keep mugs for visitors only." He tried the tea. "That's good."

My mother had always stuck to the cup-and-saucer method. After her death my father did too. One of my last most tragic memories of them, before she died, was of her lying in her hospital bed and saying to him sadly, "I do miss my china. Isn't that silly?" A nurse had brought them both a cup of hospital tea. Me too, only I couldn't swallow it.

I wanted only to escape. But I could do nothing to help her except remain at my post, with him. We used to go to the pub when visiting hours ended, or later in an interval when they had extended the visiting hours indefinitely. This is a strange and awful thing. He was with her when she died. Not me. I had had to go to the lavatory. When I came back he said, "Look, she's sleeping really peacefully now," and I thought he knew, but he believed she *was* asleep. I went and got a nurse, let her tell him. She held his hand while he cried, but he was very quiet, didn't want to distress this kind nurse holding his hand when she was so busy.

That came back to me with a terrible immediacy as I stood there and Joseph Traskul sat on the table and drank the undrugged tea.

I wanted to kill him in that moment.

The first moment I ever truly wanted that.

I averted my eyes, in case he could read them.

Outside a pigeon had perched again on the black dustbin. It seemed to be inspecting the earlier pigeon dropping. Was it the same pigeon, come back to evaluate its own previous artistry?

I felt tired. I sat in the chair.

He'd finished the tea. He put the mug down on the table and said, "Did you figure it out?"

"What?"

"Any of it. What you were asking me over the phone."

"No."

"But you realise what happened next door?"

"You said you were my son and I was your father, and I had moods during which I drew the curtains in the daytime and - I assume - might be likely to attempt suicide."

"Close enough. I thought a son-father relationship would be more compelling than the uncle-nephew scenario you foisted on me in the pub."

"That was true. You do look a bit like him. Less and less the more I see of you. He wouldn't behave as you have, either." I had decided to keep my army of invented relatives about me.

But he only said, "You don't have a nephew, or if you have you never see him. You don't have a wife."

"I have a wife."

"But she's still away."

"Her mother has been taken to hospital. I'm supposed to go over too."

"But you won't be, will you."

"Won't I? I'm your prisoner, am I?"

I thought he would laugh this off in his inappropriately urbane way, but to my dismay he didn't. As with the pans, he seemed to be considering what I had said. "Are you?" he asked me eventually. "My prisoner? I wonder if you are."

I found I held my breath. I was irrationally relieved when he seemed to gloss it over.

"But we still haven't established how I found you. Shall I let you in on it, Roy?"

"Yes."

"Tell you what. I will spill all the beans in exchange for another mug of tea. By the way, can I use your toilet?"

"It's upstairs, to the right."

Did he glimpse the spurt of possibility in my face?

If he had, it had died even as it arrived. I had nothing to hand. Though I had carried the smallest and sharpest knife upstairs and placed it in my pocket, I had not thought on my return *down*stairs to bring any tablets. Demonstrably, in spite, of my planning, I could never really have reacted to the notion of his being here in the house with me.

He swung gracefully off the table and almost *loped* from the room. I heard him go up.

One frantic moment I rummaged in my mind for anything in drawers or cupboards. But there was nothing. A mostly dried-up bottle of Peptobismal, the remains of some Cabman's Cough Mixture from January, the cod liver oil tablets I occasionally took - I did think of the bleach under the sink. But I shrank from that. It wasn't only cowardice, but the memory of the disbelieving policeman. I could picture the scene, having described it in various books, the body, the mess and bloody vomit. The police would see the evidence of an unfriendly tea-party, and conclude I had now poisoned my former lover, malice aforethought.

I therefore simply made him another tea and left it on the

table.

Upstairs the cistern sounded.

He came back into the room.

"Impressive," he said. "A bathroom with a loo and a separate loo with a wash-basin. Very sensible, if you have more than two people living together. Which you do, of course, Roy. You and Lynda."

"You were going to explain about finding this house."

"I was, wasn't I. Thanks for the tea. Odd," he hesitated a second, looking down into the mug, "has a bit of a funny taste."

He looked right at me, into my eyes. Although I had done nothing, been *able* to do nothing, my gaze quivered. I said firmly, "The milk's probably going off."

"Or you added something to it. *Did* you, Roy?"

"No. "

"Well, I'll soon find out, shan't I?" He drained the mug and slapped it down again.

It seemed to me this too could only be play. He *knew* I had done nothing at all. He would never have drunk it all if he thought otherwise.

He sat again on the table, swung one leg.

"I followed you from the pub in The Strand. Then I gave you my piano tuner card. Then I walked off. Did you look back to make sure I kept going?"

"Yes."

"How many times?"

I couldn't recall. I began to see and saw also, obviously, I hadn't looked back a sufficient number. "Not enough it seems."

"*Not* enough. There were lots of people about to hide me. I just retraced my steps and then went after you again, only more slowly than you, lost in the crowd. You were perfectly followable. When you turned round we actually passed each other, you never saw it. Then I turned round too. You got to Charing Cross and went in, and soon after onto a platform. Still lots of crowds. The train wasn't in but the time and destination were on the board. I dutifully purchased a ticket from a very pretty Asian woman, then hung about until the train appeared and you got on. Then I went through the barrier and got on the train too. I had a real fight to do it, I can tell you. The carriage was jam-packed."

"What would you have done if the train had been due to leave and I'd run for it? You couldn't get through the barrier without a ticket."

"Well, I might still have found a way to do that. But it's immaterial. I didn't have to. It was meant to be."

"Then what? You weren't in my carriage."

He looked faintly offended. "Of course not, Roy. I just simply pushed my way to the door and checked you weren't yet getting out. I'm tall, six three, I can see over people. And it became easier as the crowd thinned. I don't lie when I say I guessed the kind of station where you would alight. Not the *exact* station, just the type. And when you did, I got out too. Nothing was further from your thoughts at that time than our encounter. Rather wounding really. You didn't look round once and I, once again, merely took my time. You went out over the forecourt and I fell into step about thirty-five, forty yards behind. If you speeded up, so did I a bit. If you went slowly, I went more slowly still. You didn't look round even when you got out of the high street. Lost in your own little world, eh, Roy? The trees were useful in this street. Just coming into leaf. Shade, sinking light. Camouflage. I watched you open your door and in you went. And then I saw the passage running down a few doors up, the one that leads to the alley."

"Supposing I *had* seen you on the platform when I got off the train?"

"I'd have gone up and said hello."

I thought this was doubtless a fact.

I said, "You were in the alley behind the house. I saw you there."

"That's right. And then that fantastic owl soared over. I thought I'd leave us at that, for then."

"You were here all night. Where did you sleep?"

"There's a pub in the high street does B and B. Not bad actually. Though breakfast wasn't up to much, cereal and cold toast. I hate cold toast. How about you?"

"What about the dustbin?"

"I just bought it in the evening, a whim. There was a sort of bargain place still open, some sort of sale. They sell the beer you drink at the pub, so I got you a bottle of that too. Did you enjoy it?"

"When did you put the bin in the garden?"

"About ten to midnight. The pub goes on after it closes, regular den of vice, booze, weed, other stuff."

I thought, *I was awake at ten to midnight. But I didn't hear you. I had the radio on. I often do. Christ. I lay there and you were outside. But I'd known that already, hadn't I?*

As for the pub, I knew its reputation. It did not exactly provide B and B, even though it would, for cash, put certain people up overnight, no questions asked. I wondered if Joseph were into 'weed' or 'stuff', or both. I didn't ask.

I said, "Very well. And how did you get the phone number?

"B.T."

"You knew my surname?"

"Not then. But I knew you were called Roy, or you said you were, and your address."

"You can't be given a number without the proper surname."

"I thought that too. So first I tried your other neighbour,

Ian, the man with a tea-towel over his arm." He meant the house-husband at No 76. "I said, I'm looking for an old friend, short, thin, calls himself Roy Johnston, No 74 Old Church Lane. *Is* this Church Lane? And helpful Ian of the towel said, Oh yes, this is the Lane. Only that's Roy Phipps at 74. And I looked knowing and said, Oh, it's *Phipps* he calls himself now? Sure, said Towelly, looking a bit fazed. I added, slightly uneasy myself, But he *does* still call himself Roy, does he? Sure, said Ian. I could see he was dying to ask me why you used different names, but I thanked him, and then I said, It's really great, I haven't seen him for years. Used to be almost like an uncle when I was a kid. I'll just go and get the beer out of the car. And off I went to phone you, leaving Mr Towel to marvel as he scrubbed his Cinderellarine dishes."

Had it been so basic? It could have been. At any point the scheme could have come unstuck, but it had not.

One had an impression of the fortuitous. That this Fate had been *written*. As in my dream he had said. But I ceased to believe in God or destiny when I was a teenager. No momentous event dissuaded me. A pity in its way. When subsequent horrors did truly befall me, as most of us they do, I had nothing left to curse or turn my back on.

His use of words had struck me. Was that inevitable for a writer? He was generally grammatical, and where not only with a sort of ironic colloquial concession. And *Cinderella*rine. There was a term to conjure with. But all this was a victim's cotton wool, in which I wrapped my awareness in order to accept the unacceptable. I must be wary, not only of the amiable fiend who sat on my table, but also of myself.

Presently we went into the front room.

That was his suggestion.

He pulled open the curtains and dull evening light revealed the room. I found myself examining it, seeing it through fresh eyes. His? The faded rose-pattern sofa and the two chairs, one of which had been recovered for my parents in a plain rose-colour fabric. The blocked-in fireplace with the electric fire. The wall-to-wall carpet, quite good in its day, but that day was long past. Most of the ornaments were gone. I'd given a lot of things to Oxfam. I'm not keen on clutter, and I hadn't been sentimental over any of them. All except the red glass dog my mother had liked so much. I'd kept that on the shelf above the fireplace, with the clock that still worked, although now on a battery.

Joseph went straight over to the dog. And something in me reared up, surprising me with its feral watchfulness, as my moment of wanting to kill him had not surprised me at all.

"That's unusual. It's quite beautiful, isn't it?" He didn't touch. I was ready to shout, perhaps jump at him. But he gave me no cause. He said, "I like things like that. It's old, is it? Victorian, maybe." Then he sat down in the old-new-covered chair. "Everything's very clean and tidy," he said. "I noticed especially upstairs. You don't strike me as domestic, Roy. Not like Mr Towel."

"I have a cleaner."

"Oh, not your wife, then?"

I swore inwardly. Damn him. *Damn* him, after all that he had tripped me.

I said, "My wife does some of it, but she broke her leg last year. I prefer her not to do too much."

"Oh dear. And now she's at the hospital, waiting for you."

"Yes."

"You think I won't let you go?"

"Will you, Joseph?" I used his name deliberately. But to

use it was demoralizing to me, as if I were an extreme arachnophobe forced to say *Spider. Spider.*

"Well not just yet perhaps. I want to get to know you a bit more, first. But why don't you call her? Surely she has a mobile. Explain you may be late."

"Use of mobiles is not allowed inside a hospital."

"True. But couldn't you leave a message? She'll check for messages, won't she? No? Well, it's difficult." He seemed concerned. "I wonder what we can do."

It occurred to me it was fruitless to permit more play to him on this. "Forget it," I said. "She'll think I couldn't make it. She'll probably call."

"Probably. And then you can tell her."

"And what do I say, Joseph?"

"An old friend has turned up and detained you. Or I suppose we could both go to the hospital. Would you prefer that?"

"I don't think either Lynda, or her sick mother..."

"I could always wait outside the ward."

"Joseph," I said, "I don't want you to go to the hospital. I don't actually want you in this house, but here you are. Let's keep to that limit, shall we?"

"What if Lynda comes back?"

"She will of course come back, and my son will be with her."

"And your son's girlfriend," Joseph reminded me helpfully.

"Veronica..." the first name I could now lay mental hands on, "may *not* be coming back. Just my wife and son."

"Your son," said Joseph. "What's his name?"

My mind went blank. Then it cleared.

"I called him after my father," I said with warped truth. "William."

"But it's rather strange isn't it, I think so, that your

neighbours never mentioned your wife to me?"

"Why should they? You were talking to them about *me*."

"Well next door, for example. The old couple. I implied you weren't - quite yourself, shall I say. Wouldn't they recommend we try to get hold of her, your nearest and dearest? They might assume, quite reasonably, if I was your son, I was Lynda's son too."

I didn't reply. What could I say?

Joseph smiled.

Abruptly he said, "Why don't you stop calling me Joseph and use my preferred nickname? I made it up myself when I was a child. Sej. Call me Sej."

Something in me pressed me to ask, "Why Sej?"

For a moment he seemed enigmatic, in possession of a secret, the way children are, when they think they know something important you have no idea of. But he answered at once. "Third and fourth letters of my name, with the capital J placed at the end."

To a psychologist this might be revealing. I am not one.

On the shelf by the dog the clock now showed as twenty past five. He glanced at it. Engaging as a child - again - if not the cunning, demonic child he might - must - have been when a true child he was - Joseph-Sej asked me, "What's for supper?"

I'd forgotten them.

In a way not quite absurd, since I had taken only one, and not gone back for more. *They* were sleeping tablets prescribed by my GP for a particularly bad spell of insomnia three years ago. But that one I took, although I had forgone my nightly single whisky or glass of wine, and I had slept nine hours, made me feel nauseous and rotten for twenty-four hours after. One should flush unwanted medications down the lavatory. Had I meant to? Or had I *known*, on some ridiculous 'magical reality' inner level that, three years after, I might need to have kept hold of them?

They were in the bathroom cabinet, pushed behind the elastoplast and spare flask of shaving foam. Three years out of date, but they would still have a kick in them. They'd better have. They were all I'd got.

Of course it occurred to me he might have seen them. Opening up a personal cabinet would be nothing to one like Joseph Sej Traskul. Conceivably he'd taken the Grande Tour of the upper storey and looked in every closed-off place. Then again these tablets were fairly anonymous, and stuffed behind other items. It seemed to me nothing had been moved.

Preparation was another matter. But as I keep repeating, I write that kind of book. (Which also a police investigation would swiftly dig up. Culpable through prior plotting. At this point I did not care).

Capsules that could be broken would have been easier, but I removed six tablets, and put them in the bath. Then I got in and ground them to powder under the heel of my shoe. Lack of hygiene after all was not a consideration. I kept rubber gloves for my cleaner in a box by the basin. I took one out, scooped up and put the dust of the tablets into the thumb of the glove, tied it off and cut it free with the nail scissors. Into my pocket it went. The rest of the glove I shredded and hid in the heap of socks in the laundry basket. He might investigate there, but perhaps he already had and decidedly it wouldn't be somewhere to search from choice. The last trace of powder I wiped from the bath with toilet paper and then flushed.

Having washed my hands, I left the bathroom and went down.

He hadn't made any objection to my going upstairs. Maybe he kept an eye on the front door. Now he was standing in the doorway of the other downstairs room, reading a book. This used to be a dining-room but for years it's been my library. The book he was reading, or pretending to read, was *Treasure Island*. But he glanced up and said, casually, "You have a lot of novels by R.P. Phillips, don't you? A favourite is he?"

"Not really. People used to give me copies." Both these sentences were factual.

"Detective novels," said Joseph whom I was to call Sej

I said nothing but walked on into the kitchen.

Opening the freezer I removed a couple of steaks. I employ the microwave seldom. It had been a present from Harris one Christmas, the only time he had ever given me a present actually. I'd always been slightly perplexed by it, but it had its uses. As now.

The kitchen clock told me it was five to six. Normally I don't eat until seven, or later.

In my pocket the knife shifted, and the soporific thumb.

He had followed me in and put the book on the table. He watched me, leaning on the units. "Have you read that?"

"What? *Treasure Island*? Yes, two or three times."

"Boys' adventure yarn," he said.

"It's a bit more than that. You ought to try it sometime."

"I have. I couldn't get through it. Perhaps I should try R.P. Phillips instead."

He knew. How the hell - Ah. I recalled the dreary little photo of me, reproduced on one or two editions ten years ago. I hadn't changed that much, only got older.

He said, "You know, you ought to shave your head."

"Really."

"It'd look better. Make you look stronger."

"Oh, I doubt that."

"What are we eating, Daddy?" he asked.

This phrase, his *playful* tone, made my blood run cold. I

thought, *You're having my best Sainsbury's steak and M and S salad and red wine, if I can get you to drink it, with five or six sleeping pills.*

"What you see," I said. "I usually have some wine with dinner. Do you drink wine?"

A smile. "Yes."

"Red OK? It's over there in the cupboard. Glasses next shelf up. Get a couple of bottles. We'll have a glass now. "

"Two bottles. That's lavish."

"I don't often have guests."

If he was wary of this first crack in my armour I wasn't sure, but he lifted two of the three bottles of decentish plonk from the cupboard, and when I handed him the corkscrew he opened one, driving the spike straight in through the cork and the foil wrapper, which is what I usually do myself.

"Just a minute," I said, "before you pour." I got the kitchen scissors and used the serrated part between the handles and blades to slice off the neck of the remaining foil. Lynda had done things like that.

Joseph looked amused.

I said, "Yes, pedantic I know, but sometimes bits of foil go in the wine otherwise."

He poured us a glass each and I let him. I wondered, as I raised mine to my mouth, if *he* had dropped something in it. But I didn't think so. I had to presume he preferred me awake and on tenterhooks.

The steaks cooked and the salad was on two plates. I put knives and forks and mustard on the table, and some kitchen towel for napkins. Oh, gracious living.

We sat down either side, with the table still pushed up against the kitchen door. He hadn't suggested we move it, nor had I. It would, of course, make any escape that way harder to achieve.

The second bottle of wine stood at the end of the table, with the corkscrew beside it; I'd placed the scissors there too.

He had already consumed glass one of the untainted wine. That was excellent. I remembered how he had been in the pub, downing a double gin or vodka, setting the glass ready for more. I refilled his glass.

"Cheers," I said. I made out my swallows of wine had relaxed me a little. It doesn't take great acting, that sort of thing.

"Well, here's to your books," he said. I knew he didn't mean the library.

"You spotted the photo," I said.

"Couldn't miss it. You haven't changed much. A bit less hair that's all."

I learnt early, about twenty-five, to ride the comments on my galloping baldness.

I said, "I'm not especially proud of them, those books."

"Why's that?"

"Oh - I write them like a kind of machine, to pay the bills. I find them quite interesting when I'm writing them. But afterwards - they're hardly profound literature."

"You set your standards too high," he said. "Don't people buy them?"

"A few. Enough I make a modest living."

He ate eagerly and quickly, but in a mannerly way, just as I'd seen him do with the breakfast.

It had been borne in on me by now he wasn't starved through impoverishment, merely had a healthy appetite. He could afford after all to stay at the dodgy pub, which I had heard wasn't cheap. He could pick up on a mad whim, and follow a man, even buy him a dustbin.

This time he refilled my glass, only half empty, as well as fully topping up his vacant own. I'd have to watch that, when we came to the next bottle.

"Funny your wife hasn't called," he said.

It was time to wax a little mellow. I hoped I had calculated properly, but a move must be made.

"I'd better own up, hadn't I, Sej."

When I used his purported nickname, I glanced at him to see how he took it, both the name and my 'owning up'.

He looked smug. He might *not* be a fool, the mad cannot be relied on to be stupid, often the reverse. But he was solipsistic, over-confident - perhaps with good reason.

"So what's the dark secret, Roy?"

"Lynda left me, oh, about seven months ago. That's why my neighbours didn't mention her. As for George and Vita, if they believed you were my son they'd assume you knew, and that perhaps you had some real cause to worry about me, my state of mind. It was after she broke her leg. She met some man at the physiotherapy sessions. I also met him once. A fat chap with a long moustache and mop of hair. He was older than me, too. Nearly sixty. She told me the night she left. I hadn't guessed a thing, but no doubt it wouldn't have mattered. As for my son..." I sighed. I picked up my glass and drained it, and helped myself to more so we could finish the first bottle. "He and I haven't spoken or communicated in any way for years. The last I heard he was in New York."

Startling me, life intruding on fiction, Joseph said, "What about 9/11?"

I stared at my plate, mind racing. Then raised my eyes to him bleakly. "I don't bloody know. We did try to find out but it was too vague. There were enough unanswered questions for parents who *knew* their sons were in one of the Two Towers. I don't think, frankly, William would have been anywhere near. He didn't work, he bummed his way around, in the American sense that is. A waste. My son is a talented artist. He..."

My glass was full, I put it down.

Joseph drained his.

Perfect host, even in sorrow, I looked up and said, "Let's have the other bottle."

Before he could make a move I reached for and secured it. I sat there holding it on my lap as if I had forgotten what one did to open a bottle.

Joseph said, "Fine by me."

"Yes," I said, "yes."

And I put the bottle down and gripped it between my thighs, pulling the corkscrew and scissors towards me.

The top of the bottle was just below the edge of the table. I sat there again, looking down at it, getting the plastic glove-thumb, unseen, from my pocket. Then I took the scissors and put them to the neck of the bottle, then took them off again and lowered them against the thumb on my knee.

"Sorry, Sej. Just give me a minute. The trouble is," I looked up piteously, "you *do* remind me of him - not any nephew, my *son*. He took after Lynda. Dark, good-looking..." How flattered she should have been, the real Lynda, dowdy little thing with her flat brown hair.

But he waited. Although he looked quizzical I had bought just enough time. I snipped the top from the thumb, a tiny slice, meaningless to the uneducated eye.

Then I worked the serration of the scissors on around the bottle-neck, got off the foil, replaced the scissors on the table and drove in the screw.

I did this efficiently, only blinking as if tears were in my eyes.

My hands were rock steady. They amazed me. My legs, gripping the bottle, were starting to shake.

The cork came out. Then, the final pass. I let the bottle

seem to come loose, let it go down as if falling, gripping tighter with my legs while I grabbed for it with my right hand, now well below the table top. And crushed the contents of the thumb into its open mouth.

'Rescuing' the bottle I was able to give it a mixing shake. I plumped it back on the table with a grimace of triumphant misery. Fumbling for a non-existent handkerchief in my pocket, I restored the now-voided thumb.

Then I reached for my paper-towel napkin and wiped my face .

"Sorry. Didn't mean to get emotional."

"You need another drink."

"I don't normally drink much." I leaned over and sloshed the drugged red into his glass. Then I drank some of my own, left from the first pure bottle. I held the glass in my hand, keeping tabs on it now. I stared into it, and watched, distorted in its side, Joseph Traskul aka Sej gulp down half his new wine.

I played with the last of my steak, pushed it around with my fork.

"No. I can't eat any more."

He smiled. "I'll have it."

"Yes, if you don't mind. I hate wasting food."

"You look very pale," he said to me as he picked up the remains of the steak and neatly ate it with his fingers, dipping it in the mustard.

"Yes."

"Well don't worry, Roy. I'm not your son."

"I know that very well, Sej."

"For one thing," he said, wiping his hands, "I don't intend to leave you."

The shock of that, even in these circumstances, thrilled me with horror, as Poe might have said.

But I drank some of my wine and answered, "I don't see

how you can have any interest in me at all."

"You'd be surprised."

He drained the glass once more.

How much of the powder had been in it? Had it diss-olved properly? Had it all sunk to the bottom? So far, he seemed unaffected.

I tried to recollect how long that one tablet I'd taken had needed to become effective. About ten minutes, I thought. And that had been without the addition of four or five glasses of wine, besides anything else he might have had during the day. But he must drink more. I had to be certain. Wonderful. He took the bottle and refilled his glass. Less wonderful, he leaned towards me to top up mine.

I snatched it back.

"No thanks, Sej. I don't like mixing two different bottles in one glass. It can spoil the taste, even with cheap booze."

"What an old fusspot you are," he said, as my father might have said it, if not about this. "No wonder Lynda got fed up and took off with that walrus."

His tactless cruelty, if the tale I'd told him had been true, was predictable. But I smiled and agreed. "He *was* like a bloody walrus. You're right."

He was drinking the wine.

He said, "You're right too. This bottle isn't as good as the first. Bit chalky."

Did he guess?

I didn't react except to say, "Perhaps it's off. Shall I open the other one? That's all I've got." Say No, say *No*, this one is *fine.*

"You try it, see what you think," he said. And he held out his glass straight across the table to me.

He knew. He knew or he suspected.

I reached over and took the glass, and held it to my face and sniffed the wine. There was no suspect smell.

"It smells all right." I would have to taste it now, my God it had enough in it surely potentially to stupefy me, just one sip. But sip it I would have to. I put it to my lips and exactly then his head dropped forward, sudden, without any intent or control. He was asleep, unconscious. The lacuna lasted two seconds and then he raised his head and I observed, licking my lips, "It tastes all right to me. Not the best bottle I've ever drunk, but few of them are."

Did he realise what had happened? He seemed not to. His eyes were heavy but he thought himself apparently only a little pissed.

"Give it here," he said. And he took the glass back, now unsteadily, and once again he swallowed the lot. *Refilled* it, *drank.*

I said, "Let's have some cheese, shall we? Only cheddar, but I've got some biscuits..." I stood up slowly. I said, joking, "I'm afraid I'm a bit drunk. I don't usually have that much at one go."

I watched as his head dropped again, then again sluggishly rose. "Me too," he said distantly. "I keep falling asleep."

"*I* just did," I said. "Maybe we should skip the cheese. There's a camp-bed upstairs. I'm told it's not uncomfortable. Will that do? Maybe we should both get some..."

His head surged down again. Stayed down. His hair curtained his face.

I could hear his breathing, heavy and slow, loud and solid as thick wet steam hissing through a vent.

How much had he drunk? I took the bottle and inspected it. About three large glasses were gone. Just a couple of mouthfuls left in his glass. That should be enough, shouldn't it? Enough to knock him out for several hours, and not enough to kill him.

XI
('Untitled': Page 163)

Black worms slide through
A needle's eye.
Slick with shattered gold

THE crooked stair led up to a lofty attic of the house. As they climbed it a rat scratched enviously in the wall, and water dripped; the Master's house stood close to the river.

The general assembly had already gathered.

In the uncertain candlelight, Vilmos saw many faces he knew and besides, as sometimes happened, a couple of persons quite unknown to him. All would be sworn to the secrecy of the Order. Some would still gossip. There had been the occasional tale of events befalling one or two of these traitors. Whatever else, they never returned to the Master's house.

Reiner pushed through the throng.

"What will happen, Makary?"

"Who knows?" Makary shrugged. "There has been a summons. Here we are."

"How did his summons find you?"

"At the Tavern of the *Golden Grapes*. A boy brought it." Makary said to Vilmos, "Look at you, you disgrace. Your shirt's dirty. Is it wine or blood?"

"Blood. I fell down and cut myself."

None of the men in the room had donned the ritual robes brought out for particular meetings. None of the rare incenses burned. This anyway was not the Chamber of Revelation. That lay behind a hidden door far down in the creaking, river-damp timber warren of the house.

Vilmos said, "No summons was sent to me. Why do you think that was?"

Makary said, "The Master's messenger failed to find you. You're elusive."

"Or have I been excluded from our fine fraternity?"

"That's not for me to say."

Makary turned his back on the poet, went to a long wooden table and took up one of the greenish glass goblets, ready-brimmed with an oil yellow wine.

Vilmos also took one of these. He raised it to his lips, while his mind went on with its inner task.

> *And she lies red among the lilies*
> *Of her sullen sheets,*
> *Her sapphire soul hung wry-necked from a beam.*

A dark curtain shifted. The Master had entered the attic, and deep silence filled the air like river fog.

Slowly raising his right hand as if at first, priestlike, to bless the company, the Master pointed directly at Vilmos.

"Step forward."

"I?"

"None other."

Vilmos smiled and swung, seemingly carelessly, through the crowd of men, which drew back from him, staring with all its eyes.

"I present myself, Master."

"Take this," said the Master. He extended his left hand, and now held before the poet a broken shard of stannum tin - whose original source or purpose was no longer apparent.

Vilmos accepted the object.

He found it very cold to the touch. The contact reminded him instantly of some memory he believed he had never accrued, concerning a garden by night, with vines crossing an arbour and white stars far beyond.

"Lean closer," said the Master.

Vilmos obeyed.

The old man's bearded mouth approached his ear and the Master whispered solemnly, without emotion or any energy, "You are accursed. The Arch Beast, Satan himself, has singled you out. Take yourself away now. In one hour, return. Come to the little side door above the river. You will be granted admittance. Ask nothing. Go. *Return*."

SEVEN

Her flat was the smallest I've ever seen in my life. It was the flat of a doll.

One entered and was in a narrow hall, that angled left in front of a red and white kitchen about twelve feet by six, and on to a sitting-room about twelve by nine. To the left at the start of the corridor was first a bathroom and then a bedroom, also both very small. The bedroom window, since her flat lay at the end of the block, ran ceiling to floor and looked out on the concrete hind roof of the Co-op, and the iron stairway from the flats above. She too had 'nets'.

The oddest thing in the flat was the wallpaper. It had been there, Maureen assumed, for about twenty years, and was autographed with various blotches and scrapes, but in the hall, sitting-room and bedroom, it was all virtually the same: a tiny pattern of French *fleur-de-lys*, orange in the hall, dove-grey in the front room, pale blue in the bedroom.

Maureen didn't work for the Co-op. A friend had found her the flat; a male friend, I believe. She worked in Woolwich at Fernes, on the lingerie counter. My mother had been used to shop at Fernes. I think I'd been in the shop too, although perhaps obviously not in Maureen's section.

Aside from the bedroom I came to know the flat quite well. Sometimes on my day off in the week, she would have her half day. We would eat lunch in her kitchen and spend the afternoon in bed, eat supper, or make toast off the gas fire in the front room, watch TV, kiss and cuddle and drink gin. Have an early night.

The piano was in the front room too. That is where I heard her play and sing. I will admit, the first occasion she announced she'd play to me, I had been rather concerned.

As I've said, my father was an all right if not inspiring pianist. As for any singing, I had had at least one grim experience of the impromptu turns of friends in pubs, when a piano was present. It was pretty awful, if not much worse than the fiascos perpetrated by modern karaoke.

So when Maureen sat down and skimmed off a piece of Debussy, flawlessly, beautifully, my already engaged heart lifted like a kite.

She didn't sing to me until I'd known her nearly two months. When I heard her voice I wished I had been able to marry her, was *worthy* of marrying her. This is a fact. But then, I was young.

I was never in love with Maureen. But did I love her? I believe so.

And sex with her was what sex should be.

She *enjoyed* sex for its own sake. She made no secret of that. She'd picked me up that night because the fat man, to whom she referred only as *that bugger Reg*, had let her down. She said I had *'Something'* she liked, something she 'took to'. But if I am scrupulously honest I must suppose 'anything in trousers', i.e. reasonably OK and equipped with male genitals plus a will to use them, would have done. But she was kind, too. She once said to me she had never had a kid and I cheered her up, not that I, she hastened to add, was in anyway *like* a kid to her, but my youth she valued. "Keeps me young," she said, "being with you young ones."

She had a lovely body. Not anything like any model girls, heaven forbid, all tightness and bones. Maureen was – voluptuous, I think is the best expression. She was like a day of full summer.

On the mantelpiece over the gas fire in the twelve by nine front room were a few photographs in frames. One of these was of a fair-haired, good-looking man in his twenties, with an unmistakable Maureen, then about twenty too, on his arm.

"That's Graham," she said. "My ex."

They had married when she was eighteen. He was a steelworker and brought home a good pay packet. She hadn't had to work, and had devoted herself to tending the home. But they had wanted children, or had thought they did, and none came along. In the end Graham started on a succession of affairs. She put up with this, she said, because he still brought the pay packet in and slept regularly with her. This was during the miraculous sixties, when sexually transmittable diseases were both less known or, if they occurred, no longer lethal, and well before the universal phantom of AIDs. But it made her unhappy, of course, and in the end the last straw floated on to the camel's back. "Carol," Maureen said. Carol was the last straw. They lived in Charlton by then. *Carol* had lived six doors down, husbandless, childless, mindless, and red-haired. Carol had a russet aura that she displayed regularly to randy Graham, along with endless faulty lights and fridges he could repair, and a lot of flesh. "She just," said Maureen, "kept on smouldering at him till in the end he caught fire."

Maureen was capable of interesting phrases like this one. I confess to storing many of them in a corner of my mind, and using them years later in my work. I'm not sure I could have invented word choices of such significance.

Anyway, inevitably Graham left with Carol, while *Maureen* was left with all the bills and the unpaid rent. Somehow she picked up her life and reassembled it. I once asked her why she kept his photograph. "Same reason I keep my wedding ring, Charlie," (she still sometimes called me that), "part of my life. *My* life. Don't throw the baby out with the water, eh?"

Now she lived over the Co-op and I came to call on her once or twice a week.

She had other callers. I didn't and don't deceive myself. Again, in that era, there wasn't much physical danger that any of us knew of. If danger for the heart, we risked it, one and all.

Maureen encouraged me too with my writing. My parents had never taken any interest: I 'scribbled'. They didn't mind so long as I had a proper job. Actually I am unfair to my mother here. Left to herself I think she might have been not unapproving, in a careful sort of way. If it was my hobby, she would perhaps have congratulated me as she had my piano efforts earlier. "That's nice, Roy." But naturally my mother followed my father's example. People at work I could never have spoken to. There were enough books on the groaning library shelves, no one needed any more written by such as Roy Phipps.

But Maureen was keen to know. She used to get me to read her what I'd done. She would sit spellbound - to this moment I really believe she was - gazing at me, devouring every word with her ears, eyes, and her forthright intelligence.

"Roy - I was on the edge of my seat. Send it - look, I found this magazine advertised in the paper - try them. That really gave me the shivers."

And I would duly send, and duly get back the soulless rejection slip, and Maureen would say, "What do *they* know? You're brilliant. You'll be another Ellery Queen one day, you'll see. Then they can eat their Y-fronts."

Love. Yes, I loved Maureen. In memory I still do. She was my good angel perhaps. Just as he, Sej, must be the bad one.

The first thing I did was haul him off the chair and away from the table. I laid him out on the floor in the recovery position elaborated in so many diary-backs. He was snoring thickly by then.

I had had a set ideal of what must be done and how I must operate afterwards. I hadn't had space to plan beyond it. I couldn't now.

For one thing I had no real notion of how long he might be out.

My success in overcoming him still... *disturbed* me. He had been omnipotent one minute, and now there he lay, at my mercy. I could kill him easily. I saw that. Perhaps I had anyway, but I didn't really think so. He was young and fit, big and strong. He would get over it.

I keep all my important personal documents in a folder in the study, another 'fussy' habit of my father's, rather a good one. (He it was, on the rare celebrations when he drank it, who never liked to mix two bottles of wine in one glass, even the same wine. To me, although I never bothered to adhere to the practice before tonight, this seems to demonstrate a certain common sense. Bottles vary.)

My overnight bag came down from the top of the wardrobe.

I put in what I might need for three or four nights, the ordinary paraphernalia - pants, socks, shirts, toothbrush, shaving kit and so on. Any spare cash I drew from the box. There was only seventy pounds, but I had my cards. My passport and birth-certificate I took, and bank and building society details, including the deeds to the house. Cheque books and other financial extras were added, even the used stubs of cheques and payments to me. I wanted nothing left that he could find.

I don't keep personal letters, the very few I receive. Business emails were mundane enough but too I always delete those. Like several of my species, that is the well over forty-fives, I avoid buying or paying on the net.

From the desk top drawer I took up any discs I'd burned relevant to my work. Among these naturally was the great lumbering tome *Untitled*, plus the notes for the latest 'project'. Despite abandoning my house to God knew what, I selected none of my published books. There was only one I had ever been at all fond of, in retrospect, *Last Orders*, and that was still in print.

Then I set the computer to wipe all remaining data.

I employ passwords for every file, but nevertheless I was taking no chances.

As I've said, I'd had no plan *beyond* my plan. It might all have gone wrong anyway and never reached this stage, since he might have caught me out putting the sedatives in the wine and beaten me up, or worse.

Last prudent thought, I went next door to the bedroom again and took a sweater and a jacket. After that I went out and locked the bedroom door. It had had a key ever since I was thirteen, a perceptive unique act of *politesse* on the part of my parents. But anyone could break down a door, and anyway there was nothing there of any import. The study, with the buzz of complete deletion going on, I left open. I had everything from there either valuable or pertinent to my life. I turned all the lights off and pulled every plug, except that of the machine. Downstairs the same.

In the kitchen my guest snored on. He was quieter now. In sleep he didn't look distressed. He looked very young, softer. Perhaps I'd misjudged his age from his street-wise bolshiness, his very insanity. He could be under thirty even.

Scrupulously I emptied the last wine in the sink and rinsed out the glasses and both bottles and then slung the latter in the bin. I'd previously swilled the remaining sleeping pills down the lavatory; they were well on their way to pollute the sea by now. ("No, officer. He just collapsed, quite suddenly. Perhaps he'd had something before he came here. He did drink a lot of wine. At least six glasses.")

I disconnected the fridge and freezer next. The food, what there was of it, would doubtless go off quite quickly.

I took the sandwich bag from the drawer that contained his note, and added to it the fork he'd used at dinner.

Once I had turned out the kitchen light and the outside light, I picked up my holdall and checked my mobile was in my jacket pocket, which it was. Then, in the hall, I ripped the cord out of the telephone and smashed the receiver on the wall twice.

Going from the house on to the front path I paused a moment, looking up and down. The curtains of 73 were drawn, a rosy pink. Elsewhere I could see the steely flicker of TV screens and, in upper rooms, computers. Outside No 80 the man with the paunch who smoked cigars was indulging in one, and animatedly discussing something with the man with the paunch from No 82, whose wife had made him dig and line the lily pond.

They paid no attention to me. I could hear traffic along the high street, and further off a distant train.

I shut the door but did not double-lock it.

In one of the budding oak trees something stirred, or seemed to. Nothing was visible, even in the denuding glare of the streetlamps.

Turning away, I walked towards the Crescent, and the station.

The Belmont is one of those smaller hotels, and lies in the back-doubles behind Langham Place. It had quite a bit of gilt, and mirrors in the lifts, and jazzy carpets that to tired eyes resemble a dropped jigsaw, but it was very comfortable. I had stayed there quite a few times after various obligatory publishing do's. Now and then a particularly flush publisher had even covered my expenses there, although never, it had always been stressed, my bar bill. But my bar bills normally amount only to a glass or two of wine and perhaps a whisky; I'm so far able to pay them myself.

They remembered me at reception. I'd been lucky, for at this time of year usually they're full up.

"Two nights, Mr Phipps?"

"It may be three. I'm not sure at present."

The smiling girl said she'd make a note, but regretfully cautioned me she might have to move me to another room for the third night.

It was about nine forty-five by the foyer clock. My watch said ten to ten.

When I got upstairs to the small alien luxury of the *en suite* room, smelling of floral cleaning fluids and regularly hoovered dust, I sat down on the bed and let everything hit me like a collapsing wall.

To my appalled distaste I even cried for a moment. But that passed. Then I took out the whisky I had also put in my bag and had a couple of swigs. I'd done what I must. I'd escaped. Now there was time to think. And think I would bloody have to.

EIGHT

"Janette. I apologise for calling so early."

"Eight o'clock? That's nothing for me, Roy, I can assure you. I'm up with the lark. What is it you want?"

Though rather a good-looking woman, she has an ugly, unmusical voice, Janette, which its university-trained accent only emphasised.

"Would it be possible to put me in touch with Harris?"

"'Fraid not, Roy. Didn't you know, his father died? He's had to go over there, and I gather there are some complications."

"Yes, he did tell me something about it."

"Veronica," said Janette. "The *widow*."

"Yes, so I..."

"I really cannot comprehend," expatiated Janette, "how a young woman with so much money of her own can behave in such a peculiar way."

"It must be difficult. But I'm afraid - I have a bit of an emergency on my hands. Or I wouldn't be troubling you."

"Oh, yes." The ugly over-polished voice was now non-committal. It said quite plainly without words, *It's no use at all your telling me or asking me anything. I am not going to respond.*

I took a deep breath and said, "My life may be in danger."

"Good Lord!" She actually laughed. But I had heard and seen her erupt into this type of laughter once before. On that occasion someone at a dinner party had just spoken of finding her dog dead behind a hedge. But while I had, that time, stared at Janette, the friend with the deceased dog had also loudly laughed. "Poor old hound," had laughed Janette.

Would she now say something similar to me? No, it transpired not. "Are you ill?" she snapped with what seemed a kind of anger.

"No. It's nothing like that. I'm being - stalked."

"*Stalked!*" She almost hooted now. "*You? Roy? Seriously?* Who *by* for heaven's sake?"

Before I had called this time I had known any chance of help was slender. Even Harris would probably prove useless. But I had made a mental list of avenues to try and this was the first.

"Please listen, Janette."

"You sound like a schoolteacher, Roy. Do rein it in."

"I'm sorry. But when you speak to Harris - I assume you do speak to him now and then in Spain? - would you please ask him if he could call me, if at all possible. I'm staying at The Belmont in Prince Henry Court."

"You want him to call you in London? From Spain? Oh really, Roy."

"I stress I wouldn't bother him unless..."

"All right. There. I've noted it down." She read back to me the alleged note in a tone that managed to be both scornfully amused and irritatedly impatient: "Roy - *serious* emergency - call at Belmont Hotel. There you are."

I thanked her wanting to throttle her, and put down the phone.

Tish Ackrington, my most recent editor with the White Knife Imprint, took my call immediately.

"Hello there, Roy. Your book's doing awfully well! Really great reviews. Did we send you any? Oh dear, that's too bad. I'll get someone to. What are you up to now? Anything on your little screen we might be interested in?"

Tish was always like this. She seemed to want to cheer you up, promising things, exaggerating. I had been fooled at first, but after the initial contract nothing else ever materialised. I had once tested her with the name of an invented novel White Knife had supposedly already published, which of course they couldn't have. And she had acquiesced gleefully, "Super book! Stayed up all night with that one, couldn't put it down." However. At one of those aforementioned parties, this one organised by WKI, I had heard something about her which might now prove useful.

"The thing is, Tish, I'm doing some research in a certain area and I can't get hold of what I need."

"Oh, that's so tiresome for a writer, isn't it?"

"It's holding the book up rather. It's for quite a big house..." I named the firm, who were only less likely ever to publish anything of mine than to jump collectively from the top windows of their tall chrome building overlooking Hyde Park.

"Wow," said Tish, suitably impressed. "But can't they help you with this research, Roy?"

"Wouldn't you know it, my editor there is on holiday in Egypt for six weeks."

"Oh *God*. Well, Roy, if there's anything..."

"It's just that I do once recall your mentioning you had a friend, who knew someone who was a little bit on the shady side of the law."

A shocked silence. Naturally Tish had never confided this to me of all people. But she had confided it to someone, as it had been discussed as a fact by two or three fairly sober employees at the party. I could hear her now running a scanner over her memory, trying to find out how or why she had ever let slip such a matter to me.

Finally she said, in rather a different way, "Well actually, Roy, my friend - she doesn't see him now. He was rather - well, rather kinky, if you know what I mean." I didn't, and was glad I didn't. She said, "Not the sort of person anyway you'd ever want..."

"It was just for some background. Obviously I'd be happy to pay him a fee."

"Well I don't think - I mean, I really can't help you. Sorry. Oh *Merlin*!" she screamed, nearly deafening me. Either her Arthurianly named male PA had come in, or she was pretending that he had. "Roy - forgive me - Merlin's in a panic. I have to deal with something - big flap. Super to chat. We must do drinks sometime. By-ee."

I tried a few others. Before I could even get on to the act of confession, that was only about three sentences into a conversation, they put me off. Only Lewis Rybourne, my most recent editor at Gates, astonished me by saying, "Don't have a second now, but I'll give you a call next couple of days, Roy. You're at The Belmont, right? Talk soon." He might even do this. But also even one more day might be too late. I ordered room service breakfast, tried to eat it, and started in on my gallery of ageing friends, hoping at least for advice, some ideas.

Stanley had had another heart attack. He was 'all right, doing really well', but still in the general hospital. Matthew was divorcing Sylvia after thirty years of marriage. He was terribly distressed and we had a longish conversation, while the hotel phone bill mounted to frightening proportions, "She's had a lover," he kept saying, "a lover, Roy." And I thought of the fictitious affair of my fictitious version of Lynda. Ed Erskine was drinking again. He told me candidly he never started until twelve noon on the dot. "What else've I bloody got, Roy, eh?"

The immortal, if unvocalised line, *I have troubles of my own*, drove me slowly back towards my starting point.

I went out for lunch. I walked round by Lang Gardens and

into Langham Place, passed the Art Deco facade of Broadcasting House, and negotiated busy Oxford Street.

What a change there had been in London over the years. Elegant places had become squalid, abominations had been done up like the Ritz. By night liquid bars of coloured light washed everything to a succulent epic panoply, and from Westminster Bridge the city resembled, at least to me, the cover of a 1950's Science Fiction magazine.

I ate at the Pasta Post. Or I tried to.

Years ago someone ritually would have asked, "Everything all right, sir?"But now they merely scooped up the nearly full plate, bore it off, and offered me the ice-cream menu.

It was as I was leaving the restaurant that I stopped, petrified, and so abruptly a young man banged into me and with the scathing aristocratic stare of Black Africa, drew aside and stalked on.

I had recalled something after all that I had forgotten and left behind in my house in Old Church Lane, to the debatable mercies of Joseph Traskul Sej. The red glass dog my mother had loved.

Needless to say, that second night I couldn't sleep. Nor had I, the night before. Coming in again I told reception I did indeed want the room for three nights, and they told me, as if I must rejoice, there would be no requirement that I move to another one.

So I rejoiced that I was not required to move. At least sufficiently that they seemed gratified. For even the most superficial overlay sometimes means far more than we know.

Through the hours of the night I absorbed, through my portable radio, the turmoil of the world. I fell asleep near dawn and dreamed I was standing on a London bridge, I'm unsure which - perhaps a compendium of them all. No one was with me. The bridge was totally empty, and the river below, the roads beyond, devoid of all traffic. The lights of London glittered all about and there were many eccentric new buildings; one I recall looked like an apple made of windows, with a tall stalk lit palest gold.

During the time I stood there in my dream I anticipated the arrival of someone - something - I refused to look over my shoulder to see if it had yet come.

Waking fuddled about five-fifty, the thin light struggling to penetrate the protective Belmont drapes, I thought instantly of Coleridge's *Ancient Mariner*, quoted in M.R. James's *Casting the Runes;*

Like one,that on a lonesome road, Doth walk in fear and dread, And having once turned round walks on, and turns no more his head; Because he knows a frightful fiend Doth close behind him tread.

NINE

Showered, shaved and dressed I went down to breakfast the next day. I had decided this would do me good. I forced eggs, bacon and mushrooms down my throat and drank several cups of coffee.

I had made another decision. I was going to the nearest London police station. I was going to tell them everything, and make them listen. I would not mention the drugs I had given him, even so. Hopefully he wasn't dead, and so no post-mortem would reveal their presence or their type.

But *was* he dead?

Was it just conceivable he was? What then?

He would be lying on the kitchen floor of my house, gradually decomposing, as so many had in so many abodes during my lurid tales. Who would believe I'd had nothing to do with it?

I went back upstairs to my room, leaving the Do Not Disturb light on. I thought through all of it carefully. It was very incriminating, but there would have to be some get-out. I was nearly an old man. And I had no record of violence. I wasn't gay, had no record of that either. I paid my bloody rates and taxes - A model citizen, Roy Phipps. *Never trust the quiet ones.*

At twelve noon on the dot, as Ed would have exclaimed, I got up and went down to the hotel bar.

It was another sunny day. Some Americans without apparently a care on earth, were sitting laughing in a corner booth, drinking colas and what I took to be screwdrivers.

A smart woman and man, who looked what one used to call European, were consulting a street map in the corner of a maroon velvet banquette.

"What can I get you, sir?"

I asked for a whisky and soda and hastily added, "No ice, thanks."

The man came back with the whisky as specified and set it on a small white mat.

I looked at that, then into my drink. I was going the same way as Ed. What else had I got?

Raising my glass I drank a healthy swallow, and then gazed through the green and brown bottles along the bar into the shadowy mirror on the wall. You could see the foyer reflected there, a surge of incoming people, luggage on trolleys, a giggling blonde in her fifties, and Joseph Traskul, seated idly and relaxed, in a chair beside a potted palm.

3

It hid a cupboard, the door to the right.

Opened, that revealed an electricity meter, a plastic bucket and a tattered broom leaning sidelong in space. On a wooden shelf were two large boxes of matches, an empty milk bottle from the past, with a candle stuck in it, a London telephone directory with its cover off, a broken terracotta flowerpot.

These things looked to me like the accumulated and forgotten detritus of many occupancies. Even the matchboxes were void when I inspected them.

I had put on plastic gloves by then. The rest of my DNA would have to take its chance. I have never been finger-printed. I have no form. And today anyway, I wasn't really myself.

The other door, to the left, gave on a not unspacious room, probably about fifteen feet square. To the left side a single step went up into an open plan kitchenette.

There was a lot of light in the room, from two front windows, and from the kitchen itself, which had two side windows plus a closed, locked and keyless clear glass door, that led on to a balcony above the street.

A door to the right of the main room showed a narrow corridor, off which lay a bathroom with a suite of an intense murky brown, a bedroom, and a further, narrower enclosure that must be intended as a spare room. These three rooms had back windows only.

Outside the bedroom was a fire-escape, and below the brief back gardens of the terrace, some beautified with small trees and plants in pots, others, like this one, left to weeds and ragged grass.

After I had gone through the whole flat, I returned to the main area, and stared about again.

The walls throughout had been painted white. That must have been at least five years ago. Nothing shows dirt, as my mother had been used to say, like pale things.

The radiators, also painted white, had streaks of metal striped through.

Nowhere was there any carpet. The floors were bare boards. The kitchen space had been tiled but the tiles were cracked, and some loose, coming up as one trod on them. On the electric cooker something had spilled long ago and, over years perhaps, been regularly baked into a sort of laminate. The once trendy units were without pans or tableware.

I found one overhead bulb with a shade. This was in the bedroom. I assumed it *was* the bedroom because there was a bed in it, a meagre double, with a pillow having no pillow-case. There were no sheets or covers. The mattress was nude as the floors.

Each of the windows however had a single flimsy curt-ain, wrapped over the quaint, old-fashioned, now intermittently fashionable rails above. These unhemmed strips of material, could - supposedly - be dragged partly across to offer some privacy.

In the bathroom there was a water glass, the kind one can pick up anywhere. Nothing rested in the glass, or anywhere else. A wall cabinet, a fixture maybe, was vacant but for a dead moth.

Here and there about the flat I found other small corpses, a beetle, a couple of flies, some spiders in sagging webs that had died most likely of starvation. On the window-sill of the spare room a dead leaf. My knowledge of flora is limited, but it seemed to have fallen from a tree that had once been a flaming red. But it had curled together and lost almost all its tint.

By the lavatory in the bathroom lay the single page of a book.

I picked it up at once, put on the glasses I need now for small print, and tried to read the words. But not only was it in a language I failed to recognise, but the Cyrillic alphabet. Russian?

There was a doughy odour everywhere of neglect and inanitian - a word I use only because no editor will ever demand that I excise it.

Throughout the whole of the flat, at least during my first investigation, this was the sum of all I found. There was absolutely nothing concrete that indicated anyone still lived there, came from there, might go back there. Nothing of any sort.

XII
('Untitled': Page 191)

VILMOS was aware that the headache, to which he was often subject, was returning. Since the age of ten he had been its victim, and with the years it had increased its attendance on him. Now it arrived so frequently it seemed in fact it was his constant condition, the days without it being the curiosities. But too, strangely, when he *was* without the headache he quickly forgot it, being always filled by a ghastly shock on its reviving, and a sickened dread.

The pain invariably commenced with a stiffening of his neck muscles to the left side. Soon a burning tension began to fill his skull. Next there was the sensation of a shrill white violin string, tightening and tightening on an unseen peg, between the base of his skull and his left temple. Central to these two junctures, about the region of the parietal lobe, a large and fiery black nail began to be hammered through into his brain.

In youth he had wrenched clumps of his hair out of his head to mitigate this agony with another. Older, he had recourse to alcohol and opiates, which dulled the anguish but could not dispel it. It never lasted less than five hours nor more than sixty. In the latter, long form, it would in any case lessen from about the thirty-sixth hour. He could then feel the white string slowly slackening, melting away, while the hammered nail turned to a dying coal and went out.

This time the headache was Shosa's fault. His anger at her, the effort of slaughtering her. Perhaps even the sight of her beauty sodden with blood.

Vilmos, having once more left the stultifying venue of his

father's house, had gone back via a circuitous route to the house by the river. Only in one place did he pause, rubbing his forehead violently against the angled corner of a building, momentarily to obliterate the claw of the headache in his temple.

But by the time he reached the Master's house, he was dizzy and the string of the demoniac violin had already wound tight.

The river here ran in a wide canal, and the house perched directly above. There was no invented light at all, and only the vaguest hint of starlight. Nevertheless something white was just now floating by under the brink of the house. It might have been a bundle of washing, or someone drowned.

Vilmos turned from it and scratched on the side door.

After a moment a slot appeared. The bloodshot eye of a servant peered out at him. Then the door was opened, and Vilmos entered the house, for the second time that night.

The premises had been emptied of any crowd. Only the three speechless servants remained; two of these were already concealed, and the porter too now slipped off down a narrow dank stair. Vilmos, unbidden but knowing the way, climbed the other stair upward, towards the Chamber of Revelation.

"Enter. No, you need put on no robe. You come to me in a robe of the Devil's, and veiled in the mask of Hell. What is that blood on your head?"

"I rubbed it on a wall. I have the hemicrania that plagues me."

"And your shirt."

"Ah, that."

"Yes, you have murdered again. No, say nothing of it. The act too clothes you. You are clad in the wreckage of the Sixth Commandment. Have you brought with you the stannum you were given? Then stand here. Now we shall see."

The chamber was lit solely by a half score of glims set high up in cups of oil. There were otherwise no windows.

The Master read words aloud from a large book on a stand, then made a single pass in the air with a wand of ivory.

Gradually something began to glow in the centre of the floor, about equi-distant from the Master and Vilmos.

Vilmos had been witness to apparitions in this room before. Most of the Order, which was that of the Indian Mystery, had done so. The society was loosely alchemical in its nature, but deviated strongly in many directions. Although it claimed, as did most such sects, the primary goal of knowledge, to be demonstrated by unlocking the secrets of firstly, the Making of Gold from inferior metals, or indeed filth, secondly finding the Source of Eternal Youth, and thirdly, Attainment of the Power of the Inner Self, these god-like gifts were construed through the spectrum of an Eastern philosophy by the group, at least, called Indian.

On the floor had been engraved the Wheel of life and Death, having to do in Sanskrit with the *Seven Cakras*.

The thing which now manifested evolved within the circle.

Unlike the ethos of the *Cakras* this was a hideous image.

Vilmos stared at it through the agony in his head, and saw it was the figure of a skeletal king, crowned with a diadem of bones that dripped blood. At its back shadowy wings stirred restlessly. Its garments were ragged, grave-clothes perhaps. Through a hole both in the cerements and the being's chest, there suddenly peeked out the head of a lean, black, rat-like creature, whose eyes were like sulphur.

Colours began to burn up in the torso of the apparition. Yellow showed like the rat's eyes in the bones of the lower chest, and a surging muddy amber in its bowels. At the region of the male member a scarlet flower appeared, but a snake's head writhed in it, the jaws ejaculating sparks of poison.

Vilmos raised the cold piece of tin and pushed it against his forehead. For a second the pain sank, then flared to greater pitch. He had perceived that the ruinous and rotted king was none other than himself. It had his face. It too seemed in anguish.

A flash of nothingness filled the chamber.

Dropping the stannum, Vilmos fell forward and knew no more of anything.

TEN

I had thought, or would have done if I had ever compared it to anything at all, that the greatest and most telling shock of my life happened when I entered the hospital room where my mother lay, and my father said to me, in a kind of dreadful hope, "Look, she's sleeping really peacefully now."

In fact it was not. Inevitably I had expected her death, and therefore perhaps that something poignantly terrible would accompany it.

And now too, doubtless, I had in some form expected *this*.

I replaced the glass of whisky, unfinished, on the round white mat.

Through the top of the bar counter I gazed down and down into the abyss.

All about me rational everyday life went on. I remember, someone laughed.

But it wasn't as if they laughed at me, at my predicament. That laughter of theirs was so far removed it came from another dimension.

When I looked up again he was still there, sitting by the palm. He was reading a magazine. He wore black again today, the black jeans, and a light black sweater with a little green dart of something high on the left side of his chest, some logo.

Nobody out there took any notice of him. No, actually one of the women did, a young one with long hair. She looked round and gazed at him a moment, evidently liking the look of him, but not intruding, passing on and away.

What should I do?

There were a lot of people here. Should I grip the waiter

and mutter, *Get the police!* This seemed unreal and useless. Again, who would believe me?

Besides, I had drugged him. I might have *killed* him. Was this phantom definitely there, or only an illusion...? But the girl had seen him too. There he *was*.

Exactly then he glanced up and met my eyes in the bar mirror. (How long had he watched me before I glimpsed him?) He raised his right hand, as he had in the Crescent, a friendly, almost non-committal wave of hello. He didn't get up.

I took the whisky, put it down again. I turned and came smartly out into the foyer.

Should I now walk past? Surely he would follow. The same if I got into a lift. Did he know my room number? Christ, he'd found me here, why wouldn't he?

There was another chair facing his, I think he had drawn it over into that position. I went directly to the chair and sat down.

I heard my voice come out cool and flat.

"Well, Sej."

"Well, Roy," he said. And smiled.

"I'd better explain at once, hadn't I? We both got tired of that last guessing game."

"How you found me here."

"Exactly. I looked in your books, the most recent publication. This very year. Then I contacted the publisher - Gates. I said I was trying to trace a Mr Roy Phipps. I didn't use the landline for this, of course. It didn't seem to work, perhaps because the wire had been ripped out and the receiver smashed. Whoever did that, Roy? You should have got it fixed."

I said nothing.

He said: "I kept insisting that it was vital I speak to

someone about you. I gave your *nom de plume* - R.P. Phillips. In the end, I reached some guy - Lewis something. Lewis Ryburn, that's it."

He had the wrong name. Would that count? I guessed it would not.

"Ryburn said graciously Who is this? I said, Actually I'm Roy's son. I've been trying all night to locate him. I hadn't been, obviously, I'd been asleep. I do apologise for that, Roy, by the way. Falling asleep so boorishly. I woke up on the floor. I'm afraid I also threw up in your sink. That wine - it must have been off." Smiling ruefully now he looked at me. "Were *you* OK?"

I said nothing.

Joseph Traskul Sej went on. "Mr Ryburn was diffident at first. But I explained I'd been expecting you at Old Church Lane and was already there myself, but you hadn't turned up. I gave the address of course so he would see I knew this important personal detail, was an intimate of yours. Then he became quite concerned. He said he had had a call from you and you'd seemed rather - what was the word he used? - *flummoxed*. That was it. I said I knew there'd been some family trouble. *He* said he'd never known you had a family, let alone a son. I said neither had I known I was *yours* until comparatively recently. But we'd been due to meet and I was worried sick. After a bit more of my ham acting he told me you were here. People do let one down, don't they, Roy? My God. You ought to tell the bastards to be more careful of their authors, lucky he only told *me*. It could have been anyone."

I could just picture Lewis Rybourne, intrigued by the story, (old Roy with a son!) and also delighted to shove me off his plate on to this handy other one.

And a son again. I could hear, mentally, how plausible and winning the demon had made himself sound. Even after his sedated coma and resultant nausea.

And he knew he had been drugged. By me. What else? *Who* else?

"How are you feeling?" I asked blankly.

Smilingly he said, "I'm fine. You seem surprised."

"No, I'm not." This was in fact true. Shocked but not surprised.

He said, "Oh, by the way, I brought your mail," and lifting his tote-bag off the jazzy carpet he presented me with two business letters and an electricity bill.

I'd forgotten all about post and what it might reveal to him, but he hadn't slit open any of the envelopes, not even cleverly undone them with steam from a kettle, thereafter resealing them, I knew the tell-tale signs, having experimented with the method for my work in the l980's.

Without saying anything I put the letters in my jacket pocket.

"Where shall we go for lunch?" he said.

More or less just like the first time.

"I can't afford," I said, "to treat you."

"Don't worry. My turn. What's it like here?"

"Expensive."

He laughed. "I get the feeling you think I'm penniless."

Recently I hadn't. I said, "Are you?"

"No, Roy."

"Then why try to move into my house?"

"*Did* I? I thought it was just a visit."

"You mean you'd have eaten the food, finished the wine, and left?"

"I might have. I do have a place of my own. Up here, London. Not bad though not very cheap. Worse thing is the fucking awful music the rest of them in the building play." (I didn't think I'd heard him use a four letter word before.) "I prefer a bit of tuneful jazz - the old kind, Dixie, New

Orleans, or Bach or Handel. Do you like Handel, Roy?"

It occurred to me he had somehow heard Handel playing on my radio that night he unloaded the dustbin, noiselessly, in the back garden.

"Sometimes."

"But in the flats they play rubbish. It gets on my nerves."

Across the foyer, through the glass doors, the slender-pillared dining-room was revving up for custom. The Americans had already gone across.

"What do you think?" he said.

"I don't want to eat with you."

Benignly he looked at me. He said, "Get over the guilt, Roy. I forgive you. It doesn't matter."

I knew. I said, "What?"

"Drugging me," he sweetly said. "Don't be concerned. I'm tough and strong. It takes more than that. I knew you had, anyway."

An insane curiosity took hold of me. I found I leant forward. "Then why..."

"Why did I go on drinking your plonk? Well, I didn't think there'd be enough to kill me."

"There could have been. It could have done."

"No. You know how to judge such things, or Mr R.P. Phillips does. I read one of your books, by the way. *Last Orders*. Really liked it. Well written and no fuss. I guessed who done it, but only three quarters through - and the twist at the end was a stunner. You had me fooled on that. I'm impressed. Why aren't you much better known?"

I thought, as once or twice in my youth I bitterly had, *Because I am not part of the Oxbridge fraternity and have no influence.* But such carping bores me by now, and anyway I've come to see it's more likely I am simply not original enough, don't have enough of the slightly deranged *zeitgeist* of the modern day. Presumably too I never did. I recall one review from a well-known and influential critic, which greeted my twelfth book: "Phillips is dependable, nearly always a pretty good read if never a magnificent one."

This was when something very odd happened.

Perhaps I was already disturbed enough, but the fact he had selected the only published book of mine I personally still rated quite highly, seemed to affect me in a way I could neither express nor explain to myself. I looked at him hard, and seemed to see his face for the first time, handsome and quite ordinary, intelligent even, and couth, nothing in it to display madness or ferocity. I understood even as the feeling washed through me that this assessment was unwise. Everything he had done so far demonstrated ably enough that he was, as my father had once liked to say, off his rocker.

It was then that the woman rushed into the lobby from the street.

She was about forty, quite smart in a dry sort of way, with short thick well-cut hair. But she flew in and then halted, and like one entering in a Greek tragedy, she wore a mask of tears.

We all stared at her a second. Then most of us looked away. The English are famed for their insularity, and constipation of the emotions. Even those Brits of mixed blood and origin seem now to end up in this frame of mind, or heart. One sees displays of violence more often, of sexual passion more often too. But frank human kindness - that thing called empathy - is rare.

He'd turned his head.

In a fleeting gesture he touched my arm with his hand. "Just a sec, Roy." And he rose and went straight to her and stood there, and I heard him ask in a low, gentle voice, "What is it? Can I help?"

She started crying violently and noisily at once.

He put his arm around her, and drew her over to another

group of empty chairs, the whole distance of the lobby from everyone, including me.

Now was my chance to split and run. I couldn't take it. I was riveted. I sat there, reticence gone, and gaped at them.

She sobbed, he held her in his arm, bending forward to hear her muffled words, listening intently.

Then he let go, touched her arm rather as he had touched mine, and came back over to where I sat.

"Roy, be a gent. Can you get her a brandy?"

"What's the matter?"

"Tell you soon. Brandy first. *Thanks*, Roy."

Like the slave of chance which that moment I was, up I got, walked back in the bar and ordered it. Everyone in there was by now looking round too, and much less cautiously, the smoked glass screens giving them cover.

The waiter said to me, "What's up, sir?"

"I don't know."

"Your friend, he's helping her?"

"Yes, apparently." No point in stressing he wasn't any friend of mine.

I paid for the brandy rather than put it on the tab.

Going out I started to walk across and Sej came up to me and took it from me with a grateful nod, and bore it to the weeping woman.

She tipped back her head and swallowed the brandy whole.

Her eyes were inflamed, and if her mascara hadn't run she had somehow smeared it even so.

She spoke to him. He nodded.

Then he came over to me again and undid his bag, and pulled out a shirt. It was dark blue in colour. "That should be OK," he said. Holding it he went directly out of the hotel doors and vanished along the street.

I sat back and watched the woman surreptitiously. In fact

she was even a little older than I'd first thought, and her clothes were good, but not quite as good as in my initial impression. She sat motionless, head up. She stared through us all, through walls, through time and space. I have seen the look before with certain people. The look of sudden vital loss.

When Sej came back in he carried his shirt carefully now, wrapped around something. There was blood seeping through.

For a somersaulting instant I thought of a dead baby. But no, it wasn't that. From one end a pathetic white tail hung out. A dog.

He too noticed the tail in that moment and deftly obscured it in a fold of the shirt.

Standing by her, he spoke. Now I heard the words.

"The taxi's outside. He's OK. Shouldn't you call your husband?"

I heard her say drearily, "He won't care."

"There must be someone," he said.

"Oh." She gazed up at him with the sadness of the only half-alive. "*Must* there?"

"Then can I...?"

"No. No, you've been much too kind. And - please thank your friend for the drink. I should - I have to pay..."

"Hush, dear," he said.

Something caught inside me. My father had sometimes said that to my mother, gently in that way, if she was distressed. *Hush, dear. It'll be all right.* Lies, of course. But the human tenderness. Hush, dear. Hush.

Sej guided her out and both of them now disappeared. Beyond my line of sight he must have handed her the butcher's bundle, and put her in the cab.

When he came back in he was chalk white.

Unlike the old, who can look so young, almost childlike,

in certain situations of stress, the young have a way of looking abruptly aged. You see it in the faces of children from famine zones or bombed out villages on the TV news. I don't know why this is. Sixty looks six, and six - a hundred.

"Sorry, Roy," he said, and slumped into his former chair. "Some shit ran over her dog. Just out there. At least it must have been quick. He didn't stop, naturally. Poor little cow."

"You'd better drink something."

"No, actually. I feel a bit sick again. I had to - pick it up."

"I'll fetch some water."

I marched back into the bar and got him one of those small bottles of still water that are now so popular. When I came out he had gone, his bag too. He was nowhere to be seen.

I stood in the foyer, staring round for him. Searching anxiously, confused and made uneasy by the absence of my enemy.

ELEVEN

One can make small excuse for some things one does. And yet perhaps all such things are in some way recognizable by the rest of us. And if not, then they may come to be. And if never, possibly they should.

When Joseph returned from the lavatories, which lie off the foyer of the Belmont and are, like the entire hotel, mirrored and gilded, urinals white as the brand new false teeth of my parents' era, he was still gaunt and pale.

He sat down once more opposite to me.

"Really sorry, Roy. I had to throw up again."

My fault? Apparently not.

"I've always been squeamish," he said.

"You didn't seem to be."

"Well, you kind of put that on hold, don't you, when you have to."

I struggled not to say it, but *I* had to. "You dealt with all that very well."

"I tried. I was lucky with the cabdriver. Good man. He said he'd lost his own dog. He said drunks get in the cab and puke everywhere, so he had plastic bags... I saw to that. She couldn't. Poor little thing," he said, as if she were his younger sister. "Her husband must be a twat. But she got herself together. They went off with the dog on her lap. She said she'd bury him in a big pot, grow a plant. They don't have a garden, just this rich apartment in Hampstead. I think she said Hampstead."

He looked drained. He let his head sink back on the chair.

"Roy, I'm really sorry, now I *do* need a drink and then I need some food. Crazy I know if I was sick, but that's gone and I feel hollow. As I said, I'm glad to pay, but it has to be in the next ten minutes or I'm going to drop. I could do with your company too."

Stiffly I said, "All right. Take this water. What drink do you want?"

"Tea, please," he said. "Black, *no* milk, no sugar, no lemon."

That would have to be the restaurant. The bar ran to coffee only.

On his left hand there was a little bright smear of blood. It was on the palm, which must have been pressed to the body of the dog - washing his hands must have cleared the rest. I hoped he wouldn't see it.

I wondered what I was doing. I should have made myself scarce long before. But I hadn't, had I?

We went into the restaurant and ordered tea for Joseph who was Sej, and a glass of red for me. Then we had lunch.

He perked up bit by bit.

He thanked me several times.

What did we talk about? Not much. The food, London, nothing. We ate, I a little, all the while watching him. He ate a lot. And at the end he paid, and left them a lavish tip, thanking the waiter with an odd, sophisticated joy, as if he had consumed a slice of heaven on a plate.

At the Belmont, just before you reach the lifts on the ground floor, there is a big blue function room, which that day stood wide open.

A few chairs and long tables were left about, the latter decorated with water glasses. But the dais from which, I suppose, the officers of various businesses address their captive, pre-empted staff, stood vacant, and the mikes turned off. To the left was positioned a piano, a baby *grande*, black and polished, its lid for some reason upraised.

I saw it because he had gone back that way when he went to the Gents again, and returning, told me.

Why this time had I waited for him? But then, why had I stayed and waited earlier?

Without ducking all responsibility, partly I blame my father. He had so often told me I must try to see the 'Other person's side'. Plus I had been heavily indoctrinated in ideas of polite behaviour. Of course this is absurd, for many of us, especially from my own and prior generations, have been and were so instructed, and often with physical beatings to augment the process. My father was not a brutal man, but he had his standards and his eye could turn very cold. "I'm a bit disappointed in you, Roy." The whole structure rested on a quasi-Christian ethic, despite the fact my father was strictly agnostic. It was not to be what one wanted oneself, but what would be 'fair' to others. As a kid I had absorbed this and sometimes sobbed in combined frustration and shame - at not being understood, at the fear that I had been understood too well and found unpleasantly wanting. Countless other people, as I began to say before, in the rambling way by which I'm allowing this narrative to proceed, were lessoned similarly. But later they rebelled, emerging radiantly assured and unappeasing. Not apparently Roy Phipps.

Only in my novels have I played with the matches and the fire of injustice and utter barefaced self-obsession. And there too, in the end, a penalty is normally exacted.

All this divertissement has been solely to say that, confronted by Joseph's continued urbanity, he had bought lunch, assisted a distraught woman even though it had made him ill, I couldn't bring myself simply to run away.

I would, of course. But first civilities, the acknowledgement of his rights, must be attended to.

And therefore I'd waited once more in the foyer, and

then hearing of the open room with the piano, I rose from the chair and followed him to see.

Once I was at the doorway, Joseph went straight to the piano. He dragged out a chair and sat down. "Too high," he remarked, perhaps to me, or to the hotel in general. And then he put his hands on the keys.

"I'll play you a tune," he said, like my Maureen, all those years ago. And beauty had spread like butterfly wings from her fingers.

And with him?

He launched at once into a piece of Scott Joplin, the by now most well known one. It came out perfect, yet - flighty. Flighty. It had wings.

Once or twice, as he played, he glanced up and back at me. He didn't smile now, he grinned. He looked happy. He looked - at *home*.

After this prelude he shot immediately into one of the etudes of Chopin. My father had played this. Joseph Traskul clearly demonstrated that *'play'* was not what one did with it. Filigreed streams dashed sparkling and hopeless to a bottomless sea. A few dark chords barred their way, but died.

Behind me a woman murmured, "*My.*"

The Americans had come, drawn by the sounds, which obviously were not the everyday musak of the hotel.

They stood, seemingly awestruck, then - passing me without a look - went into the room and sat down on some of the chairs.

Joseph played.

From Chopin he passed to Beethoven, and the character of the music changed - gorgeous despair to thundering rage. I believe it was the *Appassionata*. The room rang with the notes but more than that, with the power of the composition.

Maureen had played so very well.

But Joseph played as if each note sped new-born from his brain.

Now and then I've been to concerts. I had heard this kind of quality, ability and fire before.

Never like this.

Other people kept arriving. They passed by me as if I were some doorman, some of them even smiling or nodding at me as if I held the way for them.

In the end there must have been over fifty people sitting in the room, either on the chairs or tables, or the blue carpet.

If there was a pause, they applauded. But by now his face had set in a kind of visor of intention. He played on and on, one astonishing rendering leaping at once into another, Scott Joplin to Chopin to Beethoven to Rachmaninov to Prokofiev to Gershwin.

Certainly some of the staff of the hotel had come in. The manager had apparently come down, or so I was informed, to the doors. He had meant to put a stop to this, the piano was valuable, not there for idle tinkerings. But he too had stayed a while to listen, and gone away uncomplaining.

Joseph finished with a sudden little syncopated piece of jazz, the kind he'd spoken of. I didn't know it, but I hardly know everything and that type of music, while I like it, I don't know very well. Yet I had a feeling this one was really his own.

Lightly tapping in the last note, he sat back.

He sat there with his back to us, hands down at his sides.

The room erupted, naturally. They cheered.

At first he seemed to take no notice. He seemed nearly in a trance. Then he lifted his head, stood up and, walking round the chair, bowed to them theatrically, but grinning again.

When some of them approached, crowding round, asking him who he was, where he played, he was all graceful good humour. He just, he told them, tuned pianos. And now he was handing out those cards of his. He got plenty of potential customers. The air bubbled with praise.

Finally he extricated himself and came across to me at the door.

"Well, Dad. Made you proud of me for a minute, didn't I?"

"You're a wonderful and versatile pianist. But I'm not your father."

The grin was gone. The *smile* was there instead.

He lifted his eyebrows. "Sure about that, are you?"

Lynda had had a 'scare', what she called a scare, which was her supposing herself pregnant by me. After we'd married, for indeed we did marry and are *still* married, since neither of us so far has found the need to apply for a divorce, she had another scare. This will indicate, accurately enough, that neither of us wanted children, or at least I did not. Perhaps she only wished not to have any by me. Both scares anyway came to nothing, or so she informed me. After all, I'd always gathered she was on the Pill.

We were together approximately two years. When she left, which was not because of her having fallen for anyone else, only because she had the chance of living with an aunt of hers near Manchester who had some money, which - as Lynda pointed out - we did not - it could just have been possible she was, unbeknownst to either of us - pregnant. Or should I say, *really* scared. Her leaving me occurred in 1977. I'd been more relieved than regretful. The washing-machine went on washing my shirts, and I could cook in fact rather better than Lynda. As for sex, now and then there had been someone after she went. Not very often. I'm not attractive to the opposite sex, and I don't expect to be.

However. If Joseph were about the age I'd eventually

thought him, lying there on my kitchen floor, twenty-eight-seven - he could maybe have been mine, mine and Lynda's.

Except surely she would have let me know. Not from any sense of my fatherly rights, but to get some extra financial support. At the very least, to blame me. Or did the aunt take care of everything? There was less stigma by then in having a baby without an adjacent man. Besides, we were still married. In the aunt's eyes, it would be respectable. And if the old woman liked children, perhaps this seemed a good arrangement, leaving me out of it, all the better.

But then again, could this - *creature*, this demon, who was physically so unlike either Lynda or myself, this pianistic genius - be the product of *our* midnight fumblings?

"Are you saying," I said, "you're my son?"

"Am I? Do you think I am, Roy?"

We had gone out of the hotel and were walking together along Lang Passage, up to the Gardens. When he saw them he said, "There's a park near my place. Huge trees and rhododendrons."

"I didn't ask you about the park, Sej. I asked if you genuinely believe you're my son."

We stood by the low railing and looked into the Gardens. The trees were leafing early, the sun out and shining on them. A small bird was drinking from the drinking fountain drips.

"You tell me," he said presently. "Could I be?"

"I doubt it."

"But you doubt everything, don't you, Roy?"

I said levelly, "It's often the best way to doubt."

"Innocent until proven guilty. Guilty until proven innocent. Stupid until proven clever. Purple till proven blue."

"What are you saying?"

"Nothing much. Just passing the time. That bird on the

fountain is a wren. You don't often catch sight of them in inner London. Or I don't. Did you know, they have pelicans in Hyde Park. That took me by surprise. Great big bills and red legs. What's the time, by the way?"

What to do? I glanced at my watch. "Getting on for four-thirty."

"Shit," he said. "I have to be somewhere."

"Tuning a piano?"

"Not this time. Sorry, Roy, I have to get going."

"Really."

He turned and laughed at me, then he put his arms round me and hugged me, giving me also the obligatory masculine clap-on-the-back.

"I'll see you, Roy..." he said. *"Daddy,"* he added, like a mischievous child that knows you love it and, though disapproving, won't really mind you just heard it use the F word.

Then he turned, vaulted the railing, his bag bouncing on his shoulder, and broke into a run, vanishing though the Gardens in the direction of Langham Place and Oxford Street. And I stood there, mind depleted of all coherent thought, staring after him, staring after everything.

4

My first search of 6, 66, Saracen Road had been fruitless. I went to a grimy window in the main room and looked out and down. Below, the street, and then Joseph's park of "Huge trees and rhododendrons". A few people were sunbathing there, I now saw. The June sun had brought them out like certain flowers. From up here they had a flowery quality too, already tanned and in bright colours. How easy it looked, to sample life.

As luck would have it, I peeled off the rubber gloves I had donned, because of their sticky hotness, and stuffed them in a pocket.

It was when I turned back into the room, wondering if all I could do now was go away, I heard the flat door, (already smashed and undone by me) pushed briskly open.

I thought instantly it would be him. Joseph. Sej.

Therefore, when the burly middle-aged man in shorts and T-shirt came into the room, I felt a most inappropriate near relief.

He stopped and gawped at me. He had a newspaper in one hand, and a six-pack of beer in the other.

I said, "Christ, can you believe it? Someone broke in."

"Er - yeah," he said.

I recognised, hypersensitive as perhaps I was in that moment, the voice of No 3A, he who had let me in via the main entrance.

"I came up here," I blustered on, "to deliver this bloody packet..." I pointed at my fake delivery, which now lay on the floor. "I meant to leave it by the door. You never know, do you? I mean, the table downstairs, anyone might have had it."

"You're fucking not wrong there," he rewarded me.

"And someone's smashed the glass window. Been in and taken - well - *everything* from the look. Even the carpets."

Roy was on form again, indeed he was. But I've said, I write this sort of drivel for a living. Improv comes with the job.

3A gazed round. He looked both disgusted and sullen. I sensed immediately he was not astonished, had been up here before and knew the flat was always basically exactly as now.

He said, "Like, I don't think they took nothing much. Tina don't *have* much to start with."

Touché, monsieur. Now he really had floored me.

I said, "Tina? But the name on the packet is for a Mr Trazcool. But I suppose she's his partner?"

"How should *I* know?"

How should he?

"But surely he lives here. Look..." I'd put a lot into the fake package and confidently picked it up and held it out to him.

He shambled over and scrutinised it. "Tra - *skull*, that his name?" he asked. (He could read).

"Presumably. The address is right, is it?"

"Yeah, man. That's right."

"So Tina...?"

"She's the only one lives here I know of. She gets people up here sometimes. I thought you was one of 'em."

Below us, the noise of No 5's bad music abruptly ceased.

Both 3A and I stared down at the floor.

"He's going out," said 3A. "Thank fuck for that."

3A, it seemed, didn't like 5's music either. But whether that was due to its volume or its type, remained obscure.

My mind turned back to what he had said just before.

People coming up... he'd thought I was one of them.

Was she, this Tina, on the game? A prostitute. I didn't want to ask. He too had come up here, had he not, with his paper and beer.

"Oh well," I said, with generated slight annoyance, "do you think we should call the police?"

"What the fuck for? They won't fucking come, man. If they did, what they gonna do? This place... 's always like this. Sometimes there're some chairs. Once there was a music centre - a fridge. That lasted about two weeks. I don't know how she pays her rent, but I gotta idea."

He had confirmed my own. Tina, whoever Tina was, was a whore.

"Well," I said, "I can't waste any more time. I've got things to do."

And that was when he emerged from his inertia. He squared up to me and said, quite pleasantly, "Yeah, but hang on a bit. How'd I know what you gotta do with all this?"

"All *what*?"

"The fucking door wrecked. Like what the fuck are you up to?"

"I've said, I brought his post up - or *her* post."

"Nobody fucking bothers to do that. These fucking stairs, no way. It's like climbing up Mount fucking Everlast, or whatever the fuck it's called. So if you wasn't after Tina what *was* you after?"

I hung my head.

"You've got me there. Obviously it *is* Tina."

"Then why," unfortunately astutely he inquired, "all this bollox with that letter thing?"

"Well it *was* for her flat - I found it on the table downstairs when I was here last time. Took it. Wanted an excuse to come back. Then when I tried the bell she didn't answer."

"Nah, she didn't. 'Cos she was 'sposed to be seeing me, man. Me. OK?"

"OK. Fine."

"I don't like all this," he said, sniffing at the air as if to detect, like a bloodhound, the clues of treachery. Perhaps he could. I was certainly sweating.

I said, "Look, I'm sorry if I'm in your way. I really don't want anyone to know I was here to see Tina. I don't want my wife to know."

"I bet you don't, man."

"In the past I've met her - other places. I didn't know it was your - time."

"No. OK. Right. Well, she ain't fucking here anyway is she? She's fucking off her head. You'll know." He leered abruptly. "'S'OK, man. Just wanted to be sure."

We were comrades-in-arms, love or war.

He added, "Reckon I know who done this anyhow. The door, I mean. That fucker from No 2. He's a headcase. She wouldn't touch him neither. Nasty cunt." Did he mean her? Presumably No 2. He looked at me for confirmation, so whoever it was dutifully I nodded. 3A went on, "Might pay him a little visit later. As for Tee, well, she's off somewhere. Both you and me had better make other arrangements, eh?"

"Yes."

"Give your old woman some Cream di Month or something. You never know. Might see another side of her."

"Yes... "

He had moved out of sight, back into the outer hall of the flat. I didn't dare take the package with me I when I left. It was now officially Tina's. I dropped it again, and for a second stood regarding it, not wanting to leave such evidence. But in the hall 3A swore loudly. Sounding aggrieved he said, "You walked up them fucking stairs barefoot? Trying to scare me, eh? Eh?"

On the unpapered wall I saw two vague shadows thrown, mingling and unsure, 3A's and another's.

TWELVE

Outside the BBC I watched a well-known politician sweep through into the building, with his entourage. I've seen a few well-known persons going in there over the past twenty odd years.

I did some nondescript shopping in Oxford Street. I didn't see Joseph.

Before I walked back to the hotel I went into Lang Gardens and called Lewis Rybourne on my mobile.

They told me he was in a meeting.

"Please get him to phone me. I'm at the Belmont Hotel until tomorrow afternoon."

I was just getting up from the bench when the phone made its noise. I don't have a piece of music. It simply imitates the old fashioned sound of a phone ringing.

The call was from Rybourne.

"Roy - oh, good, good. Sorry about that. She didn't know I was back. Did your boy catch up to you?"

I said, carefully, "Which boy?"

"Ah. Joseph, I think he said."

"*Joseph*? I don't know a Joseph."

"Oh, lord, Roy, I think maybe you do. He said he was - a relative."

"No. I don't have any relatives left."

"Oh come on, Roy. Your..." There was a long, dramatic pause. His voice had dropped and become intense, "...son."

I now left the interval.

"Hello?" he said. "Are you there?"

"Yes, Lewis. I thought you said *son*. Obviously you didn't."

"Of course, I shan't tell anyone. *Strictly* confidential."

"What are you talking about, Lewis?"

I could hear him breathing. Then he said, "A young man called us, said it was an emergency, insisted on speaking to your editor. Me. He told me he was your son, Joseph, and he was concerned as there'd been a family problem and he wanted..."

"I don't have a son. Who was this man?"

"I told you, Roy. He gave his name as Joseph - Joseph something or other. It sounded foreign. *She* has a note of it I think, but she's not in the office..."

"I have no son."

"All right. OK, Roy. The thing is, you'd already called me and you sounded - upset."

"I was."

"And then I spoke to this Joseph, and he wanted to know how he could trace you. He was already at your home. I made sure of the address. He knew you, and your house. Well."

"Really? That's news to me. What did you say to him?"

He breathed now like an obscene caller.

"I - er - I told him the hotel you were at."

I left a space. Then I shouted "You did *what*?"

"Roy, Roy, listen..."

"You told a complete stranger, who claims to be my son, and over the phone, which hotel I'm staying in?"

He said, with an awful meaningless contrition, "Have I done the wrong thing, Roy? I'm so sorry. I was just..."

"I'm being stalked, Lewis. Yes, I know, it's crazy. I don't know who he is, but he turned up at my house and gave the neighbours the same yarn - that he is my son. I threw him out. And yes, he has been at my hotel. Now I know who to thank for that."

"Christ. Roy - have you told the police?"

"Yes. They don't believe me, or they think something

else. And you have informed this lunatic of my hotel."

"God – Roy..."

"Think of something, Lewis. He may be dangerous. I need your help. This is your fault."

"Christ. Oh, Roy. What shall I do?"

"I don't know," I said. "But I suggest you come up with something."

I broke the connection.

To be truthful I wasn't sure how much, if any, use this would be. But the fact of Sej's pursuit of me had been established at last, with an independent and non-vulnerable source. Potential?

Having attended to that, however, I sat down once more on the bench.

The phone went again.

I looked at it.

I let it ring. I'd check any message later. Let Lewis Rybourne stew, if he was capable of it.

Meanwhile the images of the afternoon revolved slowly in my mind. I kept thinking of the women he'd helped, and the dog, its sad tail hanging out of his shirt - now ruined by blood and lost. And the piano. How he played. And how he had gone so suddenly away.

Bells were ringing from various places, including the nearby church. It was six o'clock.

I got up and walked to The Belmont. In the foyer a young woman came straight up to me, all smiles.

"Excuse me, but that guy who played the piano - you know him?"

"Didn't he give you a card?"

"Well, yes. Only I called the number and there was no answer."

I would have to bear in mind, Joseph was not only brilliant, but good-looking. This young woman was clearly smitten. I said, with a stiff smile, 'I don't know him well. Just keep trying the number. I think he's out until later." And walked to the lift leaving her there, crestfallen. Another stalker. This time *of* Joseph?

Tonight was my last night here. I couldn't afford any others. The entire excursion would already make quite a hole in what I call my Emergency Fund, that is my building society savings.

Would he come back to The Belmont? If he did, what then would happen?

I ordered dinner in my room and watched TV. Now I thought more solidly of my house and the possible damage that could have been done to it. Strangely, I didn't think he *had* caused damage. Partly too I wished *not* to go back. But I hadn't anywhere else to go. Perhaps, now Rybourne had some idea that Joseph was a danger, if the police confronted him at Gates he would have to tell them what had gone on. And any DNA test would show Joseph was nothing at all to do with me.

Unless...

Had he been Lynda's child? Hers and mine. That would make him only twenty-eight. Less? He didn't look quite that young, did he, or only when unconscious.

He wasn't Lynda's. He was neither like her, nor me.

The TV, even with its multiple channels, seemed all one chaos of unreal inanity, or desperate, unassuageable realness.

I turned in about eleven. Check-out tomorrow was noon.

I would go back, see to the house, pack a few extra things, then maybe myself head up north. I'd said I had nowhere to go, but it's cheaper there, out of the main northern cities. And Matthew lived there, all on his own without adulterous Sylvia. I could go and commiserate with him.

Before leaving however I would get some extra security added to the house. Duran, the electrician who fixed my kitchen lights and the thermostat last November, had a side line in villain-proofing. I'd gathered, from various hints, he'd been a competent burglar once, and now put former knowledge to good use for the other side. I hadn't taken him up on any of that, last time. Now I'd better. He was a tough guy too, Duran. He might have some brainwaves.

I slept well. Seven straight hours, waking at a quarter to eight, feeling drugged and out of kilter.

At reception, while paying, I heard of the manager's coming to see who played the piano yesterday. I had a last drink at the bar.

All the time I kept looking up at the mirror, looking for Sej to walk in. But he didn't. And I thought, Is it over? And a tide of relief swirled through me. And after the tide, a sort of pause. I can't describe it. It was still and quiet, without shadows, quite empty.

Less than a minute after, No 3A came back into the main room, accompanied by a skinny man with long greasy yellow hair, also in shorts, and barefoot as 3A had just accused him of being.

3A looked at me and jabbed his thumb back at the other one. "'S'im. The one I told you about. No 2."

No 2 smiled at me with crinkled grey teeth. He was about twenty-six, and his uncovered arms unashamedly revealed the tracks of needles. He stank of sweat and - sugar. A chemical smell you pick up by some chocolate counters.

"Hi," he winningly said.

I nodded.

We all stood there.

"Where's Tee?" asked No 2, smilingly bemused. "I got some lovely stuff for 'er. I get it off of..."

"Shut up," decided 3A. "This geezer don't want to know, right?"

No 2 looked deeply at me from mad huge eyes the colour of a stagnant pond. "I seen this booful car down the road. That yours?"

"No," I said.

No 2 giggled. "Tha's good. I pissed up it las' night. I bin a bad boy. 'Ere," he added, "*you* want any stuff? I got this wicked stuff off of..."

"Shut up," said 3A again. "Look, you nosed-up prick-head, Tina ain't here. She's gone off. And we're just going. OK?"

"Who bruk the door?" innocently asked No 2.

"The postman," said 3A impatiently, "he couldn't get no fucking answer so he broke the fucking door in. All right?

Now fuck off."

"That's awful that is - the postman - we ough-a get the pigs..."

"Fuck *off.*"

No 2 seemed sad. "OK, Billy," he said. "Look, here I go."

And he left us.

"My fucking name ain't Bill, neither," said 3A to me with obvious emphasis.

I nodded again.

We left the flat and went down the stairs, leaving plenty of space for the ambling barefoot No 2 to get to his lair before us.

Reaching his own flat 3A lumbered aside, went in and slammed the door. In the absence of the noisy music of No 5, the sound reverberated throughout the building.

I hurried the rest of the way to the street.

After I'd crossed the road and reached the far side of the park I glanced back. At each of two of the windows facing front, presumably those of No 2 and No 3A, a solitary form stood looking out. 3A simply stood guard there. No 2, lower down and perhaps made far-sighted by his 'stuff', raised his bony arm in a wave.

THIRTEEN

The train left soon after two o'clock. I sat in the long carriage, with its ultra narrow aisles and seats, and tried to read the Radio Times. There were only a handful of people in the carriage. The whole train was sparsely filled. Beyond the polarised windows the suburbs unwound under a dismal sky. I took out my notebook and made a couple of notes for the commissioned novel.

As each station materialised, I wondered if Joseph Traskul Sej were peering out of another carriage, to see if I had alighted at an earlier stop to my usual one.

Once a young man got off the train who bore a fleeting resemblance to him. I stared, and saw it wasn't he.

The train was slow. It took nearly forty minutes. When I came to my station I felt an edgy excitement, and reaching the platform, turned and looked round. A bald man from my carriage, in a brown shirt, had got off also. He was about forty. He looked straight ahead and went past me, down the steps.

Sometimes I get a taxi, though it's only a twenty minute walk to Old Church Lane. Today I didn't. I'd spent enough, and if I went north soon, there'd be more to fork out.

Then, walking up the high street, busy with afternoon shopping and kids on bicycles careering along the pavement, I considered that a taxi-driver might have been handy if any surprises were waiting. Although in fact, he wouldn't want to be involved. Non-involvement is the key signature for most of us now, myself included.

Just before I turned into Bulivante Crescent I noticed the man in brown again. He was about thirty yards behind me, looking in a shop window.

Immediately I was tense. Was he following me?

Mentally I shook myself.

No. Not every person I saw was likely to follow me.

Only *one* person. And he, for now, was not in evidence.

All the way up the Crescent I anticipated him. He might step from behind a tree. Out of a house even, with a friendly farewell gesture to some now-collusive occupant, whom he had conned with one more inventive tale.

When I reached 72, I hesitated. George and Vita weren't to be seen. No doubt they were at the back, in the kitchen, making afternoon tea and chatting. I envied them sometimes. Their blossoming, undemanding dual companionship.

On the path I looked round again.

The man from 88 was watering his lawn with a sprinkler. So many men are at home now during the day, even the young ones; I used to be the exception. A cat was washing itself on the wall of 73, oblivious of the yapping poodle at the front room window.

Nothing out of place.

I reached the door.

Here I had the strangest moment of *déjà vu*. It was as if, not Joseph Traskul, but my *parents* had recently been on the premises. As if it had become their house again, I only their son, lodging there, coming and going, as many sons do.

But I braced myself and put the key in the lock. The door had been firmly shut, and now it opened. The hall lay before me, with four letters scattered on the mat. To my alert gaze nothing seemed amiss. Nothing was *wrong*.

The house had an air of silence and immobility, as if the owner had been away a few days. He had.

No residue of Joseph seemed to linger.

I was certain now he had not returned here.

Nevertheless I considered leaving the door ajar. Then

thought better of it. I went into the hall. I looked up the stairs. I meant to go to the kitchen first. That was where I'd left him, where he had recovered, thrown up in the sink. Something however made me go instead directly into the front room. As I did so of course I recalled again the vulnerable dog of red glass.

Maybe this is the most peculiar thing to try to convey at this point. Standing in the door of the room I felt no shock, none at all.

I suppose it could have been because the piano, which was now installed there against the left hand wall, where the print of Monet's *Sunday at Agenteuil* had once been and was no longer, rested in virtually the same place as the previous piano during my parents' occupancy.

Unlike my mother, Joseph had set the red glass dog on the piano's top.

That night in 1974, Maureen invited me round, and she'd made me what my mother would have called a 'proper dinner'. It was roast lamb and roast potatoes with all the 'trimmings', and cheesecake from Mercers to follow, plus a bottle of decent red wine and some brandy for later.

Maureen was a good cook. She did it without any fuss either, whipping off her apron and appearing in a sexy dress. In the beginning her attire had sometimes even put me off the food I was so earnest to get her through the bedroom door.

"This is all really lovely, Maur," I said. "Thanks."

"I want tonight to be special, Roy," she said. And winked at me. "You wait till you see what I've *not* got on under this."

She was fun. Her lust was Chaucerian in its dedication, honesty and humour.

It *was* a special night.

After we'd settled down a little in bed, around 2 a.m. she sat up and lit a cigarette. I seldom wanted one. It was always, "Just take a fag if you want, darling."

"I've got something to say, sweetheart," said Maureen Parner in her pretty, Cockney voice.

"Yes, Maur..." I was half asleep. She hadn't lied about the new lingerie, and we'd done it justice.

"Sorry, luv, but you'd better listen. I really am sorry, luv. But tonight - this has to be our last time."

"What...?" I too sat up. I was wide awake, and the brandy suddenly sour in my throat. "Last - last what?"

"Our last smashing time, darling. Oh, Charlie, don't look so sad." Her eyes were full of tears.

Mine were dry and burned like acid. "I don't understand what you're saying."

"You know there've been - one or two others."

"Yes, Maur. It's OK."

"You are such a lovely bloke. Trouble is, I've met someone. And he - well he is... he's different, Roy. Roy, look, I'll be straight. I like him a lot and he wants to marry me. He's not rich but he's OK moneywise. I can stop work. We can have a bit of a good time. He's a bit older than me. Not that much. I'm pretty ancient, you know."

"*You're not old.*"

"No. But you're *young*, Roy. You've got your whole..."

"Life ahead of me. Christ. You're dumping me because I'm a kid."

Then she started to cry.

And even in my total hurt and rage and shock, I put my arms round her. I held her, and soon we started to kiss again. We made love again.

But after that, when she held me, I had the sense to know this would be, as even the song had it, the last time. I wasn't yet twenty. I'd known her just over one year. She'd put a magic spell on me, I'd changed, growing one inch taller, sloughing acne and sexual insecurity in one bound. Even selling a story to a magazine. I didn't love her, but she was my love. She was mine. My Maureen. And now, not any more. Never again.

It hit me. I stood there, stricken, the piano shining, over thirty years too late.

Not Lynda's - of course not hers. Joseph was Maureen's child. Hers and mine.

Mine. Mine and Maureen's.

She had had to marry the other older man. She hadn't wanted, being as she was, to pile that responsibility on a callow boy of nineteen with an assistant's job in a library.

Joseph was my son. He was about thirty - thirty-one-?

He was my son. Almost exactly as he had claimed to be.

When I walked dazedly out of the room I saw the letters again, on the mat.

There had been four. I'd absently counted them.

Now there were five.

XIII
('Untitled': Page 213)

TO dine in his father's house was always a custom of anathema to him. Yet here he was, seated at the long table of dark wood, the dishes set about, and his family set around them, conversing in their usual dull manner. Vilmos studied them. As sometimes happened after the talons of the 'micrania had let go of him, he seemed both to hear and to see more clearly. Like a painting on glass, his stout anaemic mother and two pale, weed-like sisters. His older brothers, big, and tonight red-faced by contrast, jested and drank, observant only of the stern patriarch. Should he frown they would lower their voices. But otherwise they were always similarly obedient to him, worked at the offices he had demanded, wed when he told them they must. At or because of Vilmos he did not frown.

Vilmos was his curse, the devil somehow borne of the consanguineous line of his house. Vilmos he paid no attention at all. That he even suffered Vilmos, his youngest son, to live, albeit intermittently, in the family home, even to sit at table with him, was due only to a horrible and parsimonious religious ethic.

Meanwhile he did not know what Vilmos had truly done. He was not aware Vilmos had killed three women in the city, and at least eight men - perhaps nine - the fate of Reiner, of course, would never be fully ascertained by any.

Had he known all this, and of other matters to do with Vilmos, how would the patriarch have responded?

Vilmos himself sometimes pondered on this.

At certain times he believed his father would, himself, have summoned an assassin, and had the troublesome

140

offspring excised from the pages of family life. But then again, his religious ethic might restrain him. Rather than murder his son, the father might only confine him in some cellar, feeding him and sustaining him 'mercifully', but never allowing him out again into the light.

Thus not only were dinners at his father's house irksome and angering, they were potentially dangerous. For that reason too maybe, Vilmos still occasionally attended them. His whole existence fled along a razor's edge, pursued by his own demons, and in pursuit of God knew what. Threat was the sea in which habitually he swam.

But now the father spoke.

At once utter stillness fell, respectful, or more properly fearful, as the Biblical canon decreed.

The three wan women, their lips parted, waited as if to receive his words not only through ears and eyes, but by mouth.

The brothers squared their shoulders, intelligent oxen ready to serve.

"This goose is dry, Saveta," said the patriarch to his wife.

"I am so sorry, Vladis. I will speak to the cook..."

"Do it. I expect my table, though now impoverished, to serve palatable food at least."

Vilmos, before he could prevent it, laughed. The patriarch did not even look at him.

When one of the brothers glared in Vilmos's direction, the patriarch spoke directly to this brother, diverting him. "I wish to discuss with you the cloth revenues. We are in arrears, it seems. Follow me to my study."

Once these two men had left the room, the women quickly got up. They went into a corner by the fire and took up their tatting.

The other brothers sat drinking. They had taken out a draughts board and now played a ponderous game.

Vilmos stayed where he was. He watched the candlelight creep on the ceiling, now and then faltering or flaring up. Two servants came in and cleared the table. The mother called them sharply. In a malicious undertone she berated then both over the goose.

Vilmos thought, with deep, comfortable melancholy, of Reiner, struggling and sinking in the river where he, Vilmos, had flung him. Reiner could swim a little. Besides debris was everywhere that he might reach and cling to. It was interesting to Vilmos inwardly to debate if his former companion had survived.

But then the image of the king, crowned with bones and with a rat in his breast, returned, slicing through memory like a knife.

In his chair, Vilmos sat upright. Something strange in the candlelight seemed to show him the king again upon the ceiling.

The colours in his torso, yellow, orange and crimson, were those of the three lower illuminated *Cakras*. They indicated appetite, greed, carnal desire. The added symbols, such as the rat and the snake, indicated blockages and perversions.

The higher colours, such as the green of the emotive heart, had not been contained in his vision. The piece of tin, when he revived and was shown it, had been burnt, apparently by some dreadful aspect of Vilmos himself. The Master was gone and had explained nothing. The servant, of course, had no tongue.

Vilmos now brooded on all this.

Few had ever attained the greater goals of the Order of the Indian Mystery. Few had seen as high as the sky-blue of the *Cakra* of communication, speech and song. And none, Vilmos thought, had viewed any higher. Unless the Master himself had done so.

Self-enlightenment, the dominion over self - and so over all other things - was reached only by unleashing the Gem of the Brow. It was the last stage of utter power. Beyond it no man could rise, save to reach up from the physical self into the Infinite, which was both Bliss and Annihilation: Death, Eternity. The Gem was therefore the ultimate state possible while yet living.

They said, not the Master but *his* Master, he who had ruled the Order before him, had done this. Armed then with the abilities of a god, he had vanished from the City.

"I want it," Vilmos murmured. He clenched both his hands on the table's edge, gripping it so hard a vibration seemed to pass through the wood.

When he went out, one of the servant girls, beaten by the cook because of the goose, wept against the panelling. She was about fourteen. Vilmos stared at her with a kind of revulsion. She smelled of grease, and her own unwashed body and hair. What wretched things humans were.

"Cheer up, my pigeon," he said to her in passing. "We're all damned. We'll all roast in the Scalds of Hell."

Her sobs choked to silence. She was afraid of him. He was the Chosen of the Devil. This notion filled him with great joy, and also with trepidation and a leaden disappointment. Why could *God* not have chosen him? Now he would never rise up beyond the genitals, the bowels and belly, the heart, the voice, into the dark blue sphere of the Elect. Unless, obviously, the Master was mistaken. Vilmos left the house thinking this. He walked through the darkness of the City to the lodging of the harlot Klavdisa. *She* knew better than to take other custom without his permission. He could practice with *her* his dominion over others, in case the Master were wrong.

FOURTEEN

Two of the letters were printed with my name and address. Two were handwritten.

The fifth, the last one lying on top of them, was different.

It was a clean, white ordinary envelope, the kind anyone could buy somewhere like Smiths, neither opulent nor cheap, empty of either name or address.

I picked it up and found it was sealed in the usual way. I ripped it open so roughly bits of it fluttered off back to the floor.

One sheet of typing or computer paper was inside, again medium quality.

Unlike the envelope, the sheet was printed, a font widely used with nothing special about it.

One word, and three numerals:

Compasses. 7.30

I use the name The Compasses for the pub. This isn't correct. It was the dodgy place Joseph had stayed at in the high street. I've changed the name.

After a while I carried all the letters into the kitchen.

The table had been pulled back from the door, which had been relocked and re-bolted. Out on the paving his black dustbin-present was now stationed neatly to one side. When presently I opened the fridge, I found he had put the bottle of Wincott's into the chiller. The fridge had been reconnected too. It was as cold as it should be, and the freezer as well.

He had washed up the dinner plates and put them to drain, and the cutlery, (all but the missing fork), was standing in its proper section. *I'd* rinsed the glasses. These he had put away, in the right place.

There was no mess. In fact the kitchen looked as clean as when Franziska tended to it. There was a faint smell of bleach too, as then.

I felt a type of nervous curiosity. I went into the library. That copy of my book, *Last Orders*, lay on the little table. A piece of paper lay on top of it with an erratically written splash of words, (his writing, already recognizable to me). *Really brilliant, Mr Phillips. Should have won a prize - or did it?*

Nothing else seemed changed. At least he had not dusted the table.

Upstairs, the computer had completed its deletions but was still on. I switched it off. Nothing was disturbed that I could see. My bedroom door remained locked and had not been broken in.

The bathroom and lavatory were virtually as I'd left them, too. It seemed he must have used the lavatory and he had used the bath. One longish black curled hair lay on the edge. I stared at it, impelled. I picked it off. It had fallen from his head and he had not noticed it, or did not care. In some crude past of banes and witchcraft I might have thought I could employ it against him. Now I truly might, if I put it into the sandwich bag with the new note added to the old one from the dustbin, and the fork he had used during our dinner, both of which I'd carried up to London and now brought back. DNA.

I had to find some access to the police that would make them listen. If he had done this sort of thing before, and they would take me seriously, they might discover him among their records, his DNA already lying in wait to catch him out. Or *was* it only me, only me as his target?

And then I sat down on the stair, the top stair where I'd sometimes sat as a child.

I held the cellophane bag in one hand, and the piece of

paper that said *Compasses: 7.30* in the other.

Suppose he really was my son? Mine and Maureen's?

Downstairs I'd been certain for all of sixty seconds.

But now?

He could play the piano even better than she had. Perhaps, like her, he had a singer's voice. His speaking voice was attractive, musical. It had that element trainers of speech would once talk about, *timbre*, the distinctive character of a voice, what Maureen herself had referred to as its *colour*. What colour had hers been? Soft pink, deep grey, silver. And his? It was dark, with a tawny edge. This is fanciful. I don't often think of things in that way.

He was mesmerizing me. Had done so. Push it off. Be sensible and wary. Even if he were - mine - he had followed and stalked and harried and *played* with me. Very likely he had an axe to grind, was enraged at me, his absent, ignorant bastard of a father. He might be capable of anything. And yet -

The phone in the hall was out of action. I used my mobile to call Duran, my ex-burglar electrician. But his wife informed me he was in Bristol, working on a big job with his cousin.

"When will he...?"

"Don't know, sorry. All he says to me when he calls me is it's going slow there. At least another month, I'd say."

The Compasses was dark, although April was turning towards May, the sun lower but still a good half hour from setting. There was oldish stained-glass in some of the windows, probably fitted circa 1930, when the pub was built. Green tiling had been kept too. The urinals seemed of the same vintage, if less pleasant.

I arrived ten minutes or so later than stipulated. Joseph played; so I did, if only a little.

And I meant to be friendly if non-committal. I meant to try to get to the bottom of all this.

The mirage that he might be my son lay like a flickering light somewhere in the murk of my confusion.

Unsettled and unsure, whether I was glad or appalled I couldn't discover.

In the doorway I looked round.

To the casual or ill-informed eye, there was nothing very odd about The Compasses. The dealers were fairly discreet. They expected you to know either whom they were, or if not to tip the barman the wink, and await an introduction.

Some couples, young or middle-aged, sat around, perhaps innocent, just passing through. Small groups of secretive looking men clustered over their pints. In the second room, a gathering watched as two men played snooker with steely concentration and the sharp clack of balls.

There was a tall black-haired man standing at one of the flashing machines, trying for a payment. But it wasn't Joseph. None of them were Joseph. Was he going to be fashionably late, as I'd tried to be?

I went to the bar. They don't stock Wincott's there, despite what he had said. I had a half pint of Guinness, and sat down in the corner under a window with pale green and red diamonds.

After twenty more minutes I was two thirds down the glass. People had gone out, come in. The dealer in the corner had approached the oldest middle-aged couple and sat down with them. They talked in low earnest voices. I kept my eyes off them. Perversely I asked myself if it were weed or crack or straight heroin they wanted, he in his baggy trousers and shirt with tie, she fake ash-blonde and floral jacket.

Perhaps this was Joseph's latest ploy. To call me to him,

see if I'd turn up, and not turn up himself. He must be watching somewhere. Where?

"May I sit here?"

I jumped.

A man stood over me. I'd never seen him before. He wore an expensive male cologne. I'm never keen on this fashion among men, although I realise I'm outdated. To be clean and deodorised is one thing, but perfumed - quite another. Yet to be fair the scent was subtle, not overpowering.

He gestured towards the chair that faced mine. The rest of the pub had gradually filled up. I could hardly refuse him. Besides, there'd be no point in my staying much longer.

"Yes, of course."

He sat.

"Warm, for April," he remarked.

He wore a collarless white shirt, loose, not tucked in at the waist band of his gun-grey trousers. He was swarthy, olive-skinned with thick black hair and a solid looking blue-black moustache.

"Yes."

He smiled and sipped his drink. It appeared to be a straight Coke, no ice or lemon. "And you," he said.

My mind had wandered. A shadow had passed the open door. But it wasn't Joseph.

"I'm sorry, what did you say?"

"Mr Phillips," said the man, "shall we get to business?"

It was then that my startled eyes, swirling back to focus on him, saw instead the man I'd seen previously on the train. He was still bald and still in his brown shirt. He leaned at the bar, watching us casually, what might be a Bloody Mary, or only a tomato juice, in his hand.

"That's Mr C," said my sudden companion. "It's quite all right." He turned his dark head and nodded, friendly, at the bald man, 'Mr C,' who nodded back and turned away.

"What is this about?" I asked. The most crazy idea of undercover policemen surged through my mind.

"No, Mr Phillips, that is to be *my* question."

He had an educated voice, with the faintest hint of an accent, which might be Greek - or Egyptian, even something farther south-east of the Med. Accents aren't my forte.

"*Your* question. What...?"

"Precisely. What is this about?"

"What is wh...?"

"No, no, Mr Phillips. Let's cut to the chase, as they say."

"Why are you calling me *Phillips*?"

"Because, Mr Phillips, that was the name I was given on your behalf."

I stared at him. "*Who* gave it to you?"

He lowered his eyes with a knowing modesty. His lashes were like a woman's, as with the Mediterranean or Middle Eastern male type they often are.

"*Someone* gave it to me," he said, "who supposed you were in a little trouble. That you might need - a little assistance."

I sat there. I noticed in a sort of blind irrelevance the black hair at his throat, a thin tarnished chain on his right wrist narrow as a hair, a wind-up watch. Although his clothes were of quality they had no labels.

Something snapped home in my brain. "When you say trouble..."

"No. It is *you* who have said the 'trouble'."

I heard Lewis Rybourne's voice in my head first. "Oh, Roy. What shall I do?" Yet somehow Rybourne didn't fit this kind of thing; I couldn't imagine it, that he might know someone from this - calling. And then instead a female voice, high, light and foolish, said to my inner ear, as it had through the phone - "... my friend - she doesn't see him now... I really can't help you."

Tish Ackrington. She'd panicked after my call. She'd phoned up her hit-man acquaintance. *Someone's found out -* she couldn't tell him it was her fault I had, not that it had been. And he must have said, *I'd better pay him a visit.* And then Brown Shirt had gone to my hotel. All the while I'd been checking Joseph Traskul wasn't on my trail, 'Mr C' had been. And now here was this one, using my pseudonym, relaxedly loose as his shirt and dangerous as an adder.

"I think - I may have been misunderstood," I said.

"No, not at all. You have someone in your life who gives you some grief. Isn't that so, Mr Phillips?"

I'd said nothing of that to Tish, but twittering idiot that she was, I reckoned it was easy enough even for her to put two and two together.

"I'm very sorry but..."

"I see," he said. He looked directly into my face and smiled again. His perpetual smiles were quite unlike Sej's. This man's smiles all had a definite purpose. They were masks.

"I'm extremely sorry," I said, "if you've been bothered unnecessarily."

"Ah well now, Mr Phillips. You see, in our line, very often we find a customer is at first a little unsure. For example, he may not be quite certain what we are able to offer him, nor if he's able to afford to recompense us for our very fine work." He sipped once more at the Coke. "We operate on a sliding scale, shall I say. And we have several forms of merchandise. If one's not suitable, it is very conceivable something else can be suggested. We are most flexible, Mr Phillips. Do please, for your own sake, give this a little more thought before making your final decision. The package can be something very small, or something of medium size. Or, naturally, our deluxe model. Everything will be tailored to your own particular needs. This can, to some extent, apply also to our prices."

I gazed at him in sick fascination. He was not like similar characters in my books. Most of those had been of the eastender sort, fists on the table and words unminced.

The *deluxe model*. I assumed this meant murder. And the other options - the packages - beating up, hospitalization, or just intimidation, a *warning*.

I looked down at my drink.

The man across from me said, "Guinness. Have you ever drunk it in Ireland, Mr Phillips?"

"No."

"You should."

He knew too much. It seemed fruitless to deny it all again.

"Er, Mr..."

"Call me," he said, "Cart."

I thought *Cart* was what he said. He didn't remonstrate when I employed it. "Mr Cart..."

"Just Cart. In this matter, I am at your service."

"At this point I'm not sure I do need your - any help."

"That was not the impression I, or my colleagues, received."

"I may have overreacted."

He wasn't smiling. Above the rim of his glass his adder-black eyes stuck to mine.

Could I shake him off?

I doubted it. I cursed myself. I, not Tish, was the idiot.

Inside some compartment of my mind also, a low voice whispered that after all, this man was one of business, as he said. He did what he was paid for. And - if Joseph Traskul were as insane as I'd first believed, to have access to this atrocious alternative - might become necessary. Or was he insane? Was he maybe only different to the rest of us, spontaneous - *compassionate*. Brilliant.

And against all that, the other thought. *And if he is my son?*

I said, "I value very much the fact you've contacted me. It's still possible I may need - but right now there have been sudden other developments."

"This can happen."

"Can I ask...?"

He waited. His eyes were gelid now. They didn't blink, or move away.

"If I required... something very slight. A *small* package."

"A thousand K," he said. "That may seem a lot, but there is my team to consider."

"And – what...?" I stopped. "It may not be necessary, but if..."

"A few little impacts," he said softly. "A little breakage, perhaps. Whatever you prefer. Nothing too serious. Enough to show the error of the way."

A lurch of nausea in my gut.

I evaded contact with his eyes.

"But if it *doesn't* come to that?"

"Then I will wish you a happy life, Mr Phillips. And you will be one thousand pounds the richer."

Perhaps I had incriminated myself enough he would now let me off.

He had seemed to be right handed, but he reached over and took my own right hand with his left. I stiffened in alarm, but he was scribbling something across my palm in black biro. He let me go and I looked down at it. A mobile number.

"You will have to call me in the next **few** weeks. After that the mobile will have been stolen, or before that, should you do something else, such as tell another. In fact, Mr Phillips, I do advise you *not* to tell anyone. For your own sake." More familiar, this. More like one of my own characters. But Christ. What had he done to Tish?

"It's not in my interest to say anything," I said. "Thank you," I added lamely.

"It has been a pleasure to meet you," said Cart. He rose and turned at once, glass in hand. He walked straight past the bar and into the snooker room. He had ugly black shoes, hand-stitched. Brown Shirt, he of the Bond-Flemingesque name, had already vanished.

Duran phoned me the next morning.

He said, "Hi, Roy, how are you doing? She said like you might need some extra security at your place. Glad to hear you've come round to it, mate. We live in interesting times."

"Aren't you in Bristol?"

"No, mate. I'm on the train for London. I can fit you in 2nd of May."

"I'm not sure what's needed."

"Leave it to Uncle Duran. We got lots of packages," he added, unnerving me utterly. "You there, Roy?"

"Yes. Look, I'll call you later this week, early next, OK?"

"OK, mate. See you."

I spent the last days of April in the ordinary way. That Thursday Franziska came and scoured through the house. She commented the kitchen was much cleaner than usual. She gave me a haughty, slightly venomous look when she said it. Hours later it came to me she perhaps thought I now had a girlfriend, some aged person like myself, and this ridiculous female had cleaned the sink and surfaces.

Franziska too made a comment on the piano in the front room.

"Should polish this," she hectored me. "Have you polish?"

"No, I'm afraid not."

"Not," she severely said, "*spray*. Will ruin the wood. And leave the lid up."

"The lid?" This was unlike the lavatories, where she always insisted lids should be left closed, which apparently was benign Feng Sui.

"Let ivories breathe."

I was taken both by the old-fashioned English expression 'ivories' for keys, and the formula of allowing them oxygen. Maureen had said that, and the piano in the doll flat over the Co-op was always left with the lid raised. Though things were sometimes untidy and dusty there, the kitchen and bathroom were always clean, and the piano dusted, though never, I think, polished.

When Franziska had gone, I sat on the paving at the back in the deck chair, drinking tea. It was a warm afternoon, the leaves unfurling fast on neighbouring trees and trellises.

The fir stood dark and unexceptional.

I thought, *I shan't see him again.*

I hadn't seen her, my Maureen, since that night of our parting those years ago.

Like most of us, after a deep but not crippling blow, I just got on with my life. I told myself it was the regular sex I missed, which was true yet not the whole picture. Months after I found myself down that way, and looking up saw different curtains in her windows. She'd been faithful to her word. She must have married her new old lover and gone elsewhere.

The following year I met Lynda Boyle at a rather flabby disco in Lewisham.

She was totally unlike Maureen. To begin with Lynda was over one year my junior. Thin, and with long limp mousy hair, she danced badly, and wore big glasses and a skimpy dress that did her few favours.

I was at the bar, with Danny Collins oddly, the *confrere* from the library I'd been with that night I met Maureen.

We'd secured our drinks, and were looking round at any talent, when Lynda came up and began trying to get the barman's attention.

Lynda was short, five foot three in her heels. No one took any notice of her, except Danny and me.

"Stupid bird," he said. He leaned across and shouted in her ear over the raucous music, "Wave a note at him, luv. He'll see that."

And she said, "I haven't got a note. It's all coins."

Then Danny said, "Hang on, I'll do it."

And he bawled at the barman, and the barman came and Lynda got her round of drinks for herself and her two friends.

"What a shower," said Danny. "Look at them."

One girl was fat and one thin like Lynda.

They huddled to one side, and sometimes went out on the floor together to gyrate to the music. But they moved like creatures whose bones have been unhinged.

There was a girl that night, I can't recall her name. She had jet-black dyed hair and she'd danced with me several times. She was one inch taller, but had taken off her shoes on realizing. Then she was one inch shorter.

Afterwards I figured it out that she was only trying to make her male escort jealous. This finally worked; he came over and shoved me aside so hard I nearly fell, lugging her off shoeless and raven-locked into the night.

Disconsolate I went out and it was raining. Danny had to catch the train, but Lynda Boyle was standing weeping under the neon sign.

"What's the matter?" I said.

She raised her raining eyes to me. No glasses now. "Someone trod on them," she sobbed.

"On - what - *who*?"

"My spectacles. It was Sherry. She pushed me. She's jealous because she's so fat. And they fell off and someone just trod on them. Look." She showed me the ruination of her glasses. "I can't afford to get a new pair, not till next payday. And I can't *see* without them."

I'd been going to get a taxi anyway. Some of them always hung around the disco after midnight, like vultures, ready to charge double and a half. "Where do you live?"

She snivelled something.

She didn't have a coat and her bare shoulders were dewed with rain. She had a nice skin, and her hair, though very thin now it was wet, gave off a pretty smell. I put my leather jacket, (yes, I had one then), round her shoulders, and when the cab swarmed up I took her home. She lived with her parents in an end-of-terrace 'mansion'. She let me kiss her outside the door. She wasn't Maureen. But she seemed to be available. She had already confessed she'd split up with her boyfriend three nights ago and was puzzling as to whether she should come off the Pill. I was nearly twenty-one. What was I likely to do? I did it a week later, having taken her, by then in new glasses purchased by her father, to my room in Brampton Way.

She refused to do a thing with the light on. But once it was off she was up and ready. She rocked the house with her noise. I was embarrassed but not unflattered. Maureen had never been that loud. But then too, Maureen had never been that desperate.

XIII
('Untitled': Page 220)

SUMMONED from the bed of Klavdisa, Vilmos followed the tongue-less servant in a daze.

The City before dawn was in its darkest and most abysmal mode. Now and then uncanny lights flitted through the black, overcast sky. Most likely they were lightnings, but for Vilmos they had ominous shapes, like those of racing greenish mares or lions, whose heads were skulls.

The Master's servant had sometimes indicated his - the Master's - purpose, by means of gesticulations and grimaces. On this excursion he revealed nothing, and when Vilmos had clapped one hand on his shoulder the dumb man thrust him off with a controlled violence that warned of strength.

"But I was called to the house, you know as much, five days back," Vilmos had protested.

Klavdisa all this while had kept to one corner of the bed, shivering. She was afraid of the Master, his alchemic reputation. Vilmos, having been with her for over three days and nights, had thought himself obscured from all search.

Truth to tell, he had dreaded that the Master would locate him now. What had appeared in the chamber, blurred as it was by his fainting, had left an impression of deep horror. And this had grown rather than diminished as time went by.

When they reached the building above the river the servant led him to its street door.

Vilmos had the urge to run away, but a line of light was showing in the east. He had an aversion to daylight, it hurt his eyes. And so he slunk inside.

The Master was seated in the main hall, in his tall chair. A fire crackled on the hearth and the toad sat there, warming itself, the Master's strange pet, which had always been about the house, so far as anyone knew. Some said it was as old as the Master himself, a creature therefore in its seventieth year. Vilmos had never beheld it before.

"I'm here," said Vilmos, affecting nonchalance.

"Oh, is it you?" said the Master, as if he had not had Vilmos brought.

"What do you want with me?"

"I? Do you think I want something?"

"Yes. I was dragged here..."

"It is the Great Powers." said the Master, terribly, "which *want* something of you. I am only their instrument."

"You have told me, jesting, I'll assume, I'm the Devil's."

"So you are. I will tell you something else, however, Vilmos. The Devil is himself punctilious and fastidious. He does not like you very much, though he intends to use you."

"Use me? Well, already he does."

"*That*? Murder and madness and debauchery? The Devil does not attend to such matters. His minor demons deal in those things. *Satanus Rex*. He's not called a king for nothing. *His* tastes are more refined."

"You know him well, then."

"All men *know* him. But he. He himself will condescend to know only a few."

Wine stood on the table in an ewer. Vilmos now, without asking, poured some into a glass, which also stood there, and drank it.

"You've said he chose me."

"So he has. But better not be flattered, Vilmos. The Beast has selected you as a man selects a piece of bread to mop up the gravy. He will use you, consume you perhaps. He does not mean to keep or cherish you."

Vilmos had drained the glass. He threw it at the toad - which nimbly hopped aside. The glass, meeting instead one of the stone pillars either side the hearth, shattered.

"I'm done with this. I'm not here for the Devil's use, let alone yours. I'm in the world for myself."

"Do you think so?"

Vilmos turned, at a loss. In the cramped windows a bloodless dawn was rising, showing the City, towers and roofs, the gleam of the dirty river, the ruined citadel on the Hill of Kolosian.

The toad had come to Vilmos's foot. It stared up at him. There was a poisoned jewel between its eyes. But its eyes also were like that. He wanted to kick it away. But he could not do it, just as he could no longer verbally fence with the Master.

"Let me go," he said.

"Impossible. You've been recognised. Not by ourselves, by That we resort to. Now you'll go upstairs. A room's prepared. Once you swore to serve this Order. Now you shall."

Vilmos said nothing.

The toad's eyes seemed to him luminous and compassionate.

To it, he muttered. "What shall I do?" But the Master replied.

"You must now undergo various rituals and observances. You'll fast and receive chastisement. When we've purified your flesh - your mind, heart and soul, of course, are beyond any redemption - you will be permitted certain pleasures. You will even be allowed to kill once more. The tally must comprise thirteen victims. After this you will serve, as you swore to do, the Mystery. Remember, Vilmos, Gold may be made from Filth. The Fount of Eternal Youth, the Enlightening of the Gem of the Third Eye, may be discovered, unlocked. The colours of the body pass up towards the Infinite. And, in the stage before Infinity, they cross into the physical threshold of Truest Power. Be happy, Vilrnos. For *you* will work an essential magic."

"But what *of* me?" he asked the toad, drearily.

It turned from him and waddled away into the shadow behind the Master's chair. Its refusal to answer seemed now significant.

Risen sun burst through a window, and in Vilmos's skull the white string and the black raw coal of the migraine woke without preamble, hungry, sinking in their fangs. He barely noticed as the servants came and hauled him up the stairs.

FIFTEEN

On the 2nd May at 8.30 a.m., Duran arrived at the house.

He isn't young, though some years younger than I am, yet he retains the air of his mature youth, which I suppose was in the Eighties.

We went round the house. He made notes on a pad from Sainsbury's in green biro.

The chat had been desultory. Suddenly, in the study by the computer, having asked me about virus-combatants, firewalls and so on - computer fraud and its prevention had also become an interest of his - he said, "So why this conversion, Roy?"

"What? The security?"

"Yes, mate. You seemed happy enough. You getting like a bit of bother round here?"

"It's a quiet road," I said. "But. Well, you hear things."

"Yeah. But you can always *hear* things. What's new?"

Of course I had had the idea before that I might confide in Duran, ask him for advice, even help. He might know - someone. But now obviously, *someone* had approached me, the unsettling *Cart* or whatever the hell his name was. And I'd put Cart off because frankly, in those moments, I had felt more scared of him and of the consequences of using his services, than of the eccentric Sej. Now however, I still felt I couldn't confide in Duran. Was it that I really and definitely had begun again to credit Joseph was my son?

"Like, Roy, mate, you don't have to tell me. Only if you felt you should. P'raps I could make you a better defence plan. For the house, I mean."

I looked at him. The words stuck. I said, "I do appreciate that, Duran. Thanks. But I'm just thinking of taking a break, going up north to visit an old friend. And the house will be empty, you see."

He chuckled. "What've I *told* you, Roy? Don't tell no one, *ever*, you are leaving your property unoccupied."

"Right."

"I mean, you don't know you can trust me. I mean, you can. But you can't know for sure."

"Almost every lock and bolt in here was your suggestion. Wouldn't you have broken in by now if I couldn't?"

"Well, you got me there, Roy. Maybe I'm just biding my time."

The other matter of Why had been satisfactorily shelved, probably let go. He was a good man, but his moral duty, even as he saw it, could only extend so far.

When Duran and I had made the 'defence plan', which would be quite costly, and included sorting out a new burglar alarm that worked - "Police don't take that much notice, unless you got one of *these*" - we fixed another date for Thursday, he had another coffee and then left. His girlfriend was eight and a half months into expecting their second baby. He didn't like having to go back to Bristol on Saturday and leaving her. He said if anything got 'stressy' his cousin would have to lump it.

After he'd gone I did the chores in the house. The contents of the fridge and freezer were low, but if I was planning to leave this coming Saturday, I only had a few days to cover. The thought of shopping, never a favourite task and always kept to necessities, exasperated me. I'd known for years that one day I'd be old and on my own and then I wouldn't manage it at all. It would be some form of modern meals-on-wheels, or deliveries from some supermarket, with half the items doubtless wrong.

But the way the world was, why assume I'd even live, or

any of us would, into our 'twilight' years?

In the afternoon I sat down at the machine and put in the disc for the latest due-to-be-written novel. It had the working title of *Kill Me Tomorrow*, which I'd lifted of course from *Othello*, but the publisher had pointed out it sounded too much like something concerning James Bond. I couldn't settle to it.

I am fairly disciplined. One needs to be in this job. But the whole rigmarole, although they'd liked and bought it, looked like twaddle to me now.

Finally I sat, staring at the words on the screen, not seeing them, and Joseph walked forward in my mind and stood there, watching me.

I hadn't seen him for days. How long? Eight, nine. But he had left an indelible impression. The four circumstances of our meeting - the pub in the Strand, under the fir tree, at my door, in my hotel - had me strung up in the certain belief he might now suddenly appear - virtually anywhere, looking in at an upper window, maybe, balanced ably on a ladder.

Or would I simply go downstairs and he'd be sitting there, in the kitchen, drinking tea?

Why had he installed a piano, if he hadn't meant to return into my life and house? Or was it a present, like the dustbin and the bottle of beer which, incidentally, I'd never touched.

He'd become bored. That must be it. His warped and extraordinary mind had abruptly swerved away from me.

I'd be glad, thankful, but only if I could be *certain*.

Or would I be glad, and thankful?

Surely, for Christ's sake, I wouldn't miss any of *this*?

Unless. Unless he was my son.

Odd perhaps, I'd kept the elements that would contain his DNA, to help protect me from him. Now for the very first I fully recognised they might have another purpose.

But then, DNA tests aren't always conclusive. And anyway, if he were mine - what would he want? And I. What would *I* want *of* him?

At 7 p.m. the burglar alarm went off, apparently because some kids were playing football outside. Later it did it again because the bicycle boy from up the road went past. It had always behaved like this. I turned it off.

That night I dreamed of Joseph Traskul as Vilmos, in the dim City of my imagination's night. He lay half dead in the upper room of the Master's house, as outlined in chapters thirteen through fifteen. In this dream-version rain was pouring in through the ceiling.

And I went into the room and stood looking down at him and he lay looking up at me.

"Don't do this, Roy," he said. "I never meant to harm."

But I answered in the Master's words, a script I had learned well, that he was for the use, not of myself, but of Great Powers beyond - yet in - the world.

And then Maureen stood beside me on the floor running with water, and she said, "He's not worth our concern, Charlie. Bleeding bugger."

And I woke, and I thought, *My God, can I wait until Saturday to get away?*

In the morning I called Matt.

"I've got to make a trip to your neck of the woods. Are you up to dinner?"

"I'm up to anything, Roy. I'm up to killing that bitch."

I thought, *This then, Matt's anti-Sylvia maelstrom of bitterness, is my alternative.* Never mind. I need to remove myself somewhere.

"Any chance I could sleep on the couch a couple of nights? These bastards aren't paying expenses."

"Why not, Roy? Have the spare room. She's had her fucking lover in there enough times. And now she's gone. So exorcise it for me."

Duran was due to come back on Thursday. On Thursday morning something happened. Someone rang the door bell, obviously Duran, yet as I opened the door I thought - *I thought* -

A woman, youngish, tall, willowy, stood there looking upset.

"I'm sorry to trouble you - but my car's stalled..." She waved in a helpless way over her right shoulder. "It's just, my mobile's out too. Could I possibly use your land-line? I'll be happy to pay."

I looked at her, and I thought now: *There have been too many things like this. Too many.*

I said, "I'm sorry, my phone isn't working." (This was, of course, true). "Perhaps try next door." I indicated 76, Ian the house-husband.

She said, looking even more upset, "I did, they don't answer."

We stared at each other, she and I.

The ultimate impasse. I didn't believe her. I was thinking, if not coherently, *This is a scam. She's up to something, this forlorn female, coming here and saying she must use my telephone.*

And then I recalled, in the most unpredictable rush, so many incidents in my life, and how curiously I had met so many characters who were now integral, even if our time of contact had vanished away. Maureen with her dramatically sloughed lover Reg, Lynda with her broken glasses - even events, for example the urge to hurry to the hospital lavatory, missing, like some cruel train, my mother's moment of death.

I mustn't be so self-involved. Everything did *not* revolve

around myself. Everything was *not* a conspiracy, a plot.

"Wait, I've got a mobile. You can use that." I turned and left her by the door. I only had to go to the kitchen table. I hadn't asked her in, nor did she come in. She didn't look particularly strong; there was nothing to steal in the hall.

"Oh thank you," she said, when I gave her the phone. "What do I owe...?"

"That's fine."

Encouraged, grateful, she did step up, just into the shelter of the doorway. She leaned by the door, and pushed in numbers.

Then she pulled a Kleenex out of a pocket and rubbed her nose, turning her back to me shyly.

I could see it now, the white car, stalled very definitely down where Old Church Lane gave way to the Crescent. Steam rose from the bonnet.

I walked off into the kitchen, let her mumble into the phone in private.

As such conversations do, it took a little while. I'd better top the phone up again, to be safe.

When I came back, she'd dropped the Kleenex on my mat and was grabbing it up. She stood clutching it and wiping her nose with it again, though now it would be less than clean. She was shaky. I retrieved my phone before she dropped that too.

"Thank you, thank you so much. It's OK. They're coming to rescue me. I shouldn't get so silly... Really, can't I pay for..."

"It's quite OK."

She went off along the path. I wondered why she was driving through these streets, where she was going, why she'd got in such a flap. She was rather a pretty woman, only about thirty. She looked sad, sad anyway without car problems to upset her. She was wiping her eyes now. What would he have done? Asked her in and made her tea.

I shut the door.

It rained in the evening. The sunset was like a squashed blue plum. I'd gone out of the back door and looked at the paving, for some reason. It was beginning to crack. I suppose not unreasonably, it had been laid some years before. Built-in obsolescence, as they say. *Bad workmanship*, as my father would have said.

Duran hadn't turned up. This wasn't like him. Nor did he call.

I dreamed about my father *that* night. He was walking with me through a dark forest full of fir trees.

"You should clear this, Roy. It's a bit disappointing,"

"But, Dad. It isn't mine."

"It's all yours, Roy. Everything is yours, ours. We just have to face it, show it we're not afraid. Never turn your back on these things, Roy. They'll only get worse."

My father had become the Master now. He even wore the robe.

We reached a hill above the forest and saw moonlight rake the acres of the trees. Above, stars burned blue. It was, as dreams can be, detailed and entirely real.

"How's mother?" I asked him humbly.

"Your mother?" he said. His voice grew quiet and tense. "She has a lover, Roy. She didn't wait for me. I'm up to killing that bitch."

When Duran phoned me at seven the next morning I was not amazed.

Nor, of course, when he said, "I still can't get anything from your landline, Roy."

"No. Trying to get them to fix it."

"Gawd. Don't hold your breath."

"I'm not."

"Look, Roy, I *hate* to've let you down. She's gone into well - we thought it was labour and she's not due till June. But they've took her in and - well, I wanna be with her,

"Yes, Duran, of course you do."

"Can I call you later?"

"Whenever, Duran. Don't worry about that. Good luck. I'm sure she'll be fine."

"Thanks, Roy. You're a king."

Satanus Rex. A king.

When I thought to look, the white car had been removed from the junction of the Lane and the Crescent.

I was fairly sure Duran wouldn't be calling me back, or if he did only to say he couldn't make it. They might send her home and he must be there to look after her, not to mention their other child, who was only just at school age.

The problem was, should I simply leave the house as it was? Presumably Joseph *could* break in. Or could he? Did his cleverness also lie in that direction? He gave off an almost supernatural impression of being able to manifest out of thin air, but in fact there were always reasons for everything he had achieved that way. He'd made sure I understood them. No, the house could resist him. Somehow he had got the piano speed-delivered and installed on that single day he was here before. Since then he hadn't come back. After all he might never come back. Presumably he had achieved his purpose, whatever insane purpose it was.

Even so, preparing to pack, I meant to put everything together again very carefully, all my documents and valued files, placed in my holdall.

At 9 a.m. this time Matt called me on the mobile.

"Your phone doesn't work, Roy." He meant the landline evidently. He sounded aggrieved. Faithless wives, useless telephones... "I tried you yesterday. Twice."

"They're being slow to repair it. As I have the mobile I'm not an emergency, it seems."

"You are to me. This call's costing me the earth. And a mobile phone, did you know, can give you cancer?" he added. Gloatingly he continued, "*She* has one. Reason I called. I can't make this weekend. Some old chums have turned up out of the blue. Every inch of space here is taken. I'll be clear Monday morning, and good riddance."

I sensed, without any evidence, he had picked up another woman and she was staying the weekend with him. Hopefully it might defuse some of his angst.

"Let's make it Monday then, Matt."

This was better, in its way. Monday would be easier for travelling up there. Saturdays like Sundays were always chancy, trains cancelled, works on the line.

But now I had tonight and two more days and nights here.

When I locked up that night the top bolt on the front door seemed loose. It had a little the previous night, but this was worse. Duran had been a bit rough with all the bolts, testing them and telling me off for using flimsy things like that still, although he had installed them himself years ago. "Yeah, but Roy, things have improved. Anyone could *kick* this door down. Bust the locks, the bolts'd just fly off."

I had told him I would then hear all that and telephone the police.

"Mate of mine," he said balefully, "he had a break-in. The cops took an hour to get there. By which time he'd chased the burk off himself. But I don't see you doing that. Not your style. Too much a gentleman you are, Roy."

I wobbled the bolt home gingerly. The lower one, which last night I'd forgotten to shoot, as I sometimes do when I'm tired, seemed conversely very stiff. I got some WD40 and squirted it, but it didn't seem to do any good. I left it and simply locked up. Then I brought a straight chair from the front room and leaned it on the door. I felt foolish doing this, despite everything that had happened. But in any case, I couldn't utilise the bolts from the outside, or the chair, when I left.

This was going to be one of my fully insomniac nights, or so it seemed. I got to bed about ten-thirty and tossed and turned until one. Then I got up, made some tea and went into the study.

Here I tried to make a start on the new novel, *Kill Me*.

Outside two cats were wauling at each other. Up the road No 98 was having a party; I could catch the thump-thump of their music.

I managed to squeeze out five hundred words of dry, formulaic crap, but it was, I told myself virtuously, a start.

Then I found myself reaching out for the disc of *Untitled*.

I put it in the machine.

Chapter XVI. Printed up, this began on page 273, and ran on to Chapter XVII, and so to the part at which I had left it, in the spring of the year 2000.

I skimmed through it, once or twice pausing, even now, to change a word, pare or extend a sentence.

Lying on the floor of the Master's upper room, Vilmos had just slaughtered a man dragged in for him from the alleys. Vilmos had performed the murder gruesomely, but without involvement. A rat had come from the corner to feast. His own body starved and tortured by the Master's minions, Vilmos lay in the blood, the stranger's and his own, his mind clear for the first time perhaps in twenty-five years, his eyes full of blue flashes, the visual product of another variation on his migraines. But the blue being very beautiful, very evocative, entertained him with its colour.

My own eyes had begun to ache.

I printed the amendments on paper, then switched off the machine. Going downstairs for a whisky nightcap, I poured it in one of the sturdier glasses from the kitchen. I felt done in, but would I sleep? Outside I heard the cats still fighting violently across the front paving. Their spitting struggle, or something like it, might fit well into the next paragraphs of Vilmos's horror. Maybe other rats could come in and these would fight. I scribbled a note and took the whisky to bed.

To my surprise I drifted after only a minute or so, into a warm and trackless sleep. Just two more days, then I'd be gone.

Waking, the alarm-clock, blurred by my vision, said it was 4.12 a.m. There was as yet no light. *Was* I awake? I thought not completely, and turned eagerly to swim back down.

That damned party up the road was still going on. I could hear the music, not thumping now, in fact a piano playing. A piano playing tunefully. Softly, pleasingly. I thought, Oh, that's only Sej. And again I slept.

I woke at half past ten. Nowadays that's unheard of for me, even after a white night.

When I sat up, a light wave of vertigo slid across my brain. I'm not subject to such things. My mouth tasted unusually nasty, chalky...

A stab of absolute fright shot through me. I'd been drugged. I had been drugged. How? The tea - no, I'd worked a while after that. It must have been the whisky. Look, I hadn't even finished it. I picked up the glass and sniffed it. There was no smell, only alcohol. But then, there hadn't been any other smell than alcohol in the red wine I gave to *him*.

This was the moment I recalled hearing the piano being played downstairs.

I floundered out of bed, ran into the bathroom and grabbed the shaving-foam. It's of the type that sprays.

Running, vertigo forgotten, I took the stairs in leaps and sprang into the front room.

No one was there. The lid of the piano was shut, as I'd eventually left it despite my cleaning girl's admonition.

The library and kitchen were also empty. There was no sign of any tampering, had been none upstairs. The windows were shut and locked, the back door also. The front door too, when I went and looked at it, was the same as I had left it, the upper bolt shakily done up and the bottom one stuck in the undone position. Both door locks were secure.

Then I remembered the chair, which I'd left leaning on the door. It wasn't there.

Back into the front room I went. The chair stood, where it usually did. Had I misremembered? Hadn't I moved it out into the hall? Had I dreamed I'd done that, then dreamed I heard him playing - what had it been? Gershwin - *Someone to Watch Over Me* - and then something else...

I walked back into the hall and, not undoing the door, pulled at it very gently.

The upper bolt fell straight down on the floor. It had been secured, this time for appearances only, by blue tac. When I'd fetched the magnifying glass from the library, knelt down and peered through it, I saw too the mass of something transparent and shiny that had trapped the lower bolt in its slot, unable to move. Superglue, probably.

I stood there, thinking over the ultimate riddle. He must of course, during the short while he was here before, have managed to obtain copies of the two front door keys. But the bolts had been fine until the night before last. Thursday. Had Sej then already somehow broken in *while I was here*? I have reasonably good hearing for my age; surely I'd have heard him? The very camouflaging of the wrecked bolts indicated he'd wanted to enter quietly, to - shall I say - *surprise* me. And the drug, if there was one, in the whisky - I'd had a glass of whisky on Wednesday night, without any ill effect. I'd slept in the usual way, not well, only the peculiar dreams, but I'd had those off and on since first I met him.

No, something had been done here later than Wednesday. And somehow I knew it hadn't been by Joseph. This was an animal deduction. My *instinct*, if you like. As if I might have detected him by odour, or a pricking in my thumbs.

Yet if not him, then who?

It was at this moment that I recalled the young woman with the stalled car. She was tall enough to reach up bolt-high easily, but had she the strength to pry the bolt loose, the skill not to loosen it entirely, only enough a slight nudge from outside would shift it? Of course she *could* have slopped the glue on to the other, lower bolt. I remembered how she'd bent down, risen with the dropped Kleenex in her hand, and wiped her nose - or seemed to wipe it - so sadly, as if holding back tears. Had there been space also for her to pop into the front room and fix my whisky?

Who was she? Why had she done it?

She must have done it because Sej told her to.

I remembered something else.

I remembered the woman with the run-over dead white dog at the Belmont Hotel.

SIXTEEN

It goes without saying that ringing both Duran's home number and his mobile got no answer. He was at the hospital. However, now I couldn't quite push off the grim feeling that Sej had somehow also got at him, and that the labour of Duran's girlfriend was a lie. The non-mad area of my brain dismissed this theory over and over. Duran would not be, let alone become, any pawn of Sej's. And yet...

Instead I called a local locksmith. I explained I needed my front door locks changed and bolts replaced.

"Sorry, squire. I'm spoken for this next month." He suggested another name and number who, politely saying much the same thing, also gave me another name and number. In the end, after several more similar calls, a nasal voice said he might be able to 'help me out'. The price he quoted was exorbitant, but I agreed. He never turned up.

What should I do?

Damn it to hell. If Sej wanted bloody access so much let him have it. I'd had to abandon the house before. It would be lunacy to stay here now. *Waiting.* I began to pack that early Saturday afternoon, and in among the clothes and other stuff, held in bubble-wrap and a small box, I placed my mother's red glass dog. Red, for Vilmos and his Order, was the colour of the lowest chakra, located at the genitals. Or blood, of course. Even a white dog could be made red that way. And what had I seen of it, that dead, white dog, I, the perceptive writer of detective fiction? A bundle out of which hung a *tail.* I hadn't even gone close. It could have been a child's *sock.* And the rest? Fake theatrical blood normally available in joke shops, if nowhere else - or even ketchup. And a small bolster.

I raised the lid of the piano after I'd taken the ornament. I thought of smashing the keys of the piano with the hammer I use to knock in the odd nail.

I also thought of poisoning every item of drink or food in the house. I didn't need sleeping pills, or bleach. Clear shampoo would do in the dry ginger. Sink cleaner, a white cream, smeared last over the frozen piece of chicken, appearance and smell obscured by the cold. Enough to make him sick again. Enough to *sting*. I toyed with these notions. I wanted to booby-trap the place but now there wasn't time. I had to get out, before everything else in the street curled up in another night, and lying sleepless and fully dressed for morning, I heard the two keys turn in the locks, as I hadn't last night. I'd piled several items against the front door again, kitchen chairs, pans and pots, the original paraphernalia plus. I'd managed to bump and heft one of the armchairs out of the front room too. Make it hard for him. I would leave by the back way, use the small kitchen ladder to climb over the back fence which, as I was light, should just take my weight as it had taken his rangier, slightly-heavier one the first time.

In a defunct plastic vitamin bottle I poured a sample of the-perhaps contaminated whisky. I still wasn't sure, there. Had I only been very tired? If it *were* a pill I'd like to know the brand name. Apart from slight giddiness on first sitting up, I felt fine. Thanks, Sej, for finally finding me the occasional good night's sleep.

I was loath to destroy the computer. To have to buy a new one would be annoying, and everything lately had taken a toll on my 'savings'. Left alone it should be useable for another eighteen months at least, and for my requirements, probably three years. I had the discs, and I'd set it to delete again.

Additionally now, I'd also pulled out the paperback copy

of each of my novels, and dumped them in another bag. I'd put the big paper copy of *Untitled* in there too, complete with the recent printed corrections and hand-written scribbles. I added my mother's Bible, the King James edition, retained by all of us for its language and antiquity, rather than any delusions of a God.

I locked my bedroom door again and for good measure, before that, myself pumped glue down the upright of the door's edge. Post locking I pumped glue as well into the lock. This was sheer perversity. There was nothing interesting in the room. I just wanted to frustrate him.

But I hadn't smashed the piano keys. It would take a lot to make me do something like that. It was a musical instrument, valuable not only as an object, but for its potential. In the same way I'd have been happy right then to poison Joseph Traskul, but not to break his fingers.

Perhaps it goes without saying I had written down the number the ghastly Cart had given me. I nearly called it twice that afternoon. But then I couldn't say exactly where the quarry was likely to be. Take it with me, and I'd have a more concrete clue that he might be *here*.

At this time I had no notion of the 666 number of Sej's London flat, only that such a flat was supposed to exist.

I'd previously checked train times on the web, and was aiming for something between three and five-thirty. The grey stone village where Matthew, once with Sylvia, lived, is like many others, all of them rather more charmingly evidenced by the famous venue in *Last of the Summer Wine*. It was a few miles outside Cheston, and Cheston. with its concluding change of trains at Crewe, would take, all told, four hours. Cheston had the Empire Hotel. There I would park myself over Saturday night and Sunday, and polish off the last of the credit on my Barclaycard.

Everything locked, bolted, barricaded, disconnected,

made, where feasible, user-unfriendly, I left the house which had been my parents' at 2.15 p.m. The bags were going to feel heavy. Having unlocked the back door, closed and relocked it, I climbed the kitchen ladder at the end fence. I intended to lower the bags over the top of the fence to the alley, trusting the packing would protect the glass dog.

The day was miserable, gloomy. No one was about. Birds sang however, and up in the fir there came the flutter of wings.

Looking over the fence I felt a fool. But there was no time for that. I lowered both bags with care; they only had to drop the shortest distance. Then I took hold of the barrier. Thank God, it at least was in decent repair. I kicked the ladder away and heard it skid along the paving, then launched myself across and down.

A boy could do that. Now and then I had, as a boy, done such things. But I'm no longer a boy. I landed awkwardly but not badly, scraping my hand on the fence, and one knee on the concrete of the alley. In the fir the birds took flight with disapproving cries. And he rose from the shadow where, unseen in black, he had crouched, smiling, and helped me to my feet. I write books. I was a book. And he had read me all before, it seemed.

Blood was seeping through my trouser leg where I'd grazed my knee like that boy I wasn't anymore.

He looked at that. "Oh dear."

"Take your bloody hands off me."

Smiling, he stepped back. And before I could think, he'd picked up both my bags. "We'll go in the front way. Can you make it OK, Roy?"

"The door is barricaded."

"I'm sure I can shift it. Don't worry."

"There's more there than last night." I didn't sound

defiant, only meaningless.

"Well, I'm strong. Come on. Won't take a minute."

I stood where I was. I said, "Why don't you leave me alone?"

"Because I like you."

"I don't - like *you*. Go to hell."

"How do you know I don't already, on a regular basis?"

An awful laugh burst out of me. I sounded madder than he did. "Right," I said. "Are you going to give me back my bags?"

"Of course, if you think you can manage."

"Give me my fucking bags."

He widened his eyes at me. It reminded me of a woman's facial gesture. Maureen had never done this. Others, especially Lynda, had.

"Take this one, then." He handed me the holdall. "But *this* one, it's smaller but it feels heavier. What have you put in here? Your secret wine cellar? Better let me carry that."

And turning from me, he sauntered back along the alley and turned the corner towards the front.

I could have let him go, run the other way - my knee wasn't bad - got out by the alley's other exit nearer the Crescent. I would, I think, have got away.

But the bag he had hold of contained my books, my discs, and my MS of *Untitled*. I realised in those seconds that I, too, was definitely unstable. In the holdall I had my passport, all crucial documents, even the house deeds - even now the glass dog. Yet I went after him. I *hurried*.

He was already at the front door using the keys when I reached him.

"Mmm," he said contemplatively. "I can feel it'll be a bit of a push. That's all right."

Just then the front door of 72 opened. Out ambled amiable George, with the big kitchen scissors he uses to trim the hydrangea on his front lawn.

"Hello, Roy. Oh, hello…" he added, beaming, to Sej.

"Hi. How are you, Mr Fulton?" politely inquired Sej.

"Oh, we're fine, thank you."

I said, "George, I need to have a word with you."

George looked vaguely concerned. As I moved forward, Sej got in my way, putting an arm over my shoulders. I thrust him off.

"George, this man is not my son. Go indoors. Call the police."

Stricken, George stood there, like a child on Christmas morning finding the presents are gone and the tree has died.

Sej spoke to him before I could do so again. "Sorry, Mr Fulton. It's all right. I think I explained a bit about this before. He'll be OK now I'm here. Just leave it…"

"*George*," I said loudly, "for God's sake do as I say. *Please*."

"Er, Roy - well, er…"

As I took half another step in his direction, he performed a most determinative action. Largely I think it was subconsciously dictated. But then, I've never known them well, my neighbours. How could any of them be sure what or who I really was? He pointed the scissors at me, the points towards my chest, and backed up the lawn, in at his door. He was still saying, almost still amiably, "Er, well, er," as he closed it.

I had my own mobile in my hand by then. Better late than never, but it was not. It was *too* late.

"Now, Roy," said Sej, not even glancing but predicting once more with total accuracy as he spun the phone out of my grasp. It hit the path. There was a crack. Had anyone else seen or heard? If they had, so what? We all have troubles of our own.

"Give me the bag," I said.

"Not yet, Roy. Let's get the door undone first."

Leave it, you fool, leave it all - sentimental glass dog, documents, manuscript, disc, book, DNA, house. Escape, you confounded fucking idiot...

But instead I came at him, I, who cannot fight to save my life and never even scrapped with anyone since I was fourteen and Ben Oggey stole my fountain pen. Ben won, incidentally. No great amazement, that.

Sej simply caught me and somehow swung me round, and as he put me down again he thrust with our combined weight at the front door. The pans went over inside with a stupid noise of armour, the chairs went too, even the armchair had shifted just enough.

The wind was knocked out of me. He pushed me in through the open slice of door, then threw the bag of books over my head and along the hallway. Perhaps he thought I'd be impelled to race after it like a stick-addicted puppy. But I merely leaned on the wall and in he came, squeezing past the fallen barricade, putting down the other bag, the holdall, which he had also somehow relieved me of in our brief non-fracas.

My front door too was shut. Outside my mobile was lying, maybe useless or not, on the path. But things get thrown on to the front gardens sometimes. There was even once, I'd heard, a whole box of uneaten pizza found floating in the pond at No 82.

"Well then," said Sej. "Let's see about that knee of yours. Then we'll have some tea."

Naturally I didn't allow him to touch the graze. I saw to it myself in the bathroom, which he permitted. I had to conclude he had permitted it, even to my locking the bathroom door. But he could break it in anyway, I was fairly certain of that.

I sat on the closed seat of the lavatory and stared in despair at the two bags I'd insisted on bringing up with me - which again, I'd been *permitted* to do.

I made another mental itinerary.

My bedroom door was locked, (he must have got copies of the front door keys by taking an impression from the locks, so might anyway have a copy of this key too). But the bedroom door now was glued shut. Study, library, front room, kitchen, lavatory and bathroom were potentially open wide.

There was very little food in the house and no phone. Apart I assumed from his own mobile, which he would still have.

Was shampoo in the ginger ale or sink cleaner on the chicken still an option? He'd be watching out now. Doubly cautious.

And there was the strong impression he might *like* me to 'try something'. A challenge, like some move in a game of which *I* didn't know the rules.

God, what could I do?

He let me take my time up there.

When I came out. I'd removed the disc of *Untitled* and also my most important documents, and shoved them in the inside pockets of my jacket. He'd see, or suspect these stiffened shapes probably, but at least this way I could run if I ever got a chance. If he took them off me, I still could. Why hadn't I already? I *had* had the chance. Not taken it.

Did that godforsaken novel mean so much? Vilmos - *Vilmos* and that invented City and all that infantile quasi-gothic rubbish, a stale brain's attempt to sparkle.

Tidily he had cleared the chairs and other things from the hall. The armchair had been lugged back into the front room and to its accustomed place, marked ready by the imprint of its legs in the carpet. When I re-entered the kitchen I saw he'd brought in the steps from outside. As in my macabre premonition, he was sitting at the table, drinking tea.

"I made a pot."

I sat down and looked at him.

"You look tired," he said.

"I am, Sej. Why are you doing this?"

"You keep asking. I keep telling. You don't seem to absorb it."

"No. "

"I like you. You interest me."

"Do you understand what you're doing?"

He smiled. "Perfectly."

He poured out tea; we both were to have milk. And neither of us took sugar, it seemed.

"Have you put," I said, "something in the tea?"

"That's *your* sort of trick."

My mind reassembled suddenly. "Apart from the whisky," I said.

He looked at me. For the first time, like a villain in 1940s Film Noir, he raised one long, black eyebrow only.

"Sorry?"

"I had a whisky last night and I slept - in a way I don't usually sleep. Actually, Sej, I'd like to know what it was. That was probably the best night's sleep I've had for about fifteen years."

And then he grinned, as he had when he played the piano like a young contemporary Liszt.

"I think I understand. It wasn't in the whisky, Roy. It was in the *glass*."

"Not the whisky glasses in the front room. I'd used them."

"No. It was a chunky glass in your kitchen cupboard. You could have put anything in it - water, Coke, take your pick."

"A glass. How?"

"I broke the tablet. It's Rohypnol, by the way. I dissolved some of it and wiped it round the bottom of the glass. Put it back on the shelf, to the front."

"So it could have happened any time."

"Truly. I wondered why you didn't come down, when I was playing you the Gershwin, and that Chabrier piece. The Chabrier was his last composition. Sheer fireworks."

I said, "Yes, I half heard it. Sounded as if you had three hands."

A look of radiant pleasure went over his face.

He said, "There are times, Roy, I *love* you. I wish you were my father."

I took a breath. I hadn't tried the tea.

Gently I said, "Am I? Tell me the truth."

"As I've said before, what do *you* think?"

"I think I am *not* your father."

He shrugged.

"Then tell me," I said, "the name of your mother."

I was calm as a piece of wood. Maybe it was shock. Now he had trapped me entirely. I was letting go all I had ever been. I had to become some other person - or some intrinsic Roy. A kind of non-effusive passion was stirring in me. I can't explain it. No doubt I was temporarily, and with some reason, mad.

"My mother's name." He looked at the table. "Let me think."

"You wouldn't have to think."

"Oh, Roy. I would. I grew up, if you can call it that, in an orphanage. Then I was fostered. I can't recall quite when, but after I was eighteen someone showed me some clandestine paperwork. And her name was on it. But I didn't want to know."

Stunned I sat there. Through my mind, irrepressibly,

went an image of Maureen, abandoning her child so her well-off old man wouldn't get angry. Had she done that?

"It's important," I said. "At least, curiously enough, to me."

And I wondered at myself for I seemed now to be two men. One knew this situation for what it was. The other - the other, less than play along, had become *engaged*. But this other me also, he had his own agenda, to which I wasn't sure I was even privy. It was as if I'd left myself below, and here he - I - sped along the high bridge above. With Sej. Most games need at least two players.

Sej lifted his head and tipped it right back this time. He looked up at the ceiling.

"Give me a clue," he said.

"First letter L. Lynda," I said, deliberately.

"No. That wasn't it."

The tea I hadn't drunk was cold. He had drunk his. "What about," I hesitated. "V," I said. "Or - J?"

And he looked at me. "Oh, Roy," he said. "We are going to have a wonderful time."

He did break in the bedroom door, later that evening. It was easy for him, as I'd have thought, although the door didn't break open cleanly because of the glue.

"What did you use?" he asked, sounding mildly intrigued.

"What she did, I expect, your woman friend who fixed the bolts downstairs."

"I see."

I'd already asked him how she had managed the loosening of the top bolt. "She's good at that kind of thing," he said. "She has strong wrists and fingers - she plays the piano, the same as me."

We had had lots of little conversations by bedtime. On

this, and that.

Once I said, "So now I'm definitely your prisoner."

And he said, "Yes. For now."

We had established this because my mobile had rung faintly out on the front path. Apparently it still worked. But when I inquired if I was to be allowed to get it he said no, and that nor would he.

It rained heavily that night anyway.

Besides, someone might steal it, simply for its usefulness, perhaps as a free gift, for it was in no way trendy.

I had also seen, during the afternoon, the tiny dark healing wound in the palm of Sej's left hand.

For one terrible moment I'd been reminded of a disgusting statue of Christ crucified - the *Crucifix*. He *saw* me see the mark. He said, "This? That's fine. I'll tell you about it later."

But I am prevaricating.

Because I don't want to put down the next section of my narrative.

Perhaps absurdly, I hadn't known I would 'block' at this point. In fact it isn't a block; I know only too well what comes next.

No one will ever see this.

No one.

Let me therefore, for my own sake, write it.

6

The second time I went to his flat, Mr C went with me.

Brothers in our shaven baldness, we were otherwise not alike. A big man, Mr C. On this occasion he wore a grey shirt. "Which one's the druggy you said?"

"Flat No 2. 3A's a possible as well."

Mr C rang the bell of No 2.

We waited, while 5's loud music thundered above. My companion seemed impervious.

There was no answer. So Mr C rang No 2's bell again, now leaning on it.

Presently a voice blurred from the speaker.

"Whah? Wha' is it?"

"Hello, sonny. I got something nice for you. What you like. You want it?"

No 2 brightened audibly. "'S 'at Col?"

"No. It's his best friend."

"Wha' you got?"

"I'm not telling you through a door. You want it, come and get it. You got one minute."

"Hang on - don' go - I'm opening the door - I'll be there..." wailed No 2.

The buzzer sounded and the door was pushed open by Mr C.

We went in and stood there until No 2 came slithering and slipping, nearly falling, down the stairs. He was as I recalled him, nothing changed, hair, garments or stench.

On the last lowest step he seemed to grasp that something was wrong here. He eyed Mr C, then me, then came back to Mr C.

"I see you afore," he finally told us both, inaccurately.

Mr C moved.

He was very quick, which I'd already witnessed.

No 2 went down like a literal bag of bones. I seemed to hear them click and rattle as he landed on the floor and Mr C knelt on him. Probably I'd heard his keys.

"Now then. We want to go and see Tina."

"All right - a' right - yeah, mate, you go an' see Tee."

"She up there today?" asked Mr C, grinding his knee into No 2's ribs so he squeaked and coughed. "Sure - yeah."

"If you're lying... "

"OK. Don' know, do I - get offa me..."

"Oh, am I hurting you, sonny?"

No 2 whimpered.

"Tell you what, why don't I let you get up and you can show us the way. "

"*He* knows - the way..." accused No 2, indicating me around Mr C's inexorable bulk.

"Never mind. Demonstrate your good manners, son. Just lead us up. Like we was blind, eh?"

"You ain't," whispered No 2. "Y'ain't blind."

Mr C stood and No 2 crawled over and coughed against the floor. Then he rose and tried to sprint back up the stairs

But Mr C tripped him and he went down with a bang on the first step, and rolled there whining, with blood on his mouth.

Above us the music roared, but I don't think anyone would have come to see anyway.

"I cut me lip - why you done that - ain't got no stuff..."

Sobbing, No 2 guided us up the stairs, sometimes faltering and coughing, once spitting red on to the step.

There was a resignedness to all his actions. One guessed he had been done over before.

Nothing else happened all the way up. No 2 ignored both his own flat and 3A's; he led us, flagging and wilting, to the top. Where no one had repaired the door of 6, 66, and it still stood ajar.

"What a good boy you've been," Mr C congratulated No 2. "Now you skitter on down to your frowsty little pen, and we'll see what Tina's got for us."

No 2 fled.

There was obviously no chance he'd call the police. Doubtless, rather like Roy Phipps, there was really no one he could call.

"I'll go first."

I let him.

I wasn't entirely certain why I'd felt I had to come back, but it had nagged me all through the couple of days since I'd been here last. I'd called the number again Cart gave me, of course by then the third time I'd done it. The response was the same. The price, on this occasion, only five hundred pounds, with a discount, too, since I'd paid ahead of the delivery.

Mr C had by now sloughed his very excellent street accent. He spoke like the well-bred Oxbridge type he apparently was. Or maybe this accent was a fake too.

The place was as I'd seen it before. Bare, empty, untouched. I'd half expected someone, some friend from another flat, to be squatting here by now. Yet no one even seemed to have come in, despite the door's having been undone. Then again, long ago any of them could have broken in as I had.

Even my unreal packet lay where I'd dropped it. Mr C bent at once and picked it up. He didn't tell me off, as Duran had done about my security, for discarding incriminatory evidence. When I'd suggested plastic gloves to Mr C he had shaken his head. "That won't be needed, Mr Phillips, you take this flat too seriously. No cop worth his salt would give a fip. "

Despite its phonetic resemblance to my surname, 'fip' was what Mr C sometimes said for fuck. So far I'd not actually heard him swear.

To begin with, once we were in he made sure the flat's front door was closed off from inside. He did this by dragging the dirty unclothed mattress, unaided, in from the bedroom, and pushing it against the entry. Its passage made strange tracks through the perhaps stranger dusts of the flat.

His search was unlike mine.

He prised up floorboards, clipped pieces out of the plaster, skirmished behind the lavatory and took the panel off the side of the bath. He used various small tools, some unanticipated, in this work. (I'd never seen a corkscrew used as a drill before).

I followed him, and when requested to hold something or move something, I obeyed without question.

I'd gathered once he had been in the police, but which department, as with the cause of his leaving, was never made clear.

The red leaf in the bedroom had already turned wan and brown. He picked it up and sniffed it with a knowing look incomprehensible to me.

"African, you know," he said elusively.

Presumably he meant something the leaf had been used to conceal, or used in the preparation of. Its floral origins, even to me, still appeared English.

Although his search was both particular and elaborate, neither did he unearth anything, to my eyes at least, unusual.

We'd been there over an hour. No one had disturbed us (5's music crashed on and on, an especially repellent opus demonstrably on repeat).

"And that door to the balcony is locked?" said Mr C.

He went to it and took a screwdriver from his pocket.

Inserting it in the empty keyhole he tried various manoeuvres. Suddenly the door snapped, shifted, and I glimpsed the key-driven bolts lifted from their sockets. He gave the door a final twist and pull and it was open.

Out on the balcony he looked up, then down.

"Nothing."

When he was back in again, I followed him along the internal corridor once more, into the other rooms, the bathroom and bedroom and spare room.

"Let's try," he said, "that fire-escape."

He shoved the window of the now-mattressless bedroom up. There'd been only a sort of snib to lock it.

Putting out his head and shoulders, he craned his neck. "Ah ha."

He helped me out of the window and we stood on the fire-escape. The metal steps uncoiled downwards to the unkempt garden. A ginger cat, chasing something small in the undergrowth, took no notice of us.

"Look there, Mr Phillips. And then up there."

Up there was the sloping roof of the house, one of the endless array of terrace roofs, all rather badly in need of re-tiling, with an independent weed or two growing out of the them, or in the tops of adjacent drainpipes.

This roof had in it a large sloping skylight. It seemed to be made of dark polarised glass. A metal ladder was fixed directly below the skylight. The end of this ladder, not quite visible from the bedroom when the window was closed, came down to the top of the fire-escape, and was firmly bolted there.

Somehow Mr C's bulk had hidden the ladder from me at first, as if he had wanted to astound me, uncovering it, pointing up.

The dark glass couldn't even be looked at. The sun hit it blindingly, a splashed broken egg.

A noise in the garden made me look down.

"I hate cats," said Mr C. "Vicious fips."

A mouse in its jaws, uncaring of censure, the ginger tom didn't give us a second glance.

SEVENTEEN

After we had the tea, or he did, Sej asked me if I'd left my bags upstairs. I said nothing, which was pointless, but he didn't press me. Instead he outlined for me what I'd packed in them, both of them. He included in the assessment what I'd also stuffed in my jacket in case I could get away.

He was very accurate.

He might have had X-ray eyes.

"By the way," he added, "you shouldn't worry too much about documents like that. Most of them are replaceable, even a passport. Your birth certificate, or a deed poll change of name, are the worst. They moved everything out of Somerset House some while back, and now you can't get hold of anything, I gather, unless you commute to some unheard of place well outside London, and search through the records yourself. It can take days."

Still, I kept quiet.

I sat and watched him.

"On the other hand, you'd want to keep any discs with you. They have to do, I assume, with your books. A paper copy wasn't necessary, surely? That has to be on one of the discs. What's on the other?"

Again, my instinct kicked in, prompting me to answer. I'd given up trying to second guess myself as to whether this was cunning of me - or placation - or the other peculiar sense of game-playing and *engagement*, which he had somehow induced.

"A future book. Not much. A pot-boiler."

"What's it to be about?"

He looked genuinely interested. But that was his way. And long ago I learned to resist the urge to spill plotlines before anyone, even the most innocuous listener. You bored them, or they ripped you off. Or both.

As I didn't reply, he smiled. "Some authors don't like to discuss work in progress. You must be one. What's the title?"

"A working title only."

"Which is?"

"*Kill Me Tomorrow.*"

Unlike the sub-editor whom I'd first informed of this, and who'd instantly wanted a change to avoid Bondism, Sej had the source at once. "Ah. Desdemona as her jealous partner slays her - *Kill me tomorrow - let me live tonight.*" He added, throwing me, "The Irish play."

"It isn't *Macbeth.*"

"No, Roy. *Macbeth* is the Scottish Play, as we both know. I mean the *Irish* Play: *O'Thello.*"

I stared at him. It was possible, if someone else had made this joke elsewhere, I might have laughed, at least - as he always did - smiled. "Very good," I said, stilly.

"Not mine. But there. So one disc is your new novel, and the other, was I right, the big unfinished manuscript now in the smaller bag - why else is it so heavy? - and which I found last time anyway, tucked in one of your study drawers under some loose blank paper."

My heart knocked.

I felt a kind of different alarm, inexplicable, together leaden and sharp. The very thing that had made me pursue the bags and so him, back to the trap of the house.

Silent, I waited.

As I now knew he now would, he told me, "I read it, Roy. It's Byronic - but more accessible, more perverse. Bit of a masterpiece. Probably, like so many of those, unpublishable. All that wonderful rambling, murky stuff about his life, the constipated family with their failed fortune, the grisly murders - which remind me of Poe, and sometimes of de Sade - that girl, what was her name - Libenka - with her throat cut, hanging by her hair from the beam, where he'd left her – until her own weight dragged the - what was it? *hennaed tresses* - out of her scalp, and she fell through the flimsy floor into the room below. And his demented visions of dogs and cattle and fiends and beasts of bone and metal. Purple passages to eat with a spoon - I expect you know, don't you, Roy, to tell an author he'd written a *Purple Passage* was to compliment him. It meant the section was unusually rich - like expensively purple-dyed silk. No, it's one hell of a book. And unfinished. What comes next?"

I swallowed.

"It stuck some years ago. And thank you, but I know it's rubbish."

He shook his head. *"Nay, do not think I flatter,"* he said, "...and that of course is the *Danish* Play about the pork butcher - It isn't rubbish, Roy. You should finish it. So there we are. The two things you should do this summer. Finish that novel and shave your bloody head. Your hair is going fast. Steal a march. Get rid of it. You'll look good, more yourself. We should all, like Vilmos's creepy alchemic Order, try to become ourselves. It's about all we can do."

I thought, What will *he* do, drug me again, then shave my hair off while I sleep?

A huge, heavy, watery terror filled me. I felt, as the Americans illustratingly say, *sick to my stomach.*

He read my mind, of course. Perhaps not so bizarre.

"I won't do that, Roy. It has to come from you."

Then he got up and walked round the kitchen, looking out of the glass of the closed door and window briefly. It was getting on by now for evening. The sky had a thickened amontillado sherry light, the fir black, its needles delineated like spikes on some giant black porcupine. By a similar light, against the fir, I had seen him here first. And earlier today, by the fir, he had jumped up to intercept my escape.

"That's a beautiful tree," he remarked. Then, cutting through me, irrational as I now was, to the quick, "You feature it, am I right? In your untitled work. The tree on the Kolosian Hill, where your hero stabs the thief."

After this he opened the fridge, next the freezer, and gazed in. No comment then. He went on to the cupboards, looked at, removed and looked at, various cans.

"Not much food."

"I was going away."

"Of course you were. Don't worry. I can go shopping. Enough shops are open on Sunday. As for tonight..." He was thoughtful. "How about a take-away? Do you have a good local Indian or Chinese?"

I rarely indulge myself that way, but there *was* an Indian restaurant at the end of the high street, the Spice Lal.

"If you want." Thought clicked. I added, expressionless. "But I won't join you."

"Oh Roy, come on. I can't drug *that*. Not if you keep an eye on me from the moment the food arrives to the moment it gets to the table. And then we each keep our hands in sight. I *still* haven't quite figured out how you did that trick with the wine that time. I'll watch you. You watch me. We'll have a good meal. And don't worry. I'll pay."

With an inappropriate abrupt rancour I heard myself say "You seem to be rich."

"Not exactly. But not poor either. Do you have their number?"

"No."

He drew from his pocket the most slender of phones, the colour of matt steel. It was more up-to-date than the last one he'd had at our third meeting. He must change them every week. "Tell me the name and address, Roy."

"Why should I? I don't particularly want an Indian meal."

"Yes, you do," he said.

I tightened my mouth. Stupid. Redundant.

Sej smiled. "Don't worry, Roy," he falsely reassured me again. "I remember a place in your high street - The Lal - yeah, the Spice Lal." Then he called one of those directories we now use, at great cost, to learn unknown telephone numbers. Next he dialled, and held the mobile out to me.

I refused to take the phone.

"I'll tell you what to order," he encouraged me. I let the phone ring in his grip, and when a voice answered I did and said nothing. I sat, he stood there, while the man's voice buzzed out of the phone, and Sej watched me. I wouldn't take the phone, or speak, wouldn't play the game. The voice ended. The connection was broken. What used to be the dialling tone sounded.

Sej's face fell. He looked both upset and resigned.

He put down the phone, leaned in across the table and slapped me violently across the side of the face with the back of his hand. The blow was meaty, it stung, numbed, blanked a second of time, brought me back to pain, my right eye watering, my right nostril running so I thought for a moment my nose bled. But it didn't.

He said, "Sorry, Roy. I'd much rather not. But we do have to get this sorted out."

Beaten women learn how to negotiate, where at all possible. Or so I've read. Any woman I've known had not been beaten, or if she had, never confessed it.

I said, "All right. I'll do what you want."

The side of my mouth seemed inert. But it was only rather like what you feel at the end of a dentist's appointment, as the cocaine is gradually wearing off. He hadn't seriously damaged me. But he had made me understand.

He rang the number again. I took and spoke into the phone. I ordered,politely, what he requested, then at his urging ordered a meal for myself. I can't remember what. I knew I wouldn't eat much of it. Unless of course he insisted.

Sej sat on the table, smiling and once nodding approval. He said, "Ask if they'll send a couple of beers, too."

I asked. They would. Then I had to ask him, for them, if he wished to pay by credit card over the phone. And airily he told me the number of his card, even the security number on the back.

But I didn't try to record it. I had also now stopped ruminating on the idea of his going shopping and maybe leaving me locked in the house, and if this offered any hope. I didn't care.

Deal done he took back the phone and switched it off. "Brilliant, Roy. Just right." He looked closely at me. "Better put some TCP on your lip - yes, just there. I don't wear a ring, but I seem to have caught you. It's nothing much but better disinfect it just in case. Then maybe, let's see, you stay upstairs. They said twenty minutes, pretty optimistic for a Saturday. Perhaps they don't get a lot of custom until later. The thing is, if you're upstairs I can answer the door. But if you stay at the top of the stair you can also watch me. Once I close the front door, you come down and we both come back in the kitchen. That way there's no chance I can mess the food up. Or you. Fair enough?" He hadn't even warned me not to try to persuade the delivery man to assist me. And I - I hadn't even considered it.

"Yes," I said.

I rose and he smiled. "You've been a real trooper," he said. My father had once or twice said that. "No hard feelings, eh? Good. These things happen. Now we can move on."

My father's advice on bullies was shit. There are many things that, unless you have either great power of some sort, or vast help from some abnormal and constant quarter, there is no point at all in facing up to, let alone trying to combat.

Denial is one of the healthiest physical states discovered by Man.

Following my scrap with Ben Oggey, after which, penless, I had to have a tooth capped, I abandoned confrontation as a *modus operandi*.

Decades after, and only with Sej, I briefly blotted my well-learned copy book. His swift action had saved me from any more mistakes, thus punishment. Meanwhile the stunning aftershock of his blow wore off quickly. The lesson adhered. From now on I would be a model prisoner.

The meal arrived in fact half an hour later. We played it as he had outlined. He was charming to the delivery man, had a laugh with him, (I couldn't catch what about), tipped him with a ten pound note. Off the man went, laughing. In came Sej, laughing, with the bag of food. He shut and double-locked the door again, with his own keys, then pocketed them.

Then I came down from my old childhood haunt of the top stair and progressed behind him into the kitchen.

Naturally he had no dread of my attacking him from the rear. Nor did I have any intention of doing so.

I remember what he ate: Chicken Jalfrezi, stuffed Naan, vegetable curry, egg-fried rice, two Poppadoms, a small tub of Raita. What I ate, or did not eat, as I've said, I have no idea.

He drank an Indian beer decanted into a tall glass. I had the same and sipped it. He'd suggested I rinse both glasses thoroughly before we used them, in front of him, which I did. The taste of the beer was appealing, slightly bitter, with a hint of chilli. In the end he finished mine too. The remains of my dinner, most of it, I believe he ate for breakfast the following morning.

There were no insidious drugs. Indeed, despite the washing, he insisted halfway through the repast we have each a few swallows from the other's glass.

He said I was to leave the washing-up, so I left it, it goes without saying.

It was after this, though rather further on, nearer midnight, he broke in my bedroom door, for me.

"You get a proper night's rest," he said. He told me he would 'crash' on the sofa downstairs. At least, he said, he wouldn't have to suffer the 'fucking row' of neighbourly bad music current in the flats, which 'got on his tits'.

Between one and two I heard the strains of Bach sprinkle from the piano.

Upstairs, the broken door leaning on the uprights to give me partial 'privacy', I sat up on the bed in my clothes, my two bags, which he had brought in, lying by the wardrobe, the light off, unsleeping, going over everything, on and on.

Our conversations of the afternoon and evening I examined now more fully.

I found I was inclined to date them BB and AB – Before the Blow and After the Blow. In fact the blow, when he hit me across the face, was neither devastating nor intrinsically dividing. It was rather, instructive, a guide-line. I'd been, on some level, expecting his violence. Who would not? It was a benchmark, not an advent.

We had also talked, superficially at least, in that most spontaneous and episodic way persons use who know each other well. By superficial I mean, of course, if we had been observed by an outsider. And now I tried, upstairs, to put *myself* outside, to look and learn. Writers do attempt that, some of us, even when personally deeply involved. The ability is a gift, and a curse.

I re-ran the conversations methodically. To begin with, I had asked him again, why he did this to me. His reply was the recurrent one - out of interest; I was interesting. We had established that he - not the girl with the car presumably, as she really couldn't have had time or access - had wiped some liquefied Rohypnol around the kitchen glass. I could have used the glass at any time during his absence.

Next we had returned to our guessing game as to whether he was or was not my son. He had said he was brought up in an orphanage, could not recall his mother's name. I didn't believe either of these confidings. Even BB I had become three-quarters convinced he wasn't Maureen's child. It might be plausible but somehow didn't fit, and definitely *AB* I refused to entertain it. He was not hers. I wouldn't allow him to be. Although naturally if he, AB, started to assure me he *was*, I would nod and agree. I would even call him my son, if that were required.

When he saw to the bedroom door he told me about the car-girl and her strong pianist's hands with the bolts. And prior to that, when the mobile rang out on the path, he told me I couldn't bring it in, nor would he. That was after the Indian meal. Even then, propped up on the bed, I could hear the rain falling quite heavily on everything, and on the mobile.

I'd seen too the tiny intense wound in the palm of his left hand. Was he prone to stigmata? I wouldn't put anything past him, even something like that, although I would suspect it of being self-induced, either by extreme cerebral concentration or (more likely) a creative use of self-harm. (Not to build this aspect up unduly, he would reveal during the next week that he had driven a long needle into his hand. He'd needed to look white and sick when he brought the 'dead dog' back into my hotel, and this was how he'd managed that. He explained too that, had I followed him to the Gents, he would have put his fingers down his throat to induce the genuine sounds and act of retching. Told this, I'd made little comment. Perhaps the authorial mind was pleased to slide last pieces of that single puzzle into place. I didn't then ask him if the dog had been real. It was AB. And also something more. I was certain by that first night the dog was *not* real, but suppose it had been? Suppose he had killed it, or she had, that other weeping woman and accomplice *surely*, suppose she had killed it *for* him? Aside from any urgent RSPCA issues, to kill an animal can, in certain cases, be the preliminary knack of those then able to slaughter their fellow men.

We had also discussed my work, of course.

Over subsequent days we would discuss it again and again. He would read my books, sitting before me either in the library or the kitchen, sometimes the front room. He read fast and with a look of total absorption that might have been gratifying, even with him, *BB*. But which, AB, was no longer so. Sometimes too he would send me off to my study. "Go and do some work, Roy." And I would go, and hack that I am, manage even to turn out some soulless verbiage, five hundred, a thousand words. In case he checked on me. But he never intruded 'uninvited' into the study, would only come to the door, with a polite knock, to ask me how it went.

My demeanour throughout was always as normal as I could make it. When we discussed my published books we did so in a civilised manner. Even AB, his criticisms were, I must admit, often valid. His praise obviously revolted and offended, but I took it with a courteous calmness, thanking him, disagreeing now and then. I had ascertained for now those areas where resistance was allowed, even wanted, as proof of our quite spurious normalcy.

There were no more blows. He needed to offer me none.

I'd said to myself I was to be a model prisoner.

It's the first thing the seasoned criminal tells you, at least those of the disempowered class of criminal. You must be obedient and respectful. Don't aggravate the warders. Take any cruelty or injustice without undue flinching or any complaint. Don't smarm, maybe flatter a bit, hide nothing but your true self, and keep your head down. As one I spoke to during my researches had once told me, "You gets a better chance to pull a fast one if you never done it before. And if you don't neither, you still get less of the crap if you behaves like a good boy." It was the same to some extent with the more dangerous fellow inmates. Unless they were 'mental'. Then probably you had problems. You couldn't predict, only stay neutral, merge with the dark.

Sej, equally jailor, criminal *and* mental, would have to be played on all three lines.

Some of our 'talks', macabrely, were actually quite fascinating. And as long as I did everything he told me to there was to be no resurgence of threat.

To return however to that first night, sitting up on the bed, I had no means of knowing he would be there through the rest of May, approximately three weeks. I had no apprehension I would have to maintain my life as a model prisoner so long.

But then, what else had I imagined could happen?

In some incoherent way, frankly, I *must* have known it might well go on. Or had I only, down in some dim recess that my swift, healthy, human talent for Denial instantly smothered, believed he would kill me? Regardless that was of my conforming and docility. I had no real notion of what other tests lay before me through the rest of May. If I had, would I have doubted my own ability to comply? Maybe not. Mortal things are generally programmed to attempt survival. Left with one plank in the sea, we cling to it. So much in life is destructive, is *deadly*, that without this built-in mechanism, less bravery than cowardice, less cowardice than resentment and rage, most of us would vanish long before my father's touch of a Grim Reaper mowed us down. Sleepless there, I must have known this too. And finally I did fall asleep, near five in the morning. I hadn't meant to, or thought I could. Sej woke me at 8 a.m. with a mug of tea, milk, no sugar, as I drink it. "*Regardez*," he said, and drank two swallows of it, to demonstrate it wasn't drugged.

By the third morning, my mobile phone was gone from the path. It had been possible to see it from my study window, which faced the front. I'd at no time thought I could get hold of it. No doubt it was more sensible for someone else to have the use of it, if it still worked. Nobody that I'd detected had called me since that first unanswered ringing. Duran, for example, would think I was now on my trip up north. As for Matt, swimming in his own ocean of depression he'd simply give up on me. What did I matter? Perhaps the woman he'd picked up had stayed on, and even if I'd arrived he would have put me off.

Sej's mobile seemed to have unlimited credit, or was paid for via bills; he recharged it regularly in whatever room he happened to be, never letting it from his sight.

He had urbanely confiscated my house keys during the initial evening, BB, asking for them in a friendly, casual manner. That was both those to the front door and the key to the kitchen door. A spare key to the kitchen door had once existed but was years since lost, by me. Sej didn't ask if there was one. Unless I wanted to try to break through either door - both of which opened inward and would be difficult - which means impossible for someone at my physical standard - my only chance was to climb from a window. But the windows, both upper and lower, refitted in the eighties and 'modern', opened only at the tops, a narrow strip that might be useable by a skinny infant or a cat. I could have broken them, if with a little effort, as the glazing was fairly tough. (I knew that because, some years before, one of the young footballers who replace each other in the Lane, and hold the World Cup there several times a month, managed to lob a ball square at my front window, which held.)

But again I'd need to put my back into it. And it would make one hell of a row.

And Sej was always there.

Despite his offhand comment on 'shopping', and my vague half-hopeful inner reaction, he never left the premises. Instead he would bring out his mobile and either he or I, on his instructions, order things in, paying with two or three of his credit cards.

Wine came, whisky, soda, dry ginger, bottled water for him, fruit juices, food and bathroom supplies, (including shaving equipment, toothbrush, and other things also for him -he'd brought nothing with him - even some jeans and shirts, socks, boxers, the whole kit. I was reminded, seeing these completely accurate stores and garments carried in by him, of my own future fears for myself as an old man, at the mercy of the careless deliveries of others. Seemingly everything Sej wanted was perfect).

At night we ate takeaways. Or he did. He never now forced me to join in, and frequently I settled for beans on toast, or a ham sandwich. Once a Chinese meal was delivered. We observed the same ritual as with the Indian, and then Sej served the food before me. There was hot and sour soup, duck with blackbean sauce, pancakes, noodles, sweetcorn and crab, Szechuan Prawns, squid with garlic. "So glad you were tempted to have some," he said, in his 'winning' mode. I did eat a little. It was very good. There were also what the menu described as Two Free Bottles of Beef. He'd ordered desert too, pineapple, toffee bananas and ice cream.

The food alone was costing him a small fortune.

After our dinners we'd drink coffee, whisky if he told me I should have one, vodka for him, a double without mixer. I recollected that from when I first saw him in the pub in the Strand.

The anti-drugging procedure was always kept to.

I prepared my own food and 'kept my eyes on it', he did the same, but mostly had his food brought in. If we shared anything at some point plates and glasses were exchanged.

Sometimes he brought me morning tea, sometimes not. He never asked me to do or make anything for him. Either he attended on me, as one might with someone ailing or very young or old, or he left to my own devices. Sometimes he would inquire if I had a preference for a type of food or drink. But that was within the limits of what he chose. After all, he was paying. I tried to figure out, in the second week, exactly how much he had spent. At a conservative estimate, well over fifteen hundred pounds.

The other elements of our relationship, if such it must be termed, went on and around about the day to day minutiae of ordinary life, however odd or opulent.

At first, what went on was, shall I say, *external*.

That is, it affected the house, its objects.

The inaugural act happened on the fourth day of his occupancy and my imprisonment. Or, more correctly, it had gone on during the previous night.

I woke at seven-thirty after a restless three hours' sleep

and smelled the acid tang of fresh paint,

I got up, used the bathroom, and went downstairs. The smell of paint intensified. The morning before I had seen some quite large boxes delivered, all taken in as usual by Sej. Although I was regularly told to make various telephone orders, Sej sometimes ordered stuff of which I had no knowledge until later. This was the case here, for he had got in the paint and brushes etc: without my knowing anything about it.

The door of the front room stood half open.

He had covered the piano over with a large dust-sheet, but not bothered with anything else.

As I stood there he turned from his position on the kitchen ladder. "Hi, Roy. What do you think?"

The walls of the room, almost finished now, were a deep scarlet. It hit my morning eyes like too bright light. I said nothing.

Not only were the walls red, but most of the sofa and other furniture, and the carpet, where paint had dripped or, more likely, been idly splashed.

"Don't worry about the mess," he said. "Come on, don't sulk. You can always get some other chairs."

The *don't sulk*, though playful, as if only trying to dispel some unreasonable churlishness on my part, was a warning I must heed.

"Why red?" I asked.

"Enlivening. We can rip that bloody awful electric fire out next and get the chimney opened up. Picture this on a winter evening, firelit and glowing."

"Yes," I said.

"You don't sound enthusiastic, Roy. Where's your spirit of adventure?"

"You paint very well," I said. This was true. It looked a professional job, aside from the ruin of almost everything else.

"Thanks. I'm not bad, am I, for an amateur?"

He flaunted himself. There was a small red mark on his forehead but his hands were enclosed in protective gloves. His hands, the piano, must come to no harm.

"Do you want tea?" I asked.

"That's all right. Had some. Want to get on. Should have it done in another hour."

I made coffee for myself in the kitchen, which also reeked of paint. The coffee tasted of paint. Even the toothpaste upstairs had done so. Through the window I watched a blackbird picking through the dead sides of my paved-over garden, and thought of breaking the glass. But I didn't trust myself to get it right, and I judged what would happen if I didn't.

He had completed the painting of the room by 9 a.m.

During that and the next day, the paint smell gave me a sinus headache.

On the carpet, curtains, and the chairs and sofa the splashed paint dried. Over the face of the old clock had run a single red drip like blood. I attempted to rectify nothing. Nor did he. I sensed, accurately, that the furniture couldn't be renovated, and it was not. I got used to the new look of the room, no longer anything to do with me, an abattoir in hell where offal and gore stayed always fresh and cheerful.

Two days on from the red paint, Sej threw out most of my crockery, literally threw, smashing it in the back garden.

I watched, as I had the blackbird, safely shut in like a wayward child who, if let go free, may rush off straight under a speeding car.

At one juncture, George emerged from 72 on to his neat back lawn, with the cherry tree and bird table.

I had a moment's hope. The activity of wreckage looked

unusual. How would George react?

He and Sej chatted in an easy way over the lowest part of the fence, where the other hydrangea was spreading the green cups of delayed flowers.

I couldn't make out what was said, my ears like my sinus had been clogged up by the paint. But both men were very relaxed.

When Sej came in, having swept the shards of crockery into two dustbin bags and dropped them in the black dustbin he'd earlier provided, he said, "I told old George you were going to make a new start. George said he was so pleased I was here. Between himself and me, he and his wife had been a bit nervous about you, here on your own in your present state of mind. They hoped I'd stay as long as I could."

"And will you?" It was out before I could contain it.

But Sej smiled. "I can stay forever, Roy, if I want."

To replace the china, some of which had gone back to my grandparents' time, Sej had ordered some thick square plates and square saucers, with large if unmatchingly round cups. All of it was pale yellow, starred with lurid marigolds. I'd never seen anything quite like it. They were less ugly and unwieldy than preposterous. I hadn't ever cared about the original china however. My only concern was that the awkwardness of the new crockery might make me drop some of it, and would this be taken as a declaration of war?

At night, when I retired to the virtually doorless environment of the bedroom, still I utilised my waking hours, or some of them, trying to concoct a plan of escape. But by now I couldn't think of anything that I dared to chance.

The night after the new cups appeared I attempted a foray downstairs.

It was well after 3 a.m. The piano, which now and then he played into the small hours, had fallen quiet just after two.

There were no lights on. Yet at the windows in the study, the narrow box room, and the bathroom where the door also stood ajar, embers of streetlighting fell into the house. The same was true downstairs, through the glass panel in the door.

Moving slowly and with care in my stockinged feet - I never now slept either in pyjamas or under the covers, but on top of the bed fully dressed - I crept downward.

As I reached the fifth step from the bottom, darkness flowed directly upward at me like a forming hill, blocking the light, barring my way.

I knew it was him, not some creature from the Hammer Horror films of my youth. But I cried out, lost my footing, stumbled into him. He caught me firm as a rock.

"What are you up to, Roy?"

"You frightened the life - "

"No, I asked first. What are you doing?"

I said, because I'd had my story ready, "I was thirsty," Like the untrusted child again.

"You should have called down. I'd have brought you something." He didn't seem angry, or worse exhibit that resignation that had been a prologue to the blow. "I'm often about at night. I sit in your library and read R.P. Phillips."

I supposed he used only the angled lamp on the table there, and pulled the door to, for no light from that room had entered the hallway.

He said, "Tea? Whisky?"

"Just water."

"You should keep some by you in a bottle, Roy. You can't keep drinking unboiled tap water, not without a filter, not anymore."

I stood marooned on the stair. Decidedly I must not proceed further. He came back with the glass with water in it.

"It's Volvic," he said, "in case you think it tastes different." And he drank a couple of swallows. "Next time, like I said, just call me."

Upstairs I went to the lavatory and poured the water away and flushed the cistern. It wasn't that I thought he had spiked the drink. I just couldn't swallow it.

Other events - *adventures* - took place during the next week.

There were all sorts of things. Some were surprising, shocking, some nearly funny in a frightful way, as had been the red paint and the smashed china. Some were on a more instantly invasive scale. For example, his nocturnal application of white paint to the glass of the lavatory window. Others were insidious things I might not notice at first, like altering the positions of the kitchen glasses, putting them where the canned and dried food and tea had been. And those commodities somewhere else again. Or when he had misfiled every book in my library. These had occupied a logical alphabetical order, author and subject. I'd worked in public libraries and this technique, less than petty, I'd found helpful when looking for things. Now I would hardly be able to locate anything without a search. That must have taken him most of a night to arrange as well. Strange I hadn't heard him, the library lay partly below the bedroom. My study he always apparently avoided entering unless he had asked me if he might. It goes without saying I never withheld my assent. Then I walked into it one afternoon, sent there by Sej to write, and gradually grew oppressively aware of something above me. Looking up I had to squint to make it out, but I at last saw the pale writing, scribbled in the lightest grey paint across the stained white ceiling, almost invisibly. He had climbed up the ladder again, perhaps balanced, incredibly noiseless and careful on the flat-topped desk where the computer stood. This time, no splashes. He must have covered it over. The writing was some of the invented poetry of Vilmos, copied or recalled from *Untitled*. If I hadn't written it I might not have been able, now, fully to read it.

Agony unended. Like the long snow it falls
And shrouds the edges of a sword
Too murderous to die from,
Too tangible to touch.
Among the webs that midnight spins
Go staggering to the doors of rotted day,
And through the keyholes, snakelike,
Spit.

This single act horrified me so far the most, worse even than his *manifestation* on the stair. But the painted poetry of course, was only my little madness and Vilmos's great one, jarred into life by Sej's spectacular insanity.

I said nothing to him about the writing, as I'd said nothing about any of it until, when or if, I was interrogated. Then I was neutral.

He didn't refer to the poetry at all.

That following night, or rather morning, he woke me from one of my piecemeal half hours of sleep. He did this by shining the light of a torch he must also have had delivered, (my own was defunct) into my eyes.

It's an old and tried schematic. I had read of it, described it in some of my work - read by him? To experience it is quite devastating.

I almost attacked him. I was just *compos mentis* enough to stop myself.

"Sorry, Roy," he kindly said, "I wanted to show you something."

Presently I went down with him. It was about 4 a.m. That I was being allowed to descend to the lower storey was not lost on me.

The TV was on, the sound turned down.

Some old film was showing, black and white, staffed with a cast of, at least to me, unknown movie actors of my parents' era. I sat on the sofa, stiff and crackling with dried paint. Although he had said he sometimes slept here, I'd never seen any evidence. Now he sat beside me. We stared at the - to me alone? - incomprehensible film. I wondered confusedly and shakily if he simply wanted me to watch television with him. Then he said, "Shall I get rid of this, Roy?"

My voice, always astonishing me recently, replied quite steadily, "Of course, if you want."

And he patted my shoulder, got up and crossed the room, and kicked in the screen.

A high hard bang sounded, less explosion than gunshot. The red room flashed purple, then white. Bits of the screen that seemed rather to be bits of solid light hailed through the air. A brief electric storm was born in a jet black hole ripped in the fabric of the room. Everything glittered, tinkled, then darkened, while from the TV plug in the wall a white ray, shaped like the classical lightning bolt awarded to the god Zeus, was flung to the ceiling and died. After this all was blackness.

Sej murmured, "You hardly watched anything, did you? I think you said the news gets on your nerves."

He threw a kind of shadow, lighter than the dark, but he himself was now invisible to me.

"Yes," I said. "I didn't often watch."

"Oh well, better get you back to bed."

He led me up the stair. At the top he turned to me, and now I saw him in the vague orange light from the street-lamps.

"Didn't scare you, did I - I mean, doing that?"

I gazed at him. I said, "What you do is your business, Sej."

"Yes, Roy. And so are you. My business."

He let me go through into the bedroom alone, and from the outside adjusted my door slightly, to permit me more 'privacy'.

Through the pretended barrier he called after me softly, "You haven't tried to get away. Or not properly. Why's that, Roy? "

"Too tired, Sej. At my age, you get fed up, running about."

His voice was now so soft I had to strain to catch it as I stood there, rigid, in the non-electrified dark.

"Do you, Roy? That's a shame. Not sure I entirely believe you, you know. You're not that old, either. Young as you feel. Sleep tight, old sport. Tomorrow is another day. "

I stood by my bed in the darkness for about another forty minutes after he had gone, or I thought he had. I didn't sleep again that night. I thought what prisoners must often think, that to continue in this way was not bearable, and that I could only bear it, having no alternative. And I thought dispassionately of some callous miracle - George hammering on the door calling for assistance - Vita with chest pains - an ambulance - some logical development which might allow me to evade my captor in two or three freakish moments of unexpectedness. And I thought finally of the stupidity of my situation, and that I ought to be able to get free, there *must* be some solution. But I could conjure nothing.

Into darkness I stared, the memory of the explosion of the TV screen sometimes igniting in my brain before my inner eye, truly a *flash*back. I wished him dead. That was all I had that I could do. I wished him dead, but it was unreal to me. And I believed I'd reached the end of my road.

7

He went up the ladder first, and I reckoned I would leave it to him. But when somehow Mr C, standing on that ladder some fifty-five to sixty feet over the back gardens, both hands employed in screwdrivering access through the skylight, had raised the window and it was open, and he leaned inside, looked back down and spoke to me, I knew that I too wished very badly to see into the place above. I wore trainers. I put one foot on the lowest rung and hauled myself up quite efficiently, ignoring the idea of the distance to the ground. I felt different in my 666 role, shaven headed, in jeans and T-shirt and trainers. I felt unencumbered. I felt I too could climb the dangerous ladder. And climb it I had. When I got into the attic room above Sej's flat, both Mr C and I paused, looking round. I was nonplussed, although I quickly saw he could not be. Given his wide experience surprise would be rare, and then no doubt only associated with types of extreme violence.

He had already informed me no one was in residence. He had checked every corner of the long, wide space, and opened the single door to reveal a long narrow bathroom.

"Well, it's an eagle's nest but he does himself proud," said Mr C. He sounded more amused than intolerant. "Not like the lower quarters, is it?"

Decidedly it wasn't.

The attic room, a sort of English loft apartment, began under the slope of the roof, where even *I* couldn't stand upright. But after a few crouching steps someone of six and a half feet could have done so with ease. At the centre the spine of the roof allowed standing room of at least twelve feet. This area extended for maybe twenty feet square. Even where the tapering down began, the roof sloped gradually. Once one was fully inside there was no sense at all of constriction.

The beams and joists were on view, but clean and varnished. Above them, a high plasterboard ceiling. It was painted a pale creamy blue. The brickwork of the walls behind the wood was also closed in plasterboard and painted, this a very light apple green.

On the whole floor-space lay a blue carpet, immaculate and with a deep pile. Furniture was set here and there, armchairs, tables, two large couches that Mr C told me were what we used to call put-you-ups - able to be converted into large double beds. Everything not plain wood was upholstered, sky blue or light royal blue, or various greens.

Bookcases, six of them, ranged along the edges of the room, crammed with books. There were two wooden cabinets. One had cutlery and dark green plates and mugs, and long straight blue glasses. The other cabinet contained cleaning materials, a Dyson. Above on shelves packets of tea, coffee, canned goods, matches. Towards the back of the room was a large piano, lid raised, and a guitar and a mandolin hanging from two hooks in the beams. A music centre rose behind the piano. Several carousels below revealed CDs of many classical composers. A lot of it was piano music. There was some jazz too, and R and B.

No radio or TV were visible.

The lighting consisted solely of table-lamps with parchment-coloured shades. Mr C had turned them all on.

Set back in one wall was a small kitchen annexe, that had a stalk-thin fridge-freezer, a small expensive-looking washing machine, a microwave oven, a miniature electric oven with two gas hobs, and a toy-size sink and drainer.

In the narrow bathroom, which was white and very clean, as the whole upper space appeared to be, were a long bath on lion's paws, a lavatory, a bidet, and two washbasins under a wide mirror. An ultra-modern shower cubicle filled one corner. From rails hung clean crisp towels, all of them white. White soaps, still in plastic wrappers, lay by basins, bath and shower. Another cabinet revealed several Lilliputian shampoos of the type found in hotels, a selection of chemist counter painkillers, such as aspirin and paracetamol, elastoplast and tubigrip, and a large plastic container of hydrogen peroxide.

There were also two hampers in the bathroom. One was empty. One held more clean white towels, white sheets, pillow-slips and blankets, all neatly folded.

"What's in the fridge, I wonder?" said Mr C.

He undid the door and we looked in.

There wasn't much. Some black truffles in a box, some strong cheddar in white paper. The wine rack held one bottle of Dom Perignon, one of red wine, (French) and a single bottle of Dutch geneva. A couple of two litre bottles of Volvic occupied the lower shelf.

In the freezer compartments were bread, pork sausages, steaks, chicken breasts and chunks of free range salmon. And a big carton of chocolate ice cream. None of these items had been opened.

Neither Mr C nor I were apparently tempted. Though sealed, it could all have been poisoned after all.

"That skylight is definitely polarised glass. Bullet-proof too, I'd say. But the lock..." He sneered and snapped his fingers.

The apartment was quite dark, or had been until he switched on the lamps.

"What do you think?" he asked me.

"He lives here."

"I would entirely conclude he does. Or it's his HQ. Basic nutrition, doctor supplies, hygiene, sleeping facilities. Not bad, for an amateur."

Below us even now we could hear the mindless blundering of flat No 5's music. It was much fainter, but still intrusive. Sound rises, like scum.

"Have you seen enough, Mr Phillips?"

"I - yes, I suppose so."

"Do you want me to do anything?"

I thought he meant smash it all up, unplug the fridge-freezer, score the CDs and tear up the books - God knows. I said inanely, "I'm baffled."

"Are you?" said Mr C. "I'm not. Your man's a nutcase." Then he reverted to his alternate accent. "A total nutter, our Sejjy. And that sort - I'd wipe 'em off the arse of the world."

EIGHTEEN

May was moving towards June. The weather changed for the better. It was warm and usually bright. Upstairs, I was told, I could/should open the small upper panels of the windows.

This was the time when regime change happened.

I had been obedient, subservient perhaps.

Each night I slept only a couple of hours. But I hadn't slept well, had I, for fifteen, nearly twenty years.

He had never intruded, that I knew, on my slumber, despite the bedroom door's being off, aside from that one striking time with the torch. Since that night I'd been very careful of him. Which is a crazy thing to say, of course. I was already careful of him. And it had done me no good.

And too I'd formerly taxed my brain, trying to find ways to outwit and deal with him, evict him. Destroy him.

I was hampered, naturally, by my authorial brain, which went too far. Frankly, my scenarios ended often in his maiming or death. They were fantasies. They were not possible to me. Either I am an indoctrinated pacifist, (my father, always think of others) or merely an utter coward - by which I mean, in this context, *squeamish*. I don't boast of any truly moral wish to spare his life. I can't lay claim to any saintly fastidiousness of that sort. But the end of the road was before me, and still I could think of nothing at all.

The wasp entered my life two days after I started to leave the upstairs windows open.

This had happened during other summers. Even given a notable dearth of insects constantly reported in the news, and put down to human vileness and global warming, intermittent moths, flies and wasps had always penetrated the house. Like, if not in the same spirit as my kindly mother, I tend to catch them all and put them back outside. Even wasps I spare until the autumn, when the damn things will perish anyway. I'd been stung sufficiently to know I wasn't allergic to them. But also I was aware that, if they got into the mouth and stung, they would cause a swelling in the soft tissues and membranes which, closing the throat and airway, might result in death.

This wasp was obviously young and inexperienced. I caught it easily in the glass from the bathroom. *Having* caught it, I decanted it into a large empty jam jar I'd retained in my study to house spare biros. On top of the jar I placed a piece of card, pierced by me with air holes. Did they need to breathe? I had to assume so. Would it also need food? I dropped into the jar some crumbs from the breakfast toast I'd carried upstairs.

My wasp crawled about in the jar. buzzing in blind, automaton-like anger. Then settled on a bit of the toast. I stowed the jar in the bottom of the bedroom wardrobe. Perhaps the wasp would go to sleep. Perhaps it would die. I might find no opportunity to use it. I might let it go.

And if Sej discovered it? I'd say with the purest truth I did rescue them and then release them in summer. But, (now lying), this one had seemed comatose, so I'd given it crumbs and let it rest - and then unfortunately forgotten it.

One thinks sometimes, wrongly often, madmen will accept other madmen and their quite dissimilarly insane actions.

By this time I had been told by Sej both of his flat and its address in Saracen Road. The residence had come up once or twice in our communal post-dining phase, among the coffees, whisky and vodka. The 666 aspect of the number seemed never to strike him. He said little about the flat either, only that it wasn't worth the money, but all right. Aside from being blighted by loud bad neighbouring music. He described the outside more than the inside, (including the glass panel in the door), and in fact said nothing I afterwards recalled of internal appearance. The small park he mentioned several times, the trees and shrubs. And why had he given me the actual address if not to point out its Satanic twist? "You'll have to pay me a visit one day, Roy. Flat 6, top of 66, Saracen Road. It's a big white terrace, or it used to be white, back when."

And I said, "I should visit you?"

"Why not?"

"Won't you still be here?"

And, "Oh, I might even be, Roy. You're right."

The day I caught the wasp and hid it, around eleven-thirty I went down to the kitchen, as during daylight hours I was seemingly allowed to, and through the library door I saw him asleep in the corner chair.

A book, not now one of mine but Milton's *Paradise Lost*, lay open on his knee. Over by the power point in the corner, his steely slice of mobile rested on the floor, re-charging.

I froze in the hallway. I stared.

It didn't seem impossible he might really have nodded off. He was young and would be able to fall asleep, and needed sleep more than I, no doubt. If he kept watch for me so much of every night, ready, playing Chopin or a Brahms Rhapsody on the piano, wasn't it quite likely he might suddenly flake out with no warning?

But *did* he sleep? *Did* he?

His breathing had the sound of a sleeper's. But things like that can be acted, and Sej, if he could do anything, was quite an accomplished actor.

There I hung from the thread of his tyranny, glaring in, transfixed, a stone.

And he opened his eyes without even any of the slightest sleeper's momentary dislocation, and smiled.

"Hello, Roy. Making any tea? One for me, please."

So I made the tea, and found my hands shaking so much I nearly did drop the bloody yellow and marigold cup. When I took it in I swallowed the regulation two gulps, and passed it to him.

"Sit down a minute, Roy." I sat. "I've had an idea."

Then he drank the tea. He didn't say what the idea was, I waited. I waited while he drank all his tea.

Then he put the open book and the empty cup aside and stood up.

Going out ahead of me he called back lightly, "Come on. We're going upstairs."

I followed him. He climbed the stair. Docile, I climbed at his back. He had left the phone to recharge on the library floor. Had he forgotten? I decided not. It was another tease.

He preceded me into my study on this occasion. Neither had he ever done that before.

The whole surface of my skin was prickling. My eyes seemed stretched to the size, if not the square shape, of the hideous new saucers.

Something else that was new was about to happen, and I was to *see* it happen, be a part of it. It was like the smell of smoke, of burning, like the sick marzipan odour that still hung in the front room round the gutted TV.

My jacket and the two bags he wanted arranged in the middle of the room, by the desk.

He had suggested, ("I suggest, Roy") that we both open them up now. He wanted to know, he said, if he'd guessed correctly what I had in each - aside from toiletries and clothes that I would have unpacked for use on my 'return'.

I unloaded the jacket first. There was no sense in evasion.

He'd been right on everything there, almost. He hadn't itemised, however, the house deeds. He was quite impressed by my having included those. "Are these copies? They look like the originals. Well done, Roy. Your parents must have paid off their mortgage. Those were the days."

"Yes," I said.

Then we did the bags, and it was all as he had said, aside from one or two things that he joked about, as if I had entertainingly put over a clever trick on him. "You weren't taking any chances were you, old sport?" Reminding me, as before by his abrupt use of this antiquated expression, of the eponym of Fitzgerald's *Great Gatsby*. The DNA samples, including the fork, seemed to fox him a moment. After that he realised and laughed. "Not bad. Not bad." Eventually he opened the small box and pulled off the bubble wrap. "I'd wondered where it had gone. Your parents', right?"

"Yes."

"Lovely." He stood caressing my mother's red glass dog tenderly and I wanted to snatch it. I wanted, as now I did so often, to kill him. Impotently and despairingly, need I say.

Carefully he placed the dog on my desk.

Not once had he glanced up at the writing on the ceiling.

"Well," he said, "that's that then, all cleared up. Got anything else hidden, Roy? Anything you want to confess to?"

I stared at him, blanking from my wide eyes and mind the glass of wasp in the bedroom wardrobe.

"Well," he said again. "Then I think it's time for your bath."

Even I, even then, even like that, did a kind of physical double-take. "What?"

"Your bath."

"What are you talking about?"

"Yeah. I know you're a nice hygienic guy. Clean shaven,

all but that cobweb arrangement on your head. Teeth your own and all flossed and brushed, the rest showered, ready to face the world. But I think today, take an early bath. Or a shower, if you prefer."

I said, hollow and estranged, knowing it was not so simple, "If you say so."

"Yes, Roy. That's it."

I half turned.

"No, no, sorry, Roy, should have explained. We'll see to the water in a minute. Just take your stuff off."

"My - stuff."

"Clothes, Roy. Shirt, pants, your Y-fronts or whatever you favour. Shoes and socks."

The shock this time came externally from far away and wrapped around me as if I were something dead that could not feel.

I didn't move. My brain had nothing inside it but rushing and white noise.

"Oh," he said. Contrite, he lifted one hand. "Again, *mea culpa*. I should have made it clear. This isn't sexual. You have nothing to fear, that way."

I didn't move.

"Oh, come on, Roy. Do you want me to help?"

I must have backed a step. The filing cabinet tapped my spine.

"Yes, OK," he said, reasonably, "why am I telling you to do this. Because it has to be *faced*, Roy," (Oh Christ, shades of my father), "it just has to be dealt with, here and now. Clothes off. All and everything. Or I will help, Roy," His voice was quiet and a faint hint of worry was in his expression - not yet quite the upset and concern that had heralded the blow. But enough.

"Give me a minute," I said.

"Sure. I'll time you." And he started, at an exact pace,

softly aloud to count off the seconds.

My mind sent me a message that he was checking to make sure I had nothing 'concealed on my person'. My mind was trying, apparently, to make sense of what was either senseless or had another meaning it refused to confront - to *face up to*.

I knew, despite the business with bags and jacket, that Sej wasn't checking for anything concealed. Unless it was my concealed flesh. My body.

And no, it wasn't sexual.

At school, when the showers had been installed for use after games, (games - the misnomer of all time, nothing playful about them), one or two things had gone on here and there. I have no problem at all with homosexuality, so long as I'm not expected to join in. To me, even when presented in the best of literature, it seems silly, a sort of invention. I've no doubt this is a flaw in my intelligence - not of course that I find myself 'straight' as they say, but to be incapable of grasping others may find non-straightness not only the only option, but enjoyable. Or maybe even, as a boy of my own age, then about sixteen, once coaxingly said to me, my alienation is my defence against finding out my *true* feelings. Most if not all men are supposedly quite adaptable to enthusiastic sexual acts with their own gender. Generally however, at school or elsewhere, I've seldom been propositioned. Nevertheless I seemed to know enough to believe that he, Joseph Traskul Sej, had no inclination or interest that way. And at the same moment a burning dominance radiated from him. There was no route out of this. As with everything else, I'd better give in.

It goes without saying, I've had to strip in front of strangers before, once or twice in tense and difficult situations, as when I'd had a cancer scare two and a half years previously.

I didn't wait until he reached sixty in his counting.

Off came everything, as he had stipulated, watch and shoes first. I hung the shirt and pants lightly over the back of the desk chair, left the rest on the floor.

He sat in silence, watching me.

I didn't glance at him.

When everything was off I stood there by the desk, looking out of the window. And he got up, and came and looked me over, front and back, at a distance of about four to six feet.

During this he said nothing. Neither did I. It took about five minutes.

"OK," he said, "let's run the bath, shall we?"

Now I was to walk first. I went into the bathroom and realised I did not want to bend over in front of him to put the plug in the tub. Something so trivial. And curious, too, if I felt - and I didn't - no sexual threat. Yet threat of course I *did* feel. I simply couldn't codify it. It wasn't that I was merely embarrassed. I was not embarrassed. While my body has little to recommend it neither am I deformed or spectacularly scarred. I've been neither blessed nor cursed in any physical area. I am a short skinny man, generally average, nondescript.

Having no choice anyway, I leant forward and shoved in the plug, then turned on both taps.

He meanwhile walked past me and letting it down, sat on the closed seat of the lavatory. He kept on watching, observing.

Then he said, "You were circumcised."

That sent another jolt through me. Not the reference, just the impact of his quiet, flat tone.

Again I said nothing and he added, "It's routine in some hospitals. Evidently the one where you were born, as I don't think you're Semitic." When I didn't speak now he added "Or are you?"

So I must answer.

"I haven't a clue. My parents weren't."

"You're a bit underweight," he went on, as if musing, "gut a bit flabby. Nothing much." The bath was full; I turned off the taps. "Get in, then," he said.

I got in. I sat down when he gestured to me to sit, in the warm water.

"Well," he said, "just carry on."

"What am I supposed to carry on with?" I said.

"Your bath. Just do what you always do." He paused and then said, in the most indescribable, vaguely humorous, *terrible* way, "Don't mind me."

In prisons of war or kidnap, guarded by jailors indifferent, sadistic or murderous, men have had to do this. They have had to urinate and defecate and vomit, also under the keen eyes of these enemies. Would that be the next step?

The soap was in my hands. I began to wash.

Still I hadn't once looked into his face, let alone his eyes. Not looking at him, even though he never took his eyes from me, seemed peculiarly to leave me a measure of privacy, perhaps safety. This is irrational, and afterwards became meaningless.

With each ordinary everyday move I made, I wondered what would come after.

He said nothing for a while.

He watched.

When I'd performed these ablutions, sluiced myself over, then he said, "Don't you ever lie back for a minute in the water?"

"Not often."

"So that's all."

I thought, He is going to instruct me now to do something else. To play with myself, perhaps. Or to sing a song. Am I going to do that? Either of those? I suppose I'll have to.

I stared at the light shining on the chrome taps. They weren't very clean. Franziska hadn't done a very good job, but to be fair too, that had been weeks back because he'd made me cancel her visits. The agency were very understanding about the emergency journey abroad he'd told me to say I had to make. I could have rung another number, pretended, let her arrive. But what would she have done anyway? Besides, I'd imagined him telling her he was my son, and how deranged I was, she'd been lucky. Even playing the piano to her, asking her for a date, God knows.

"Well, Roy," he said, breaking in on these random thoughts, "the water will be getting cold. Better get out now."

When I was out again I reached for the towel, but before I got hold of it he said, "Now leave the towel. First I want you, just for a minute, to stand there and look me in the face."

It wasn't chilly in the bathroom. It was nearly June and the sun was out.

I raised my head and looked directly at him.

Only I couldn't. Somehow I couldn't. My eyes slid off his face. I tried to make them stay - less for any affirmative reason of my own, than in order to obey and so appease him. And I couldn't. My eyes began to water. This was not fear, or tearfulness. It was the *strain*, as if I forced myself to stare into the sun, or hold up some huge weight that was going to break my back.

"OK," he said then. With the edge of vision I saw he smiled his smile. He threw the towel to me. And walked past me and out of the bathroom.

I heard him go down the stairs.

What happened next surprised me. I pushed the door shut and locked it, then I lifted the lid of the lavatory and was sick. The bath was still gurgling as it emptied. Perhaps he didn't hear the noise of my nausea.

I stayed in the bathroom after this for some time.

I believed, even if he'd heard nothing, even if he came to 'check' on me again and I made some excuse as to why I was still there - cleaning the bath perhaps - even so he guessed, had calculated and foretold how I was.

I advised myself I had been very afraid that something frightening, a thorough assault, a beating, was about to be perpetrated on me. Even after all male rape. But I knew I hadn't thought that. And I had been convinced also that so long as I did as I was asked, there'd be no violence. My subsequent physical reaction, and my mental one still, were not caused by actual anxiety or terror. It was something else.

On the floor by the basin I sat on the damp towel, thinking, thinking of this. Thinking of how I had been naked.

It was a very minor ordeal. Nothing dramatic or ghastly had occurred. It amounted to nothing.

But my brain held it. As in dreams sometimes I do, I saw myself as a separate person, and viewed from above. I saw myself standing before him, then in the bath washing, getting out and standing again in front of Joseph Traskul, unable to meet his eyes, unable to look at him. I knew that once more clothed, I would remain unable to look into his face.

I found too I didn't want to leave the bathroom. I wished to stay there, by the basin, seated on the floor, not focussing, staring inward, thinking about myself seen from above as another person, naked. Or rather, this was not what I wished. It was all I could do. Even to move my left leg, the foot of which had gone to sleep, was beyond me. My mind was filling the room, and the house outside, with a kind of cerebral fog. In this Sej vanished. He *would* not therefore come up to the bathroom, knock, break down the door. Nothing would happen. Time had stopped.

NINETEEN

When I went downstairs it was almost 4 p.m.

Outside birds sang, and a couple of lawnmowers droned. Now and then a car went up or down the road. Everything was completely normal. But there was no sound in the house at all. I might have been alone there.

He was lying on the paint-splattered sofa in the front room, the shattered TV to his far left, a cushion under his head, reading Milton.

Without looking up, he read to me.

"'Som natural tears they dropd, but wiped them soon,
'The World was all before them, where to choose
'Thir place of rest, and Providence thir guide:
'They hand in hand with wandring steps and slow,
'Through Eden took their solitarie way.'"

I said, not looking at him, or no further than the book. "I'm going to make something to eat."

"Go ahead," he replied.

I walked out and on into the kitchen. There was no smell of food, and no crockery either in the sink or washed and draining.

From the fridge I took out the last of the ham and cut a couple of slices from the uncut loaf, spreading it with margarine. I thought of mustard too, then decided that might be too strong.

I had put on the same clothes from earlier. Just one addition. Something in my pocket.

While I'd made the sandwich, I had kept an ear and an eye on the hall. But Sej hadn't moved, he didn't come to see what I was doing. Generally, if I made myself food, he ignored me.

I took a couple of bites out of one half of the sandwich. I was almost hungry, which startled me slightly. When I'd swallowed them I opened up that half of the sandwich again and dropped in the wasp from my handkerchief. It barely reacted and seemed mostly dead already; I'd reckoned any mustard would kill it outright. I replaced the top slice of bread gently, not to crush the wasp. Then I coughed loudly and started to swear.

Sej didn't come to see what was the matter.

I went quickly back up the hall, carrying the plate, and into the front room.

He glanced up. This time I met his eyes, mine bulging. Now it was bizarrely possible.

"What have you done to this?" I shouted.

He raised his eyebrows.

"Tell me what you've done to it. You've put something on it - God knows what - it tastes like - cough mixture..."

"Oh, Roy. I haven't done a thing. You're the one tries to drug people."

"What about the fucking Rohypnol?" I ranted.

"Well, I'll tell you a secret, Roy. I lied about that. Yeah, I lied. There wasn't any Rohypnol in your glass. You must just have been rather tired and gone to sleep. But you were so keen I'd done something I hated to disillusion you."

"You've put poison on this bread - or the ham - That wasn't the deal."

"OK," he said. "So I've poisoned you. With, what was it? Cabdriver's linctus. Oh dear."

"*Taste* it," I roared. My face was hot. I had absolutely no trouble in glaring right at him. It was easy, almost - pleasing. "That's the arrangement. You taste my food, I taste yours. If you haven't done anything..."

"All right. Give it here. If it'll calm you down."

I shoved the plate at him. He looked amused.

Supercilious, as if at all other times we led a happy low-key life together. "This piece?" He lifted the half with the wasp and put it to his mouth. And bit down on it.

Something happened in his eyes. I was staring now so intently and fixedly I saw it, like a spark, as if he had said *"Ah - but wait..."*

And then he gave a cry. The plate went flying. The two portions of the sandwich fell off and the bitten half opened. I couldn't see the wasp.

Sej was gripping his mouth. He had jumped up.

"What..." he said though his hand, "burns...?"

Then he made a noise as if he were retching, just as I had done earlier upstairs.

I said, "I told you so."

And I turned and walked out and straight into the library next door. His phone was still lying on the carpet. I detached it from the socket and stabbed in the number, ready memorised, that Cart had given me. I shut the library door and leaned on it.

Next door Sej was coughing violently, on and on, perhaps beginning to choke. I couldn't bank on that, or perhaps I could. But could I bank on Cart?

And it was only then I remembered that Cart had said his number would be available only for a 'few' weeks - was it too late?

After three rings an accented voice answered. "Bizan poos," it cheerily, incomprehensibly said. I must risk it. Had no other choice.

"I have to speak to Cart." I said, "quickly." I was almost whispering. Probably Cart was gone. Probably - The voice had heard. If this was still the right number - maybe they were used to panicked whisperers.

"Who is asking, innit?"

"Phillips. Say R.P. Phillips."

"Phillip."

Next door now there was a soft thud.

Another voice came from the phone. I knew it.

"Mr Phillips."

"Cart - I need you at my house - your man knows where. How quickly can you..."

"Quite quickly. An emergency, yes?"

"Yes."

"I have tried to warn you, Mr Phillips."

"The front door's locked - can't open it - need to break in - I'm his prisoner. And there's no money here to pay you." I added, "*You* can hold me hostage until my bank opens."

"Mr Phillips, have no worries. We will always accept a recognised credit card."

The line went dead.

I felt a deadly triumph and a sickened fear. If Sej was still conscious or able-bodied, how long would I be able to survive him? I dropped the mobile back on the carpet and reconnected it to the socket. I went out again into the hall.

No one was in the front room - he had gone.

Christ -

From the kitchen I heard water running.

I should get upstairs, barricade myself in the study. The desk and file cabinet, if I could lug them to the door, should keep him out a while.

"Roy," Sej called. His voice was a little roughened, that was all. He was there then, standing in the doorway. His lip was bleeding. "Something scratched me," he said. "Burn's like hell." Neither his mouth nor his face were at all swollen.

I stood my ground; I had begun to shake now, and getting up the stairs was going to take longer than I'd planned.

"I said..." I repeated.

"*You* put something in it, didn't you?" he asked. His face

was neither enraged nor did it have that dangerous quality of concern. "And I fell for it."

"If I put something in the fucking thing why would *I* have been eating it?"

"Well. I didn't *see* you eat any, did I?"

Where before I had been unable to look into his face or eyes, precisely as a few minutes earlier I found I couldn't look away.

He came out into the hall.

"Let's go and inspect it, then," he said, "your sandwich."

Perhaps the sting hadn't yet had a chance to build up to its proper toxicity. In the cases I'd heard of asphyxiation, or at least incapacitation of anyone stung in the mouth, happened inside a couple of minutes.

We both walked back into the front room.

The undone sandwich lay there, bread and ham and the smears of the margarine. Nothing else. The plate hadn't broken.

Sej went over to it and toed the food.

"What's that?" he asked. He bent forward and I saw the tiny blackish curled up corpse of the wasp lying under the rim of the plate.

Now I had better turn and run as fast as my watery legs would carry me.

A loud crunching crack sounded from the back of the house. A chair went over in the kitchen. Feet were pounding like a train up through the hall. Something pushed me aside.

There were two of them, both in black jeans, T-shirts and trainers. One wore a baseball cap pulled low over his eyes, the other had a mop of brown hair.

I'd staggered back and reached the wall.

I saw Sej standing there with his eyes wide and then they had him. One blow thudded home in his stomach. As he doubled the brown-haired man grabbed his arms from behind, and swung him away to the wall beyond the window. There, screened from the street by the drapery of one of my mother's curtains, the other rhythmically began to sink fresh blows into him.

"That's enough," said the brown-haired man presently. He looked over his shoulder at me. "We'll do a bit more work later, somewhere else. You'd like him off the premises I take it?" He spoke with an Oxbridge accent. Under the cascade of hair, I identified Mr C in a wig. I'd never, then, heard him speak before.

The other man, one I didn't know with a young bony face, was examining Sej as carefully as a doctor. "He's out."

"How did you - I mean - so fast...?" gormlessly I said.

"Cart knows your type, Mr Phillips. And your friend here's type too. We've been watching. Just round the corner. Come on," he added to the other man, "we'll take him out the back way. Vehicle's just along the Crescent, Mr Phillips. You'll need to get your back door fixed. But this one won't be bothering you for at least ten days. Say twelve days, by the time my colleague has had enough room to exercise his full powers." The other one grinned.

"How will you...?" I said. "I mean, someone may see you."

"They won't see him," said Mr C. "We have a big roll of carpet out there. Ever heard of Cleopatra?"

I nodded, stupefied.

The other man said, however, "She was carried unseen like into the presence of Caesar, tied up in a carpet. And that's how we do it, place like this. 'S nice carpet. And look, no blood to mess it up." He winked. "Not yet."

They dragged Sej out.

I followed them in a kind of dream state to the kitchen. The door was intact but the lock had been nimbly forced. A large roll of carpet lay on the ground. They pulled it through into the house and I wondered if George and Vita were watching.

"My neighbours..."

"Suspicious? You'd be surprised, Mr Phillips. Any questions, someone bust your back door when you were out, or having a nap. Stole some carpet. They get confused you see, witnesses," said Mr C. his voice taking on a differently accented twang. "Carpet came in, and went out? Nah. Just went out. Elderly couple I think they are, right? Saw 'em the other day. Both batty from the looks of 'em. Guy the other side too busy hoovering. Likes a bit of weed an' all, *je pense*. Not reliable."

They put Sej into the carpet, rolled him up.

I stood there watching.

I kept wanting to laugh, but also I needed to be alone. I wanted them gone. How didn't matter. Nothing mattered but solitude.

"And he won't - be back."

"Not for a while. And of course, if there's any more trouble," Mr C was Oxbridge once more, "we can always arrange a larger delivery. By the way," he added, as they efficiently raised the bundle, "best to pay HQ inside twelve hours. It's more polite. Looks as if you're pleased with the work."

Weakly I said, "The man said a credit card - is that right?"

"Affirmative."

Out they strode, carrying the carpet. Limber as squirrels over the fence they went. They must have a van. I closed the door and found I could after all jam it shut. Immediately I called the number again on Sej's mobile and got the one who answered with the mystic words *Bizan poos*. But very smartly he acknowledged delivery of my 'order', and took the details of my card. I was warmly thanked.

Only later did I realise both entries to and exits from my house were now barred to me, I was still trapped, the back door jammed, the front door locked and no keys left, for Sej had them all. But the keys came, both sets, next morning, put through my front door in a plain white envelope. And the day after that Duran, flushed with the joy of successful fatherhood, mended the back door and enhanced every aspect of security in the house.

TWENTY

Collapse. That happened on the third day. Until then I'd kept going, carried by a sort of transparent bubble of buoyant un-caringness, the kind that can result from certain types of trauma, or alcohol.

Duran hadn't been quite fooled by it, I felt, less fooled than I was, probably.

"You OK, Roy, mate?" he asked me several times.

But then, he'd seen the gutted TV and the red paint all over the front room.

Knowing now I couldn't spill a single bean to him, I spun him a version of the story Mr C had suggested. Vandals had broken in at the kitchen door while I was away up north in Cheston. They'd stolen a few bits and pieces including, for some reason, a spare carpet. They'd also destroyed my TV rather than nick it, and broken a lot of crockery - hence these peculiar cups and saucers, which I'd borrowed, I blithely told him, from Ian at 76. Painting the walls of the front room bright red was pretty warped I had to admit.

"Yeah, and they ain't done a half bad job," Duran agreed. "Looks professional - apart from the mess. But I've heard of worse."

I said I hadn't had a chance to try to clear up yet. It would undoubtedly mean replacing the sofa and chair covers, even the carpet and curtains. Funny the piano wasn't messy, he said. I said this had struck me too. If he noticed the pale painted words on the ceiling in my study he said nothing. He asked if I'd called the police. I told him I had, but got nowhere. He nodded in gloomy belief.

I liked Duran. I couldn't rid myself of the urge to get him off the premises, as if some poisonous gas cloud lay in wait inside the house, and no other must be exposed to it. Also an intense need remained to be on my own. Normally he didn't get on my nerves, but this time, once he left, I broke down. I snivelled for about a quarter of an hour, and then I slept, inside my newly bolted and barred fortress. I dreamed my mother was in hospital and I had had to go to the lavatory, and coming back into the room I found I stood there, a grown man and naked in front of her, but she only said, "Don't worry, Roy, dear. I'm dying. It won't matter."

I'd checked the call register on Sej's mobile.

All calls were deleted, except my pair, of course. I myself for some reason deleted these. Then I smashed it to pieces. On the morning of the third day I made myself go out. The security of the house was now impressive. Even the alarm worked. Beyond the fortress however, might Sej still lurk?

My common sense told me he would be in no fit state to do anything of the sort. The little I'd seen of the pasting Mr C and his 'colleague' had given Sej assured me he'd be out of action for some while. After further 'work' I doubted he'd get far at all for two or three weeks. And he wouldn't come back. No. Even he, even he wouldn't come back for more.

I kept seeing him in my mind, when awake, the way the blows had gone into him - this always recaptured in slow-motion, whereas at the time the whole sequence had been blurred by speed - and the way he was when they'd finished. Which was like a very life-like dummy, life*less*. Even when I had drugged him he hadn't looked this way. The man in the baseball cap was correct. There was no visible blood. They hadn't marked his face. It was hard and yet, conversely easy, to put his two personas together - the lifeless bundle of limbs and hair and face, the dominating tyrant AB, who had made me strip and take a bath in front of him.

And that was strange to me, too.

Because this last act I had had to perform seemed to have unlocked so much implacable horror inside me, and still I couldn't analyse why. I wasn't some virgin Victorian girl. It was nothing, that thing I'd had to do, *nothing*.

And yet. It had been the pivot.

On that, my bid for freedom had turned.

My excursion to the high street and back went almost without event. I bought some food and various other necessities. I even bought some mugs and plates from the expensive shop which sold them, plain white. (The ordinariness of the high street both reassured and disturbed me. My 'adventure' must have gone on in some other parallel world. Not a ruffle on the surface here. Irrelevant).

As I returned up Old Church Lane, I was feeling a dull shaky elation. Then I saw George Fulton was out, slowly mowing his front lawn.

What would he do, I wondered, when he saw me? Turn and run like last time, pointing something sharp in my direction for good measure?

Besides, what had he seen of my paint-and-carpet 'vandal break-in'?

Better take the bull by the horns.

"Hello, George."

He glanced up, switched off the mower and eyed me carefully. Carefully too he said, "Hello, Roy. Feeling better?"

I'd previously made a decision on how to handle this.

"Yes, I'm fine now. He got in a state and blew it out of proportion."

"Your son."

"He really isn't my son, George. I used to know his mother a long time ago. I hadn't seen him for years."

"No," said George doubtfully, "I didn't think we'd seen him, Vita and I, not before. He said something about that. I can't remember what..." George paused and regarded the mower handle. "Why did you ask me to get the police, though? You did, you know. And your - your young friend told me you insisted he smash all your plates."

So that was how Sej had covered his actions in the back garden. *My* fault again.

Nor could I in turn incriminate Sej. Not now.

"Yes, George, I did, I'm afraid. I'll tell you the facts. I've had to take something for years for blood pressure." (George nodded inadvertently. I knew, so did he have to). "This new stuff the doctor put me on can have a very funny effect on the brain. The dose was wrong too. Frankly I'd like to clobber the man, but in the end it's been sorted out. I'm fine now, and I apologise for worrying you."

George's eyes looked nervous. He said, very fast, "But what are you taking? It's not Captopril, is it? Only I take that, you know, have done for years - I mean, you hear these things don't you, and I'm not as young as I was..."

I nearly laughed. I controlled it. All George really cared about, like most of the human race, was how he might be affected, and if he might even suffer symptoms like my own invented ones.

"No, you're OK, George," I said. "That wasn't what I got fobbed off with. Your medication is one of the best, or so I've been told."

He loosened and gave me a little smile.

"Well I'm glad you're better, Roy. And your - he - has he gone?"

"Back to his own life I hope, George." One truth anyway.

I opened up my newly complicated door, went in, closed and re-locked it. Then I took the groceries and other things into the kitchen and put them on the table. I'd just filled the kettle from the tap, still half sneering at George, when my legs went from under me. They gave way.

I'd heard of this.

I sat on the lino listening to water drip, and thought. Brace up, Roy. It's over now.

But the kitchen reeled, or something in my head did so.

And I thought, *He's done something to me - some other drug - something - he's in the house - he's here - he's standing in the doorway...*

But he hadn't, he wasn't.

I was alone.

The collapse lasted for about ten minutes, after which I knew I could move again, and cautious as old George I got myself up and sat on a chair.

Finally I rescued the kettle and made the tea and drank it in a white mug. (Why had I bought three of these?) It tasted of a bitter nothingness.

About four-thirty I went to bed.

I dreamed of Sej by night floating down a river, perhaps even that black river in Vilmos's City. He was presumably already dead, but nevertheless I hefted a large stone, using unusual strength, and dropped it on his body. He sank. Without a trace.

8

Mr C shook my hand before we parted. This was on the far side of the park, after we had left Sej's flat in the roof.

"Don't worry about him, Mr Phillips," said Mr C in his university accent. "I really don't think you have anything to bother about now. He was - shall I say - well cared for."

I looked him in the face. "Hospital job," I said.

Now he shook his head. "Best not to ask. He's alive. He'll get over it. Lesson learned. All you need to know. Nice working with you, Mr P."

I'd called Cart's number again, some way on from the day of the collapse. It was after I'd destroyed everything Sej had brought into the house, just binning some of it, like the toiletries, smashing and binning some, (such as his phone, which I'd already seen to), tearing or cutting up garments and binning them. I'd have made a fire and burned them if I'd lived elsewhere. But I could just imagine Ian and George and Vita if I got an incinerator and started it up out the back. Actually the black dustbin was what I used, put out the front for what Lynda used to call the rubbish people.

Sometime I must also acquire a new landline telephone; for now my current mobile would be adequate. While in a few more days I'd go into Woolwich or Greenwich and check out places for fresh carpet, covers and curtains. My 'emergency fund' was almost gone, but once I got *Kill Me Tomorrow* properly on track, written, delivered, I'd have enough. Sometime too I would sell the piano. I might get a couple of quid for that, but I'd need to shop around. Until then there was the other credit card. Never before had I been so profligate, but now I had no choice.

I had cleaned the house too.

The faint writing on the study ceiling I left. I had a phase of sitting in my desk chair, staring up at it. One night, in fact the night before I called Cart's number again, I wrote a little more of *Untitled,* the first onslaught I'd made on it concisely for years. The idea that I shouldn't be doing it, that I should be working on *KMT,* seemed to have revitalised the 'project'. Or. Something had.

But I had started to have a recurring dream by now. I kept dreaming of his flat, at that point unseen. It was always different, but always *there.* I'd walk up endless wooden stairs to reach it, or stone stairs; it was always *upward* I had to go. And sometimes in the dreams I'd force a door with the glass panel he had described, often ornate, the glass stained, or it would already be forced, but inside I would find not a flat, but a garden with fountains, or a wasteland with a mirage of sun, or a dripping cellar, or a flooded municipal library - countless varieties of symbols, secret ciphers, of my id, or his. God knew. And so at last, rather than seek the furnishing departments of Woolwich, I went to central London, to Saracen Road, and broke in. And then I came back, and called the number and returned to the flat with Mr C.

Once halfway rational again, I'd been a little puzzled Cart's number had been and was still available. This was far more than a 'few' weeks. I decided on a simply theory. Maybe everyone was told the number evaporated in that time, a precautionary lie. After all if you used them you were implicated. And who could prove anything? However odd the name announced to callers, it was a business, and perhaps had a front that legitimately was. They took credit cards for Christ's sake. How would it show on a statement - Bizan poos...

Now anyway I knew about the apartment in the attic. I'd

seen it, climbed up to it in waking reality, by the ladder, and climbed down knowing its nature.

All the way home on the train from Charing Cross I thought about that place, its greens and blues, its ambience of money and impermanence. It was like a camp in a wood. A middle-class bivouac between battles. Stocked with straightforward nourishing proteins and edible delicacies, bandages, painkillers, areas for not-quite-ordinary R and R. A hidden sanctum. What else? We'd found no weapons.

Some of my neurasthenia at being outside the house had gone. I walked home from the station, up Bulivante Crescent, along my own familiar road.

When I was almost there I saw the eccentric car, a 1930's Morris in shiny condition, parked by the curb.

This car I knew.

But I couldn't recall from where, or why.

Then Harris Wybrother opened the driver's door and got out, looking round uncertainly at me, this hitherto unseen shaven-headed, moustachioed Roy all in black.

"You look really well," he told me, pummelling my hand and arm. "More than you'll be able to vouch for me, I expect."

Astounded, I could only say, "This is a surprise."

"Yes, old boy. Janette got some bee in her hairdo, the day I got back - last Friday - she thinks she had a message that you were having some kind of dodgy squabble with a publisher."

Shaven house-breaker, employer of hitmen, Roy shook his head with a thin smile. "She misunderstood. It was a personal matter. I'd have liked to ask your advice. But that's in the past."

"Oh, she tends to get things wrong. Wrapped up in her own multi-tasking. She's in Strasbourg till tomorrow. I thought I'd run over and see you. I can do with a breather. So this is your domicile?"

We both stood and looked at my house, semi-detached, inadequately paved, unimpressive, slightly run down - aside, of course, from its brand-new security locks.

"Somehow I didn't picture your pad like this."

My pad.

"Come in," I said.

"Glad to," he said, "I'm done in, I can tell you."

He looked all right to me, despite a yellowish half-formed tan which he tends to put on at the start of an English summer anyway. Perhaps Spain had been overcast?

"Oh the weather stank. Hot, and storms. They put it down to the usual global hoohah. And they're still in a state from the terrorist stuff."

We had gone in and I guided him through into the kitchen; the door of the front room was shut and the curtains I had drawn. He glanced at the shut door but made no comment. He was already telling me about his father's funeral, which apparently had had to take place in Spain, according to Veronica the thirty plus child bride, and also to Wybrother Senior's will. "The official crap - you've no idea, Roy. It wasn't red tape - more like red bandage." He had declined coffee or tea so I fetched the whisky, shutting the door of the front room again when I came out. The old bottle had already been emptied, this was a fresh one. "Christ, Roy. You have no idea."

"You had a bad time." I felt remote as I said this. I felt, actually, contemptuous.

"Bad's not the word. And that bitch Vero - that's what Dad called her, apparently, Vero. So now she's Vero. Sounds like some US brand of energy drink, doesn't it. Vero took me aside the first evening, after I'd bought her quite a lavish dinner at my hotel. She put it to me very clearly that most of the money, and any property outside the Hampshire place, was hers. I'm sure you grasp, Harris, she said, I'm entitled to that. I've had to put up with quite a lot from your father. This with him on his bloody slab not two miles away."

"It must have been tough."

"Yes. And I went down with food poisoning, or some Spanish bug..."

Somehow I couldn't resist. "A fly, perhaps?" I asked mildly.

A month ago he might have got that and laughed. A month ago however I doubt I would have said it aloud.

"Flies? You are correct. Everywhere. The air conditioning just made them frisky."

He continued to fill me in on his saga.

I pictured him, racked with worry and the unadmitted grief or fear I'd glimpsed in his eyes that day in the restaurant in Holborn. And stuck there in the luxury hotel, with his still current expense account from the firm, via which, I had no doubt, he had financed Veronica's lavish dinner.

"And there'll be death duties I'll have to pay on the damned house. Can you believe it, Roy? I mean, that crumbling wreck of a place. Hampshire! Miles from London. The dunnies don't even work properly. For God's sake."

The light was darkening. It looked like rain again.

"But you haven't told me anything about *you*, Roy."

I hadn't had much chance. "I'm fine."

"So this personal stuff of yours blew over."

"Yes."

"They have a habit of blowing over, don't they? These nasty little troubles. I suppose even all this shit with Dad will blow over. And you're OK with Gates - old Lew Rybourne?" (Lewis was at least twelve years his junior).

"Yes."

"Working well?"

"Fine, Harris."

I poured him another drink. He was already leading us towards the last third of the bottle, although I'd only had a couple.

"Are you seeing anyone?" he asked suddenly. There was a kind of sly subterfuge in his voice.

"You mean a woman. No. Not at the moment."

"You're a wise boy, Roy. Wish I had your bloody self control." He then launched into a monologue on 'someone' he had met on the plane back from Spain, which rhyme he included several times, like a chorus. "I mean that is a dire little flight. Don't know if you've ever done it - the plane from Spain? No, well. Not missed much. Too short to get stuck into anything, too long to manage not to get cabin fever. But then *this* plane from Spain had this girlie on it. And I got lucky. Or she did. Sat side by side. Really bright girl - oh," as if I'd asked, "about twenty-nine or so. Could be a bit older - don't you find women don't look their age now. Until they hit about forty-five, and then - everything falls, as they say in Venice. Anyway. We got on, shared some champagne – Look, Roy, would you do me a completely priceless favour?"

"Why not?" I said, smiling.

"You're a diamond. Jan is a bit suspicious. Don't know why. She never used to bother. Her age, maybe, she's coming up for the big four nine this year. Tonight I'm going up west, and my plane from Spain friend and I - well, you can guess, I have no doubt. Doesn't need one of your sleuths to solve it, does it? But Jan's due back tomorrow and I may not make the airport to collect her. Not that she needs me. If she left her car in London that's her look-out and she's perfectly well able to call a taxi. But you know what they're like. Could you back me up if it comes to it? That is, you and

I had dinner tonight, it got late so I kipped in your spare room - you do have one, don't you?"

Kip. His word – Sej's word had been the more modern *crash.* Kip or crash. Crash...

"I've got a spare bed. Yes. I can say that, Harris. If you want."

Rather than feel any fleeting gladness that Janette was to be deceived, or that I'd been involved in it, I felt a strange rush of oblique anger at him. Not *because* he wanted to involve me. It was far less logical. I was remembering how his brief flare of panic and distress during our last lunch had unsettled me, and sent me ultimately into the pub in the Strand. Where Sej had found me. Was *found* the right word? Dreadfully, maybe it was.

"That is so kind, Roy. I don't want to upset Jan, you see. I mean this thing is just a passing - fancy. She's too young for me, this chick off the plane from Spain."

Chick.

Was Harris becoming his father? Is that how we fill the niches where the dead once dwelled, not like the ancients with their sacred bones or carved semblances, but by transforming ourselves into their image?

He downed his drink then.

"Well, it's been good to see you. You look really good, Roy. I like the punk style. You ought to get some new publicity shots. I know a really splendid guy. I'll send you his name and email. I can just imagine some tasty ladies in their forties really liking the look of you."

Forty-five-year-olds, no doubt, the poor collapsed old cows.

I smiled.

We went out to his car.

"Why are the curtains drawn in there?" he asked me. "I meant to say before."

He had indicated the front room.

"Some decorators painting it. It's a mess at the moment. Stinks of paint too."

"I know what you mean. Veronica - ah, pardon me, *Vero* - was having the villa painted. I've seldom seen a white so *green*. You know, I long for the good old days when you could hire a witch to cast a juicy curse."

I smiled.

We shook hands.

"And you're OK," he said, "about that little thing with tonight?"

"Yes, Harris."

He got into the Morris, careless of the whisky. He waved, and drove off down the road.

The only reason he had come to see me, evidently, was to establish his alibi. But whether I upheld it was really down to me. Doubtless I would. He was still partly my agent, after all.

XVIII
('Untitled': Page 319)

CANDLELIGHT had revealed the face of Reiner.

He had survived the river. He was alive.

Having been dragged, about midday, into the Chamber of Revelation, Vilmos stood on legs that did not belong to him, made of strong stone like the supports of the Flavel Bridge. Planted in life's rushing black water, they never shook.

Vilmos's upper body too seemed to have its own physical if quiescent strength. He stood straight, his head held up, his arms and hands motionless at his sides. It was not either that he had been frozen and was too cold to move. It was that his body itself had decided it would not want to.

There was feeling in every limb, and in his torso and head, but though striped by severe flagellation and bruised by blows, pain was not all-consuming. He had no headache, had not had it, he thought, for more than twenty days - which was unusual. Awareness only was paramount. His mind worked intelligently and quickly.

Sometimes he did turn his head a little, for his head permitted him to do this. His eyes allowed him to move them freely. He had noted, his heart-beat was uncongested if rather slow, his breathing regular and deep.

Thus, seeing Reiner who might have been dead, slipping here and there through the crowd of men in the Chamber, Vilmos knew at once that Reiner had simply swum to shore.

Such an idea amused Vilmos. He felt for Reiner unfettered contempt. To survive now seemed, in some innate, inchoate sense, more slavish and conventionally drab than to have given in and drowned.

The *import* of the revelation did not strike Vilmos for a while, during which he continued to peruse the robed gathering of the Order of the Indian Mystery, as he stood upright in the centre of the room within a great new circle representing the Wheel. It had been made about him, its execution beginning in the late afternoon and proceeding through several hours. Those who had seen to this task had frequently grown exhausted. Some swooned and had to be replaced. Vilmos on his stony supportive limbs, his spine a reliable column, remained tall among them, watching the ones to the front and a little to either side, *listening* to those who worked behind him, since his head did not intend to let him to look over his shoulders, just as all the rest of him did not countenance the act of his fully turning round.

They had drawn the Wheel on the floor with the spilled blood of creatures brought in cages, from salt and liquefied silver, from ordure, which had been dried to powder and did not stink, or not greatly, and from the contents of vessels of milk. This last, according to what was said, was of three types. Firstly that of a virgin cow inspired to produce it by giving her a calf to foster, secondly of a whore who was feeding, or had been, her own baby, thirdly of a pure mother whose spouse belonged to the Order. There were other things also; chips of bone and splinters of wood, which Vilmos assumed had been hacked from reliquaries. Dusts ground from precious stones had been added in miserly quantities. But too there were other commodities. Some - many - Vilmos did not recognise. His mouth, tongue and throat did not wish to be used, and so he could not inquire.

The Master oversaw the entire labour. He chid the artisans, once or twice struck them with his staff. Those that fainted he chose to inspect. In some he found virtue. Others not. One he spat on, saying the fool smelled of drink and had perhaps upset the ritual. But in the end it seemed not;

the old man was satisfied.

He had rarely glanced at Vilmos. He must know how Vilmos was, and that he had been primed to his present condition and use.

Vilmos did not even feel any anger at the Master, let alone entertain thoughts of revenge. Revenge, of course, could not enter into the equation. When all this was - done, Vilmos would be no more. As some other foreign poet had once described it, Vilmos was to be their torch, and like a torch they would not light him for himself. He would kindle and burn up, and reaching the sixth stage, the point of dark blue fire, his purpose for them would be accomplished, and his own life snuffed out.

Yes, for all these lumbering and inadequate imbeciles, for these talentless lesser things, he was to attain and instantly freely render up the power of utter dominion over the inner and outer spheres: Mastery of Self, Mastery of All.

This it seemed the Devil granted to the Order, having become sick of the idiocy of mankind. For Satan loved God. He longed hopelessly only to be forgiven and raised.

And Vilmos felt neither fear nor struggle in him. He did not care anymore what became of him.

Like Satan, Vilmos was sick of the world and all its works. And if God did not want him, neither did Vilmos want any part of God.

And then. He beheld Reiner.

And a little while after, perhaps two or three minutes after, Vilmos saw what this meant. And also he saw that none but he had seen it - either Reiner, or what his presence suggested. The rest of them, the rabble in the Chamber, the educated and wise, virtuous acolytes chosen of the Master, the cripple-hearted Master himself - none of them saw or knew.

The very fitness of Vilmos, and his use to them, was

predicated upon his having killed men and women to the number of thirteen. For this reason had they not brought him here another man to slaughter, while the girl they brought for his carnal release they swiftly removed after congress, in case he might offer her also death - and so *increase* the number of the slain.

But Vilmos, since Reiner lived, had formerly killed in total only eleven, and now, with his single murder here, only twelve.

After all, something salient in the rite was out of alignment, a broken bone sticking from the skin of the spell.

TWENTY-ONE

Lynda left me, not only because of her well-off aunt near Manchester. I haven't been quite honest about that either in these pages or with myself.

Lynda left me because, the night she put it to me that she - and I - might go up north, where things were cheaper and the aunt presided, we had a row.

We'd often fought. When I tried not to join in it only made her more furious, I think. Certainly my neutral answers and refusal to lose my rag seemed to provoke her at these times to greater acrimony.

"Oh, you just sit there, Roy. Just sit there with that book. Don't you understand I want something a bit more than this rotten little flat and working for that horrible old rat, Christmas..." She meant her boss, a Mr Christmas. "...and your *stupid* hours at that library and never having any money or doing anything exciting. Oh, you just sit there. You don't care, do you? Long as your dinner's on the table, long as I've washed and ironed your clothes."

In fact we shared a lot of the chores. But for some while, Lynda had seemed to believe my late nights at the library, compulsorily working until six-thirty or eight p.m., were my choice in order 1) to get out of cooking a meal or helping clean the flat or 2) to avoid Lynda.

"But why do I *bother* to say anything? *You* won't try anything new, will you? You're like a bloody old man, Roy, you're like some old guy of forty-five."

"I'm sorry."

"You're not sorry. You're *not!*" she screamed. And then dropping back to a tone, which even she herself would describe as sarcastic, "But it's no good trying to shift you, is it? No good being sarky even. You have to have your own little way, don't you, Roy? Roy knows best."

She was always on about my liking to have my own little way. I've mentioned this before. It rarely failed by now to get on my nerves.

"I'm sorry, Lynda. Why don't *you* go and visit your aunt? I can't take any holiday now, you know that."

"*Yes*. I *know* that." Her thin lips squeezed almost white. The hard fluorescent kitchen strip shot lightnings over her glasses.

"Look, I need to go and try to finish that story in a minute - there's a good chance they'll take it but I have to have it with them before next..."

"That's all you do, isn't it? You're out all bloody day and half the night and then you're off to write some story. Some rubbish. How'd you know they'll publish it? They didn't want the last one."

"No."

"Oh, but you go *on*. You have your own little way. I don't know why I bother to come to bed. You sit and read, or scribble, or you're in the lounge typing till midnight. I can't even watch TV in there. And it's been two weeks since we last - since you know what."

I put down the book and looked at the back of it, unseeing. I couldn't say to Lynda that I found her by now unappetizing. That I really needed to be - well frankly very ready - before I could make love to her. And to make matters worse I'd had a bit of a thing about a woman at work. She was a few years older than me, quite pretty and very happily living with a man. Obviously I'd been aware I stood no chance, but I'd enjoyed her being there, working with her. We got on well, saw eye to eye on a lot of things. She'd read a story of mine published in one of the magazines and praised it, (I published under my real name

then). She said I shouldn't be working in the library at all.
About five days before my row with Lynda this woman, I
won't put her name, had been transferred to another branch
nearer her home. She was delighted to go. I'd wished her
well. I'd kissed her cheek and shaken her partner's hand.
She said they'd be looking out for my first published crime
novel.

"Lynda, I'm tired."

"Not too tired to *scribble*. Not too tired to type and turn
the lounge into your *office*. Paper everywhere. Books. A *tip*."

"Lynda..."

"Oh, shut up!" She surged to the door. "*You* do the
bloody washing-up. I'm going to bed. You..." She paused.
"You can *sleep* in the lounge." We had no couch. She meant
on the floor or in a chair. "You can go to hell!"

I got up. Although we fought, somehow I had never
really lost my temper. It was as if, even for rowing with her I
had to be in the right frame of mind. But now I was.

"Fuck off to bed, then," I shouted. "And if you want to go
to your aunt's so much just fucking go. In fact *I'll* go. I'm
leaving. Get out of the way..." I pushed past her.

Now she ran after me into the bedroom. "What are you
doing?" she bleated. But she could see. I was shoving a few
clothes into a bag. Next I went to the bathroom and got my
shaving stuff and toothbrush. "What?" she kept saying,
"What?"

But I didn't speak to her again until I was at the front
door. "Right. What you do, Lynda, is up to you. If you're
still here when I come back we can discuss it. But I hope you
won't be." The flat was rented. She always had most of my
wages to date and all her own. She would manage.

She said, crying now, her glasses dripping tears, pitiful
and revolting, "What shall I do?"

"Whatever you like. Fuck off. That's the best thing."

I went out and downstairs and let myself into the street. It was after ten at night and raining. I felt a gust of relief flare through me, like raw cool oxygen. As if I could breathe again. It was less getting away from her than escaping the surge of potential violence I'd sensed suddenly present inside me. I have never physically hurt a woman. That night I felt I might have done.

One of the fellows from work was in the pub I ended up in, and he let me sleep on his sofa. "Good thing Jenny isn't here tonight. She'd never put up with it."

When I went back to my own flat two days later, crestfallen and feeling rather bewildered, Lynda had gone. She had left me a four page letter, written in her over-ornamented handwriting with plenty of misspellings and wrong grammar.

The gist was she had her Pride. Her father had always told her that if a man didn't want her she must not want him, And she could see I no longer loved her, so she would indeed be "going up to Auntie's." She had taken her things, "like you would expect me to." Actually she had taken quite a few of mine also, including some of my books - dictionaries and a thesaurus. She couldn't possibly have wanted them. She must only have wanted to deprive me of them, I assumed, as I'd seemed to prefer them to her. Which of course I had.

Her father called me the night I left the flat, migrating back to my parents' house for a brief stay, as I sorted out my financial affairs. "A great pity," he sternly told me. "I always thought of you as rather a steady chap. I wouldn't have let her marry you, Roy, if I hadn't."

I apologised for not being what he had believed me to be.

One wonders sometimes how often one has had to do that.

Since then I've never seen Lynda again. I never saw the

other woman, from the library, again either. She was a bit like Maureen, not to look at, more her manner, although her accent was better and her voice not quite so musical or warm.

When Harris Wybrother had driven away I sat in my kitchen in Old Church Lane. I'd made some filter coffee, bought that day, an indulgence I don't often allow myself. There were some chocolate biscuits too, and I ate four.

Something had puzzled me about Sej's flat in the roof. Only I hadn't quite realised what at the time. Now it had come to me.

The apartment had many things in it that were quite large, such as the piano, not to mention the couches that could be transformed to beds. And there were things that would have needed either careful packing or delicate handling - glasses, plates. The flat was also able to produce water in the kitchen and bathing areas, had radiators, and lights and a music centre which would require electricity.

How had the breakable or heavy items been got into the apartment, how had the washing machine been plumbed in and cooker connected? Only the freelance limber or foolhardy would chance that ladder up from the fire-escape. Certainly no one from the electricity board or the water services, let alone anyone delivering a piano.

There had to be, did there not, another entry and exit from the flat. But neither I *nor* Mr C, the expert, had spotted one .

At nine that night, just after I'd finished off the Vilmos chapter upstairs, someone rang the bell.

I went down and I thought, *This won't be him.* But before I could decide what I felt, let alone open the door, the letter-box flipped up. George called through, "Roy, it's me. Just a little something."

I had no inclination to open up for George, but established habits linger. Or was it that? I unfastened the door quite swiftly despite its new bolts and locks.

The sun had only just gone. The sky was a broad silky blue, high clouds catching a peach afterglow, fading.

And there was George with a plate, and on the plate a round dark fruit cake.

"Vita, you see," he said, with an abashed vaingloriousness. "She baked this afternoon, and she thought you might like this one."

I stood at a loss again.

Belatedly it had occurred to me how I had been hoodwinked before by George and Vita, Sej using them to gain access. Now too he could have been out here. He could have been. But he was not.

The cake smelled good. My mother had sometimes baked, but not so successfully as Vita. My mother's *forté* was jam tarts, her fruit cake tended to be merely laxative.

"That's much too kind, George," I said. I took the plate. "Wonderful. Please thank your wife very much."

"Just look after yourself," admonished George. He managed to convey this cake was not a reward, but a tick for effort. I still needed to keep up the work.

He plodded back and went in. I stood holding the cake looking up and down the road.

The bicycling boy bicycled past. The prancing poodle was being taken for a walk by the new man in the life of No 73.

Going in myself I shut the door, and re-secured it.

In the kitchen I put the cake to one side. After the coffee and biscuits I didn't want it. I wasn't sure I wanted it anyway. Too much contact with my neighbours could prove time-consuming and draining.

Besides, I hadn't forgotten George and the scissors.

Poor old sod. It hadn't been his fault.

I closed my mind to him and went upstairs to back up the last chapter I'd done of *'Untitled'* on the machine. I supposed I should be pleased with it. It seemed to me I might suddenly have concluded the thing. But in a way I found that uncomfortable. The novel had been with me so long. And now what was I to do with it? No one would even want to glance at it. Writers, if they have any success at all, are always expected to remain in their handy and clearly-labelled ghettos A pseudonym? But all that was hypothetical. Probably tomorrow I'd want to rewrite that last chapter entirely.

Ten minutes later the door bell went again.

I was disinclined to go down. It must be George, or Vita even, coming to see what I thought of the cake. There'd been a similar visit over the last piece of cake she'd awarded me, years ago.

Idly I went to the unlit study window and looked down. George was there, standing on the paving talking to the paunchy man with cigars from No 80.

I drew back and took out the sheets of *'Untitled'* from my printer-tray and left them lying by the computer.

The bell went again. I ignored it.

I ran a bath and lay in it listening to the Third Programme. By which I mean Radio 3. It was Rachmaninov, the Third Symphony, or do I mean Symphony 3?

As a boy I'd found him too emotional. But that was insanity. Every age of one's life seems to carry some particular intellectual failing. If we learn one thing we seem to have lost another. Or probably only most of us. Some, surely, truly do grow up. But they are rare.

He returned into my life a couple of evenings later.

It was slightly less time than Mr C had promised. More, perhaps, than I had originally instinctively credited.

XIX
('Untitled': Page 323)

TO be on fire, to burn, was neither an agony nor alarming. The fire was cool, and although he felt it moving upward through his body, it had a certain familiarity. He seemed to have experienced its passage once or twice before. Then, however, it had given no light, and so he must not have known what happened to him.

Nothing of him had burned away. Still he stood, motionless in the centre of the Wheel of Life. No other light but that within *him* now illuminated the Chamber of Revelation.

It had begun with the deepest rose red, which flooded not only the lowest area of his belly and the area of his loins, but shone outward there and through his thighs. The veins and arteries in his calves and feet were also lighted with this colour. One could not be afraid of it, the gorgeous redness. It seemed life-giving.

Despite that, and the fact the chants and magical gesturings of the assembly had caused it to ignite, a concerted groaning gasp had risen from them all when the red fire began.

Vilmos had gazed down at it, his head bending a very little and so enabling him to see. He was delighted, intrigued.

He knew very well what now must follow.

He felt in fact a curious, perhaps inexplicable excitement, as the ruby colour seared upward and in turn awoke the intense shade of fiery marigolds in his bowels. In *this* light the faint shadow of his intestines appeared. How fascinating they were, labyrinthine coils and the tiny secret cavities between, like a thousand serpents mating in a cave. But the flame rose ever upward and next became the colour of the palest yellow topaz. The sack of stomach, and the shape of another organ, maybe the spleen, hung like ripe fruits in the morning glow. The liver represented an amorphous landmass, or perhaps a cloud...

Vilmos was perfectly conscious the fire would next pass into his heart; already arteries in his hands and arms were catching faint streaks of amber and saffron and now the reciprocated hint of emeralds. The heart was green. It was a leaf in latest spring. Beyond the heart lay the cornflowers of the throat. He would be able to see this blue aspect of the fire *only* through its reflection outward.

After that the flame must rise into and through his head, his eyes and brain. On his forehead the blue of it must darken. For there the fire would turn to indigo. And in that moment, Vilmos, the prepared alembic, would become the final crucible. Indigo would open to him a knowledge of All Things. Indigo would remake him and he would rupture, he would crack and explode, as had many of the alembics and the crucibles of the Order. But now, from him, the genius of knowledge would burst forth and cover everyone in the room.

Vilmos was unafraid.

When the red fire started he had begun his own soft chant. Over and over, nearly laughing, he whispered it inside his mind. His mouth and tongue could not be operated; he could not say anything aloud. But the chant within him was now so forceful and so sure he seemed to hear it dinning in his ears like a trumpet. Even the fire, ever rising, ever changing, pouring upward in its rainbow, red to orange to yellow, yellow to green to blue, even the blue fire reaching now, stretching upward, seemed to flicker in rhythm with the voiceless chant of Vilmos.

"Twelve not thirteen. Twelve not thirteen. Twelve not

thirteen."

For, since their ritual had been flawed by their own ignorance, the Moment of Revealing was to be also his. The supreme Moment of the passage through to indigo initially would be his *alone*. For one instant he would contain the powers of spheres and ages and dimensions and angels. Dominion.

After all he could touch God, even if God then shied away and shattered him.

And he yearned for it. He welcomed it. He *rejoiced* in it.

"Twelve not thirteen."

The fire soared, clearly visible to every watcher in the Chamber, even to the ancient toad crouching by the wall, at last blue - to indigo.

To Indigo.

TWENTY-TWO

The sky was overcast that evening, it rained, and by six o'clock the sun might as well have set.

I'd been doing some clothes in the washing machine. I was thinking I'd have an early dinner and decided, rather than cook, to order in pizza.

Some of the streetlamps prematurely had come on. The darkness was dreary. The sound of the rain oddly put me in mind of marbles dropping into wet cement.

When the bell sounded I wasn't thinking of anything much. I'd glimpsed a man in a raincoat going up and down about twenty minutes before, canvassing for something, miserable and unwanted in the rain. It seemed ridiculous to me, even as I undid the front door, to do this only in order to tell him I didn't want double glazing or a new look for the house, or to sponsor someone to lie in a bath of jam for charity. But I opened the door and there he was. Joseph Traskul. Sej. Standing in the rain in blue jeans and a deep blue shirt, his hair rain-plastered to his head.

He said nothing. He didn't even smile. Perhaps to smile would hurt him: there was a bruise on his right cheek despite what Mr C had said.

The way he stood too, slightly bending forward. He had a denim jacket over his left shoulder and it seemed to weigh him down a bit. His ribs, I thought, bruised too or cracked, on that side.

Nor did he stride forward, try to push past me.

He just stood there, over seven feet from the door. Looking at me.

I had known he would come back.

He was like a machine you could not turn off, however

often you threw the switch or pulled the plug or hacked through the electric cable. Although demons don't exist in any supernatural sense, they are here. They are among us. They are called fellow human beings, and Sej was one.

I said nothing to him. But I must make this quite clear, I easily had time to slam the door, bolt and lock it. If it came to that, once safely inside, I could have activated the new burglar alarm.

But both of us simply stood there, watching each other,

In the end, he spoke.

"So you shaved your head."

When I heard his voice I felt the most peculiar rushing sensation inside my gut, the cavity of my chest. This wasn't disturbing. It was more like circulation spinning back in a foot or limb that had gone to sleep. A shutter seemed to fly up in my brain. I blinked, and seemed to see not only Sej but everything, with a bright abnormal clarity. It felt, and I use this phrase with dismay, as if my eyes had been cleaned like windows. I wasn't frightened. It wasn't like that. Perhaps I'd felt something like it before, but if I had, misunderstood and so forgotten it.

And I stepped aside and said, "You'd better come in."

In the kitchen, where the light was on, he sat down gingerly on a chair.

I made some tea. If he scrutinised this I didn't see it particularly. He didn't tell me to taste the mug I handed him, nor did I offer.

"*White* mugs," he said. "What did you do with the others?"

"Oxfam."

"Very wise," he said. He stretched his legs out, and regarded the revolving washing in the chugging machine. He said, without much expression, "They knocked me about a bit. Nothing terminal. The hospital assured me I'll be fit enough in a month. Till then, I must just be careful. Lucky that. I came to in the hospital car park, about 1 a.m. No one in A and E. Can you believe it? It's normally packed out. Someone did ask how this had happened. I said, Personal matter. Girl I shouldn't have fucked. Did I want the police? I said no, I'd probably deserved all I got. And how have *you* been?"

"Here," I said.

"How's the book? I mean *Kill Me Tomorrow*."

"Going quite well."

"Glad to hear that."

I too had sat down. We drank the tea. The chocolate biscuits were on the table. I pushed them over.

"Thanks." he said. He took out two and ate them, also as if being careful, now, of his jaw.

I didn't ask him why he had returned. He didn't tell me. We both knew, at least both of us, I assume, *thought* we knew.

The machine finished its cycle. I got up and put on the drying programme.

"Funny that," he said, "the comforting noise of a domestic washing machine. Never like that in a launderette."

"So you use launderettes," I said. I was thinking of the flat in the roof and the washing machine that couldn't be there unless there were another way in and out.

"Oh, now and then. You meet some weird people in launderettes, Roy." It was the first time now he'd used my name.

"I expect you do. I expect," I added, "*they* do, as well."

"Me, you mean? Yeah."

He smiled. I did.

"I was going to order pizza," I said. "You've got me into

bad habits - junk food, takeaways."

"I did, didn't I. Yes. Pizza would be extra comforting. Only tonight I can't pay. Sorry."

"Oh, that's all right. You bought so much last time. Just one thing though, Sej. Now I answer the door. You can stand on the top stair if you like, and keep watch."

"Oh," he said, "I trust you."

We both ordered the Pizza Double Plus, which had pepperoni, bacon and steak on it, along with mushrooms and olives, tomatoes, mozzarella and ricotta cheese.

It arrived around seven. I paid and brought it in. We sat in the kitchen, the windows dark as if it were January, and the washing machine chugged on, and we ate pizza and drank a bottle of decent if not wonderful red wine.

Afterwards I brought the slab of dark chocolate I'd got myself out of the fridge. We broke this up and ate it too - I noticed he let his melt a little in his mouth before he'd bite - dental work? A broken tooth? I made more of the Brazilian filter coffee and brought out the last of the vodka, which I'd never poured away as I didn't drink it. There had been little conversation - comments on the food, the weather, London, the world. As before.

But reaching the coffee-chocolate-alcohol stage: "So," I said, "now tell me about yourself. Tell me who you are."

"Joseph Traskul."

"I know that. At least I know you told me that. Last time you told me too you were in a children's home. True?"

"Did I? Well yes. It *is* true."

"Prove it."

"I can't, Roy. But. It was shit. Look." He rolled back the left sleeve of his blue shirt. "See?" I *could* see a long thin old scar. "I have a few of those. Someone there liked to use me as an envelope. He, you understand, was the letter opener.

Bloody letters."

"And you learnt from him," I said.

"Learnt from *him*? No. I just learned."

He leaned back in the chair. He was looking at me, and all at once he was crying. The tears ran from his eyes.

I thought, with great compassion, he can do this at will. But how and from what has he learned *that*?

He said, "Roy. Life plays with us. It *plays*. Cat with mouse. And all we can do..." He spread his hands, lowering his eyes. When he looked up they were dry. "*We* can play, Roy. Play. Roy. If there's a lesson, that's it. Learn how to *play*."

We sat in silence, as we often had this evening. The rain and the washing machine, now at work on the towels, filled the gaps, marbles in wet cement, domestic chugs. We drank the coffee. I poured him another double vodka.

"I shouldn't drink this," he said. "I'm on prescription pain-killers. But vodka is better."

"You'll be OK."

"You should know," he said. He smiled, but it wasn't like the other smiles he'd always used. "You arranged it."

"Arranged what?"

"I wonder."

"Did I? So you're angry?" I asked. "Resentful?"

"No. I said. I deserved it."

I must justify nothing.

"You can always sleep here. I have a put-you-up bed. It's not too bad."

"I remember. Only last time I couldn't use it, because I had to watch you."

"Well now you don't have to."

Bluff? Double bluff? Double Plus Pizza bluff?

He said, quietly, "There are people staying at my place. I - have to let them do that. I've got a couple of couches that turn into beds. But I can't stay there. These people - need some space."

"This is at your flat, 66 Saracen Road?"

"Yeah."

He put his arms down on the table, and rested his head on them. This lasted about two minutes. I drank my coffee. At last he looked up, sat back.

"Thank you for dinner. Perhaps I should just get out."

"Well, if you prefer. But - why don't you play the piano in the front room. I used," I said, smiling, "to like that. My father used to play. And a woman I loved. She played the piano - not as well as you, but very well. I loved it. I loved *her*, Sej. I thought she might have been your mother. Only she wasn't."

"No, Roy. No. My mum's name was Ashabelle." He spelled it. "A.S.H.A.B.E.L.L.E." He laughed, deadly. Not like any of his other laughter. "She was about fifteen when I was born. So she was carrying me at fourteen. It's too young. I don't know much about it. Only that she shat me out and dumped me. Ashabelle. Is that black?"

"You don't look as if you have black blood."

"No. God knows, Roy. Do you," he paused, "do you really want me to play?"

"Have another vodka. Play the piano. Then - crash on the other bed. You're safe with me."

"Am I?"

"Nothing sexual," I said, "I can assure you."

"*Touché*," he said.

I made more coffee and tipped the last triple measure from the vodka bottle into his glass.

He explained about the wasp after I'd opened up the front room and turned on the standard lamp covered in splashes of red paint.

"I ought to explain," he said. "I mean I don't want you to think you have to be guilty about putting it in a sandwich. Or too triumphalist either, I suppose."

He'd sat on the painted sofa, still nursing the vodka, and I on one of the painted chairs. The curtains had stayed drawn. He had been right about the red walls. In lamplight they did glow. If everything else had been OK, it might have a wonderful effect, modern yet warm, different.

"So you'd found the wasp before I used it. You knew I *would* use it."

"Thought you would."

"When did you find it? I only put it there that morning."

"I'd been on the look-out. One or two of them had got into the house. I had a feeling it might occur to you. But I let the ones I saw out of the kitchen window. It was after your bath," he said. And flashed me a dim shadow of his former impervious smile.

"When I stayed in the bathroom."

"It happens," he said. "So I had a look upstairs. I looked in your wardrobe as a matter of course. You hadn't concealed it superlatively well, Roy. For a writer of detective fiction... I can tell you though, the beast was angry. I let it go at the bedroom window and got stung in the process. But I never have much of a reaction to wasp stings."

"No," I said. "So the wasp I found later in the glass was another one?"

"A dead one. Much less lethal. I'd found it on a windowsill in here. The paint smell probably killed it."

"It was dead?" It had seemed to me the wasp in my glass had still had some life in it, if not much. No doubt, in the state I'd been in, I'd imagined the slight vestige of response, expecting to see it.

"It was dead. Then I waited, and you put it in the sandwich, between the top slice of bread and the ham."

"But you didn't bite down on it - did you?"

"I was looking out, Roy, remember. When I took the sandwich about which you'd made such a scene... I could *feel* the wasp through the bread. Poor sod felt like a prawn. So I bit well clear."

I recalled the corpse of the wasp, undamaged, lying under the rim of the plate.

"Then your reaction was one more fake."

"'Fraid so."

"Your mouth bled. I saw it."

"Ketchup, Roy. When I went into the kitchen."

I burst out laughing. I couldn't, myself, tell if this were genuine mirth at the madness of all this, or an actor's laugh, used for effect. Something of each, maybe. I recollected he, like most of us, liked flattery. "You're a genius," I said. "Did you train at RADA?"

"Oh, sure," he seriously acquiesced, smiling a little, still not in the old ways. "A year. I was expelled."

"RADA? Expelled? Why?"

"Not good enough."

A lie. Or not. Either was unlikely - that he'd been there, that, being there, he'd be thrown out.

I said, "You could act Olivier or Jacobi or Sher off the stage."

"No I couldn't. But thank you. The world's my stage anyway, Roy, and all the men and women merely players." He finished the vodka.

I said, "There's only whisky now, I'm afraid. I can taste it for you, if you'd like some."

"Trying to get me drunk again," he said softly.

"You'll get a good night's sleep. Or you can leave, as you said. I don't take prisoners."

"No?"

"No."

He rose. "Anyway," he said, "I'll play for you, before I go. What would you like?"

"Your choice."

He paused, looking at the piano; then he turned and looked across at the mantelpiece. I'd known he would. I had known.

"Where's the glass dog?"

"Oh that. Still upstairs. When I get the room fixed, I'll bring it down again."

"It means something to you, doesn't it, the dog?"

"Yes. My mother loved it. It reminded her of the past, some happy memories, and she said to me once, When we're gone, Roy, whatever you get rid of, please keep the dog."

"It's nice you had a mother," he said.

I said, "Wait a minute. I'll get it."

He looked tired. For a moment he looked, as I've said, as we all know the young sometimes do, much older than he could possibly be, whoever's son he was - Lynda's, Maureen's, Ashabelle's - Mine.

He sat down before the piano and opened the lid, and ran his fingers along its keys, stumbling once, a false rill of notes, which I'd never heard happen in his playing before.

I was upstairs, the red glass dog in my hand, when I heard him begin a Rachmaninov concerto - a transposition which perhaps he could effect spontaneously. It was the Second, the most beautiful and therefore the most hackneyed of the opus; the breaking melody of the second movement. When you hear this, for the first, or if you *listen* even after long familiarity, it has the power to shake the heart, even the dullest or the darkest heart. Unlike the Third Concerto, which is virtually perfect, the work of a supreme genius, the Second is imperfect, yet has been, as they say, dictated by God.

I stood at the head of the stairs with the dog in my hands, and I listened as Joseph played.

What was he? *What*?

But through the melody stared all the rest of what had been, and what he was otherwise. And I had known from the beginning, from before even he had come back to my door.

Returning into the room I sat quietly behind him, back on my chair, holding the dog. I rubbed my fingers over the smooth glass, and Rachmaninov poured from the piano.

No mistakes now.

In the upright wooden shell of the instrument, where the strings stretch unseen from keys to hammers, like the hidden muscles of the emotional body itself, I could see his face reflected. Lowered towards the keyboard, intent and pale, only the dusting of the bruise under his cheekbone. His eyes seemed closed. He lived and expressed the music.

I remembered how I had known I couldn't harm his hands.

Some trick of the light, the redness of the room, cast a red glimmer across his forehead. It was where the smear of paint had been when he worked on the walls. Red, the lowest chakra, reproduced at the exact region of the higher sixth chakra, the Third Eye, Vilmos's focus, the goal of his corrupt Order, (Indigo), inner seeing and self-knowledge and thus the dominion over All Things, but firstly of the Self.

Slowly I got up again and moved quietly across, as if drawn forward by the music and wanting to watch the movement of his hands up close.

I stood behind his left shoulder, as the Devil does in some Mediaeval woodcuts. *Retro me Satanus*...

Yes, he was entirely absorbed in his playing, and I too could become so. The rapid dance of his fingers and the waves, black to white to black to white of the keys, were mesmerising.

I went on watching, until the aching melody had almost reached its end. Although the ultimate theme of the last Movement is the greater, this Second Movement premonition of it is perhaps more pervasive. Unheralded, it invades. Unfinished, it haunts and echoes on the corridors of the mind.

But he would stop. He was tired and in pain. He might have to.

I stepped back a little, and half turned away, and stood almost with my back to him.

My reflection too would be in the upright wood.

I changed the position of the red glass dog in my right hand.

Steady as a rock. Nothing in me felt frail. I wouldn't falter.

The stream of music was running to its close. Now, then. It would have to be now.

Turning round again I struck him violently on the back of the head, with all my weight - and if undersized and slight - still I'm a grown man - behind it.

The dog was heavy, solid. I felt the point of its nose connect with the parietal lobe to the left of his skull.

Unlike the scenes in so many films, there was no discordant clash of chords. His hands slipped noiseless from the keys. His body jerked once and slumped forward, his head striking again, the frontal lobe now, on the wood of the piano.

I'd believed the dog would shatter. It hadn't. Instead, very neatly it had split in two sections, breaking just behind the neck. I bent down and retrieved the smaller piece, the head, examined it and quickly saw I would be able to superglue it back together.

XIX
('Untitled': Page 333)

THE cataclysm that had destroyed the Chamber had been visible to Vilmos only for those six or seven brief seconds, when he seemed to hang in space between earth and sky, day and night, life and eternity. Then came the locomotion of a colossal fall, worthy of Lucifer's it seemed to him, although later he spurned a comparison of such ineptitude. The *end* of the fall, its destination, threw him feet first through the collapsing cellarage of the Master's house. He found himself then, abruptly, as if just waking from a vivid dream, floating comfortably on the broad bosom of the river, a bridge before him that was not the Flavel, the moon, thin as a cat's closed eye, squinting down from above.

He knew the water would buoy him up, carry him. There was no need to struggle. The river did so and presently bumped him home against the bank.

The stone jumble of the City was sparse here. A tree craned to the water and Vilmos caught its lowest bough and hauled himself in with little effort.

It was not cold. Already his garments seemed to dry themselves in the extreme incandescent energy which still radiated from his body.

The lights of the mystic *Cakras* had faded from him, at least to the physical eye, but every part of him felt charged and effulgent.

Vilmos was well aware of what had happened.

Twelve, not thirteen.

They had made an error in the formula of their spell, and this had warped it. And so he had been able, on reaching the indigo instant of utter power, to claim himself back from them, and so wrench free. The power he shed, meanwhile, when this took place, detonated instead in the room.

He doubted any of them had survived, but now, standing on the bank and gazing back along the curve of the river, he saw a livid rusty glare, and a solid black cumulous of smoke that was rising up. It came to him this went on about where he would expect to find the Master's house. And that therefore, not only had it been shaken down, but it was on fire, and burned.

Imagining the crowds of neighbours in their nightshirts springing out in horror on the street, gazing at this in frightened awe and malign disgust, Vilmos smiled to himself.

Without questioning or reticence, he knew that all the might of the ritual and the alchemical surge had entered and refined only him. What now then might he not do?

On an impulse he turned, and with a *look* struck a flame on the black river. It lit at once and blazed there like a lily of phosphorous. He had done this by his will alone.

Notions of Satan and God had become superfluous.

Vilmos was his own man now.

Just then the Master's ancient toad pulled itself out of the water also, and squatted on the bank, staring at him. As the engendered flame was extinguished, Vilmos saw both the toad's eyes, and the evil jewel between them, had kept the terrific dark blue of the Indigo Instant. Only the toad and he had escaped alive. And perhaps it too had been able to garner some power.

In all his life no single human had either joyed or contented Vilmos. But he might benefit from a companion.

"Come then," he called to the toad, and like an image of black jade, understanding him, it lifted itself and approached. "Which way shall we go?" he inquired of it. The toad reversed itself, and Vilmos saw that over there, in the east, dawn was commencing. He had no need to fear light any longer. Nor dark, if it came to it. "East then," said Vilmos. And eastward they went.

TWENTY-THREE

At first I thought I'd killed him outright.

When I pulled him back from the piano, his face was pallid and slightly puffy and I couldn't see him breathing. But there was the vaguest pulse in his throat. Still alive then?

Unusual strength can be accessed in times of stress. I'd read of it, even written about it. Now I found it to be true.

I dragged Sej off the seat and from the room, along the hall into the kitchen, without trouble.

What I did next was a precaution. It was my more pedantic side, making certain, covering all possible eventualities. A writer's action, or the deliberate murderer's.

Having got him on the floor, leaning by the table I pulled him forward, and cracked his head, the back of it, a second time very hard against the table's corner. Then I allowed him to fall.

Still I couldn't see any breathing. Yet the pulse in his neck stumblingly kept on.

It didn't really matter, did it? He wasn't going to interfere in what came next.

Perhaps I should note my state of mind during all this. I was flatly calm. I was rational, unexcited and concise. I might have been organizing my washing, or checking over an especially-to-me boring proof chapter in one of my novels. This mood had opened up in me like a well of cool water the moment I saw him standing outside my door in the rain. Partly, at the beginning, I'd wondered if it would suddenly desert me, leaving me after all unsure and panicked, unable to make a decision. But it had not. And in some odd mental fashion, I'd known from that same first moment what I must do, and roughly how I would do it. As if, as with the plots of my stories, I'd already written out a careful synopsis, and only had to consult that from time to time in order to construct the book.

Once I'd seen him sprawled on the floor, I went upstairs and got ready.

I was particularly facile at packing by this time. It was after all my third attempt to escape. On this occasion however, I didn't pack all the documents, only birth certificate, passport, bank details and those of my savings, plus their necessary various cards and other safeguards. Some of these things I might legitimately take with me when travelling. Some of them I could, if I had to, claim to have mislaid years ago, as many of us do. While some of the items now left out would, after tonight, be redundant anyway.

Naturally I packed more clothes, more toiletries. Again legitimate. I was going to stay with my poor upset old friend at Cheston for quite a while, wasn't I? Duran believed I'd gone up there before. I'd mentioned Matthew's frame of mind post his 'betrayal' by Sylvia. From the brief picture I had then, perhaps innocently, painted, Duran definitely wouldn't be astonished I'd been begged to go back. As for George and Vita next door, those two silly old fools hadn't seen me for days during Sej's last sojourn, and only had his word for it I was in the house. While, as Mr C had pointed out witnesses, (especially elderly ones) were unreliable.

None of this might help, of course.

But it was reasonable for me. After so many invented third-hand literary alibis and get-outs, to fabricate something now.

When I had everything ready in the two larger bags, including the two bits of the red glass dog, carefully wrapped, I came back downstairs.

I bent and touched him again. He felt very cold and lay totally inert. I couldn't find any pulse now. But being no doctor, I couldn't rely on that.

From the freezer I took a pack of pork sausages. The remains of the pizza and the wine, mugs, glasses, plates, the coffee, still lay on the table. On the hob I put an over-full pan of oil, and placed four of the sausages in it. Just the sort of late snack a young healthy man might fancy, particularly if depressed, even after all the pizza eaten between seven and eight o'clock. The cake was still on the side, too. It should burn very well.

It wouldn't be a problem that the sausages were frozen; just slow everything down a little. Which was a good thing, given the circumstances.

I lit the hob, kept it very low.

Outside the kitchen the night lay ink black, a few stars showing dully like wet grains of sugar.

I hoped the fir tree wouldn't be affected. Probably not. Long before the wooden fences went up someone would have heard or smelled something wrong at No 74.

The cooking oil I sloshed liberally round the kitchen, the table, and over him. How lucky I'd bought an extra bottle. There was enough to trail along the hallway and the bottom of the stairs; even the library carpet got a sprinkle. But books burn beautifully, as Ray Bradbury let us know in *Farenheit 451*. That is, if we'd missed the history lesson that began even before the great Library burned in Alexandria in the time of Caesar and Cleopatra.

In my bag I had the MS of *Untitled*, plus the disc, including the last chapter, XIX - if such it was - work in progress, that was the file and disc for *Kill Me Tomorrow*. I had *Last Orders* too, in its paperback form. My favourite. But why shouldn't I take that to read over on the long train to the north? Quite legitimate. And writers often travel with their work, picking at it in odd moments. I'd be able to use Matt's computer, wouldn't I, if I could persuade him away from his twenty-four hour blog, which he'd started to describe Sylvia, if under another name, and all her slut-like wickedness. He'd told me during our short telephone conversation about this blog, and how he was getting hundreds of 'hits'. Men - and women. *An Age of Traitors* he called it.

Going back to put the emptied bottle of oil in the kitchen bin, I was careful not to tread in any of it. I'd been especially careful not to splash any on my clothing. I washed my hands at the sink. Like Pilot.

I did glance at him before I left the kitchen, leaving on the light, as I'd left on the light in the lavatory and the study upstairs. (I had got the spare bed out and put it ready too, placing blankets and sheets and a pillow on it, all prepared for Sej's never-to-be-realised crash).

Sej lay exactly as I'd left him. A little line of blood had run from his nose. I didn't know what that might mean, but it could hardly auger well.

My bags were already by the front door. Again cautious where I stepped, I let myself out and relocked the door, both locks, then slid the keys back through the letter-box on to the floor, where he might casually have dropped them. Because naturally, if he were minding my house while I was away, he would need them. For what it was worth, I kept the other set, those he had copied from mine. I had de-activated the burglar alarm, too, for the liar's reason that Sej might have trouble with it.

My previous dialogue with the police, asking for protection, also had an explanation. I'd been afraid of this sudden stalker. Then found out he was the son of a woman I'd known years ago. We'd sorted it all out, and even though he was a little strange, I'd had a fondness for him, because of her, and because I'd last seen him as a child. Obviously this was my gullibility. I'd accepted the yarn he spun me. No doubt the police would eventually point this out. Whatever else, I'd had to go to Cheston to visit Matt. I'd left Sej in the house because he'd told me he was upset, needed a bolt-hole. Some woman he'd got into difficulties over. (If he *had* told that tale at the hospital, I might have extra back-up).

On the other hand I didn't really trust any of this to bale me out for long, if the proverbial shit hit the fan. And presumably it would. Matt for one was a doubtful ally.

Old Church Lane seemed in its normal night-time phase. The rain had gone, leaving a cold sparkle on the edges of things. The clock on the church was striking ten-fifteen. All around, the usual flick and flutter of TV and computer screens through glass or drawn blinds and curtains. No lights were visible at all over the road in 73. Perhaps at the back, where the bedroom was. A black or dark blue car had been parked outside No 80. A tall girl and a young man were leaning on the side, embracing, locked in a prolonged kiss. What must that be like? Did I recall? Yes. Oh yes.

I walked across the paving to 72 and rang their bell.

It was late for them, but some lights were still on upstairs and down.

Perhaps they wouldn't answer, however, already into the bedtime routine, dressing-gowns and cocoa, or whatever they drank last thing. In this day and age even George and Vita probably resorted to a tot of alcohol and a sleeping pill.

Then someone shot the bolts.

George opened the door, virtually as I'd pictured, in a port wine paisley dressing-gown. "Oh - it's you," he said.

"Sorry to disturb you." I was factual and restrained. "I thought I'd better let you know. I'm off again," (the 'again' was deliberate), "that pal of mine up north. I can't really say no."

George looked baffled and slightly offended.

"The thing is, in case you hear sounds through the wall, Joseph - is there. He's staying over for a couple of days. He needs - well, somewhere to get away from it all."

Something had happened while I said this. I had grasped I didn't know if George knew Sej by that name, or the other one, Joseph - or by some *other* name entirely. Had I ever heard him call Sej by a name? Had Sej ever mentioned what George knew him as? I didn't think so. And certainly George still seemed baffled, and now uneasy. I added, "Joseph. That's the young man who said he was my son. My friend's boy."

"I see."

"Actually, he's pretty depressed." I made myself sound world-weary rather than confiding. "Some trouble with a young woman. I wish it was that easy with my chum Matt, up north. His wife," I said, "has let him down rather badly."

A sort of flicker went over George's face. He seemed caught between a wish to get all the gossip, and a wish to be rid of me.

I granted the second one.

"Anyway. I should be back in four or five days, a week at most. I can't keep running up there to hold Matt's hand, can I? Take care. Best to Vita."

I turned and he cleared his throat.

The outrageousness of his next question, one which I not only had to answer, but to lie about, nearly stunned me. "How," he demanded angrily, "did you like her cake?"

Much later, I did consider that my semi-detached house, when it caught alight, possibly even with a small explosion, might endanger George and Vita. The brief mental sketch I'd made still inclined me to think the fire would be smelled if not heard, seen even - smoke billowing - early on. Even drugged by whisky and whatever else, Vita would wake up, her hearing wasn't bad. Failing that neighbours or the fire brigade would alert them.

But to be quite honest, I didn't care.

I didn't give a damn.

Long ago, before modern forensic techniques, and also given the inattention to detail only displaced now and then by a real life detective of the type of Sherlock Holmes, I could have got away with it much more easily.

Finding Roy Phipps' house burned down and a burned male corpse inside it, very likely said corpse would have been taken for Roy Phipps.

Not now, of course. By no means.

They would learn if not who, then who he was not, inside a few days at most. And despite the ruse I'd set up and the care I'd taken, any police force not completely composed of morons would instigate a search for me.

I had decided to make for France, via the popularly-named Chunnel.

To access the train times of Eurostar would have taken too long tonight. I'd opted to catch the last Ashford train from Charing Cross. There were a couple of hotels in Ashford. I'd pick up the Chunnel train tomorrow as early as was practicable .

My French was adequate. Besides, two years before, when I went over there on some business junket with Gates, (signing books and so on for an affiliate French company known as *Lisez-moi!*), I'd found even the Parisians, notorious for their hauteur, had come to speak English, many of them. Maybe only in order to disgrace us by talking in our language more elegantly.

The train going in to Charing Cross was almost empty. It was by then about eleven.

I sat in the carriage with one of my bags squeezed into the uselessly narrow rack overhead, the other bulkier one on the next seat.

The thick yellow light was both somnolent and unrestful.

For the very first, finally, I began to feel a hollow terror at what I'd done. But it was far off. For now at least I could ignore it. I took out the miniature of whisky I'd bought en route, and downed a gulp.

The train presently made its pneumatic hissing sound and we stopped. I don't recall the station, although at the time I noted it. The couple of people already sitting back along the carriage got out, and someone else got in. I heard him give a sigh. And then he walked up towards the front of the carriage. I smelled an exclusive male fragrance I had met before, and quite recently. I couldn't think where. Then his shadow crossed over me and I found I looked up quickly and in alarm.

There was nothing in my head. I had no forecast image of a policeman, plain clothes or otherwise. Nor of Sej. Sej, I knew, was in no position now to have caught this train with me.

"Mr Phillips," said Cart, and sat down facing me in the dark yellow light.

My first, and probably not utterly inane thought, was that the credit card company had refused to pay out on my 'deliveries' from him. I hadn't checked my current credit, thought I'd paid a lot off the last card bill. (I'd not yet received the one which would show me what name Cart's outfit traded under).

I stared at Cart. He wore a dark raincoat.

"Now," he said, "Mr Phillips, you seem dismayed. Please. You have been an ideal customer. That's the only reason I now seek you out."

"What for?" I said. I had felt very sick, but after a second this went off.

"It is about the unusual apartment your dangerous young friend was in, at Saracen Road."

I didn't know what I could say, or what I needed to say. I said, "How did you know which train...?"

"Oh, you were followed, Mr Phillips, like before. I have received the text at the proper moment, and come at once to board the train too. Aren't you curious," he went on, smiling a little, "to know what is my interest in the apartment of Mr Sej?"

In the false light his thick blue-black hair, eyebrows, lashes and moustache seemed made from some lush material that couldn't, any of it, be hair. He looked manufactured.

Unzipping the pocket in my bag, I took out the whisky and had another swig.

"Ah, a whisky man," said Cart, all approval. "So *I* am, Mr Phillips. The purest alcohol there is. Vodka is poison, and wine - the dregs of vinegars. But a fine malt may not be rivalled."

I felt bleak. I was afraid. "Tell me about the apartment."

"Very well, of course. Our good friend Mr C has discovered something of great importance about it. This we felt you should learn also, as it may be to mutual profit."

His English, which had been fairly sustained before, tonight seemed a bit less sound. How I noticed this I'm not sure. But it can happen. As when going blind, other senses compensate, the faculty of logic enters some other area when shut out of the main stream by fear. In the same way, apparently, condemned criminals can often describe in minute detail a pebble or a drop of dew, glimpsed on their way to the gallows.

"All right," I said. I put the whisky back in the zippered

pocket, although I needed to take more. There wasn't much left by now.

"It seems there is another door into the flat. Mr C was concerned that some heavy furniture, a piano and so forth, were in the loft, and only an outdoor ladder to be going up."

I too had thought of that, had I not?

"And so?" I said. My voice didn't sound shaky. Even my hands had been steady on the whisky. The shakes were all inside.

"Well, Mr C has cleverly located the other door to the apartment. In light of this, perhaps you would like to go back there? I mean, accompanied of course. And free of all charge. It seems he - your enemy-friend - is elsewhere." (I almost blurted something when he said this. But I didn't). "Perhaps we might go there tonight. As you are already on your way up to London."

"I have a business meeting."

"*Do* you? So late." Silky, he looked at me. It was a flirtatious look, which said, *Oh come now, I know you have nothing of the sort.* "Just an hour from your urgent schedule. He pronounced this *skedule*, as Americans do.

I thought, *This is some form of so-far unfathomable blackmail. I'd better agree. I can delay the journey, start early tomorrow from Waterloo... pray no one is looking for me right there... If I offend him, refuse, God knows.*

We'd stopped at two or three stations meanwhile, and gone on. I hadn't noted them. We might have been in a foreign country, not France: somewhere I couldn't begin to decipher the signs. Hell, perhaps.

"OK," I said. "If you want."

"It will, I am sure, be mutually helpful."

In the window's black night glass, our shades sat in the amber of the light. I didn't look afraid, I saw. But then, I didn't look quite like me either.

He said, "That's good, you see. Now we are coming into Waterloo."

What was striking was the silence of the flats. I'd been expecting blasts of bad music, even though now it was almost midnight.

A few dim lights were on in various rooms. Everything however, the terrace, the street, the surrounding city, seemed still and relatively silent. Among the shrubs and trees of the park, old rain glittered, catching streetlamps which, here, had stayed shell white.

Cart had brought us here by cab. He himself had paid for this. Now he produced a key to the main door.

I'd anticipated keys, for no doubt the talented Mr C would have managed that.

The door undone, and discreetly shut behind us, we walked up the flights of stairs, I carrying my two bags.

Reaching the landing where flat 5 showed its door in total noiselessness, Cart, surprising me if I were yet capable of surprise, knocked lightly on the wood.

After a moment the door to flat 5 was opened.

A big man, overweight and ruddy, with thick greying hair, looked out at us. He wore a dark blue T-shirt with two lines of script which read: *Tell me how long you've been a swan.*

Cart laughed. "Hi, Leo."

"Hi, Cart."

"This is our Mr Phillips."

"Hi, Roy, good to meet you," said Leo who wanted to know about swans. "Come in. Liberty hall here." He had a London accent and clear diction. He knew my first name.

I went first, because Leo stood aside and Cart waited for me. As soon as I was in the flat's hall I got myself in over the threshold of the larger space of a big room. The layout was not dissimilar to No 6 above, the empty flat that lay below the roof apartment.

But Leo had furnished this one, and the hall too, what I'd seen, in an uncluttered, comfortable style. He had the things one expects people to have who live in the Western world - carpet, couch and chairs, TV and obviously powerful music centre, even shelves with books, and a fruit bowl with oranges and plums and a bottle of diet Coke standing on a table. "Like a drop of the hard stuff, boys?" asked Leo.

"Sure," said Cart.

"Roy?" politely asked Leo.

I didn't speak, and Cart said, as if proud of me, "He is a *whisky* man."

"Great. So'm I. Best drink you can get. I'll break out the new Scottish malt." To me he added, "Just dump your gear anywhere." He meant my bags. Tired by now of holding them, perhaps wanting my hands free, I let the bags go. And he went into the kitchen, which here was through a door, and had white and pine units and clean-looking lino on the floor. He returned with an unopened bottle.

"See this, Roy," he said, showing me the label.

It was highly prestigious. I'd heard of but never tasted it in my life. So far as I'd known, you couldn't even buy it, over the border.

"I am of the Clan McCallum," said Leo. "Friends in the Highlands." And suddenly in broadest Scottish, "Ye'll no be averse t'a wee dram?"

Cart laughed again. "To listen to him, we must think he is truthful. In fact he's no more Scots blood than I."

"*Huish*," said Leo sternly. He had got the bottle open and produced three clean glasses from a place on the bookcase among paperbacks and volumes with old black covers.

When he handed each of us a filled glass, Cart said solemnly, "One moment, Mr Phillips - see, I drink. Now, you take this glass, I yours." And handed me the glass he had sipped from twice.

That was when I knew.

I knew it as the tidal wave is known, rushing in. Without syntax, without hope.

Leo called the toast. To me it sounded as if he cried "Hrarnaschy!"

And we drank. Bottoms up.

It was a good, a beautiful whisky. If I could have tasted it.

It was about twenty minutes later that Leo let us all, (me holding the bags again, refusing his offer to carry one), through the door at the end of the corridor in flat 5, the area that, above, was occupied by the small spare room. The stair was quite wide, with sturdy shallow steps. It would have been a challenge to get a piano, or the heavy couches up, but it should have been possible, and demonstrably, had been.

At the top Cart knocked once more on another white door.

The woman who flung the door dramatically open was known to me, but I had been waiting - if not for her - for one of them.

She wore a dark blue dress that looked like satin, pinned with a blinding brooch on one shoulder, feasibly diamonds. Her hair was done differently. Now, smiling and glamorous, not in tears or beside a bundle of bloodied shirt and dead dog, she seemed the perfect hostess.

"Hello, darlings. Come in, come in."

Leo opened a bottle of Dom Perignon. Marga told us, reassuringly, there were ten more of these in the other larger fridge (This was the one on the landing outside the upper door into the attic). She added there was a roast of lamb in the oven.

The smell was appetizing and corroborated the statement. In the kitchen area potatoes waited and a transparent bowl of green salad. But she also handed round plates of crisps and nuts and cocktail sausages.

I was seated on one of the green and blue couches, the bags at my feet.

Cart sat on another couch with Leo, and Marga in a deep dark green armchair.

Bach was playing softly on the stereo.

Cart had remarked, "Better than that shit you play, Leo."

And Leo said, "Either you like it or you don't."

"Are you all right, Roy?" asked Marga in a little while. "Shall we start to explain now? Please, I *know* this isn't simple. We've all been through it. Haven't we, guys?"

"You betcha," said Leo.

"Mmm," said Cart, and drank a little champagne. He had removed his coat, which was also blue.

Marga lifted her glass, a flute I hadn't spotted here before. We all had one. "To Roy Phipps, aka R.P. Phillips."

They drank to my health. I didn't.

I put down my glass on the polished coffee table.

"Tell me," I said. "When does Sej arrive?"

"Oh, Roy," painfully said Marga. She put her hand to her mouth. But this time she didn't cry.

Leo said, "Look, Roy, he's in the hospital."

"Really. But he always gets over that," I said. I felt as if I had been frozen inside old ice. I was miles off. But also, here.

Leo looked round at me. "Roy, feller, you did a very good job. The last text I got from Liss, Sej may be going into theatre for an op. You seem to have fractured his skull, Roy. Didn't you know?"

I sat there.

I sat there.

"But you could be lying," I said. Or the thing which

spoke for me said it.

Leo said, "Only I'm not. Hey, Roy. It's OK. He *knows* - we all *know*. It can happen. You play this game, you put your life, and anything else worth anything, on the line. If the bus goes o'er ye, ye've none ta blame than yoursel'."

"And he would never blame you," said Marga. "None of us would."

Like a stone I said, "What happened to the house?"

"C and Liss and Sid put the fire out. Hadn't gone far. You'll need some new carpet, though. Then they got him off to the hospital. Apparently," said Leo, "some old guy next door called down out of the upper window, what was going on? C said they were friends of Sej's. He needed looking after. The old guy said he wasn't sure, he thought he ought to call the cops."

"And so Sid said," helpfully interposed Marga, "that was maybe the best thing. If the old man would be kind enough to give the police all the details when they came, in about an hour or so. But meanwhile they needed to look after Sej. They'd be at so-and-so. Obviously that wasn't where they went."

"No," I said.

Marga said, "Leo, Cart, should you tell Roy how C and Sid and Liss knew what was going on?"

"They were watching the house," said Leo. "I mean, he'd said, this was almost certainly the night,"

"The night," I said.

"The night you got there."

"Where?"

"Where we go."

I thought, *Can I get out of this room? Is it still conceivable I can get away?*

She, Marga, said quietly, "Roy, this is the hardest bit. Trust me. Hang on. It gets so much better."

The door into the attic, seen from *inside* the attic, was painted dark blue. A faint tang of new paint clung to it, barely discernable in the aroma of cleanliness, polish, and roasting lamb. A panel in the pale green plasterboard had been pulled back to reveal it and give access. Normally this panel would close flush to the wall. And a bookcase stood there, or had done previously, now moved on up the room by about five feet. I would never have noticed this panel, as it had been. But someone like C - Mr C - must have done so. He hadn't needed to find it, however, had he? Evidently he'd already known of its existence, as he knew about everything else in the flats, both below and up here. He had probably stayed here, now and then. They might all have done, all this gang - this *team* of mad people who were the accomplices and friends, perhaps the lovers of Joseph Traskul. Should more than one person stay at a time, there would be little privacy for them here, of course. If you slept here you would then sleep, if not in the same bed at least in the same room. And there had been two wash basins in the bathroom, a shower and a bath. Imaginably other things could be seen to in pairs, or groups.

They had no secrets from each other, that was no physical secrets.

And the way they spoke about him, it was familiar in the truest sense. It was *familial*. They were his family. Siblings, incestuous or not, brothers and sisters.

They told me things in segments, listening to any questions I asked with grave attentive faces, answering gravely, yet sometimes laughing too, appreciating, they said, my clever gambit with the sleeping tablets and Duran's new locks, (which C and Sid hadn't, even so, found particularly difficult to undermine. I'd kindly turned the alarm off for them, too. They were also amused by that. C could have neutralised it in moments anyway, they reassured me. He had been a policeman, did I know?) They congratulated me too on my last tactic, presumably the meal or they had heard the piano from outside, that which had so lulled Sej and resulted in his fractured skull. How did they square this with their demonstrated liking for, admiration of, *love* of him?

"Roy," said Marga, "we know what it cost *you*. We've all been there," she said, "I told you that."

"You mean," I said, "are you saying - he's done to all of you the sort of things he did to me? He drove you so far towards insanity that you attacked him, meant to kill him? Is that what you're saying?"

"In a way. Yes. But it isn't towards insanity."

Leo said, "You should have seen what *I* did to him, Roy. I threw him down a flight of stairs, broke both his legs. His right leg's full of metal."

"No one blames you, Roy," said Cart, the first time he'd used my Christian name.

"I don't care if you blame me," I said woodenly. "You rescued him, you took him to a hospital - if any of this is true."

"It's true."

"What about the last time? That beating up, C and - who is he? Sid?"

"No, he didn't need the hospital bit then. The doing over - some was real - most faked," said Leo. "Really just the first blow, that was genuine, to convince you. Then stagecraft. The way actors learn to do it. It would look good, like it did in movies before the digital stuff came in and made all the stunt-men redundant. C's taught us all a lot of it. Marga's an actress too. She still has contacts. Even I have now been to drama fight school. I could fight for real before, you understand. Had to unlearn quite a lot."

They cracked another bottle.

I still hadn't touched my first glass.

No one pressed me now to eat or drink.

About 2.30 a.m. by my watch, the man called Sid came in via flat 5 below, to which they all had keys. He was the young one with the bony face I recognised now not only as C's companion hit-man, but the tall man kissing tonight the tall girl by the dark blue car in Old Church Lane. And she had been the one called Liss, the girl whose car had originally 'stalled', allowing her to glue or break my door-locks. Tonight's blue car had been her white one. They'd simply resprayed it. (I'd asked. They'd told me).

Sid now wore dark blue also, a dark blue pullover with a white 0 on the right arm. This seemingly represented his full name, which he told me was Obsidian. "Obsidian mate, innit. But just call me Sid."

He told us Liss was waiting at the hospital. The op hadn't happened yet. Surgeons were discussing X-rays. Liss had said could one of the others relieve her before 4 a.m. C was still there, but she needed to get home, she had to work tomorrow. "I'll do it," said Leo, "haven't been out all day. I'll give the car a run."

About ten minutes later another man arrived. For a minute I didn't think I had seen him before, but I had. He wore a dark blue suit, Armani it looked like, a dark blue Italian tailored shirt. His shoes were possibly worth two thousand pounds.

Dark blue. All of them wore that. The car had been sprayed dark blue, even C's van, I'd gathered, which had waited round the corner in the Lane and which I hadn't spotted. Certainly the inside of the upper door into the attic.

Dark blue: indigo.

He had read the MS. The colour was one more game played against me, the rules made up so no one new could learn them. There *were* no rules. In fact, that was what you had to learn.

Marga said in the '90's she hadn't had work for three years and her husband was a bastard, but a rich one. He still kept her on as insurance against any of his 'tarty birds' trying to force marriage. Divorce, he told them, was out of the question. He couldn't harm his wife like that. Once one of the birds, crazed with jealousy mostly of the bastard's bank balance, got the address of his and Marga's huge flat in Hampstead. "She came round with a gun. It was only a toy, but I didn't know and I passed out. Scared her, I suppose, and she took off. A couple of months after Sej homed in on me out of nowhere. I nearly went mad with fear - only it wasn't. The worst thing," she said, serenely, "was when I had to strip naked. I was over forty. Too old to be very confident, and with few reasons to be, either. I hoped even so he'd make love to me. Hoped *that* was what he wanted. But he didn't. He doesn't, Roy. He's - celibate, so far as any of us know." (I thought, *He gets his jollies from this game he plays.* But I didn't say it. Although she was an actress and this was likely only one more performance, her stillness held me there.). "So that was why *I* tried to finish him off. Do you know what I did? I stuck a carving knife in him."

"But you got it wrong."

"It struck a rib. Apparently a common mistake for the novice assassin. Yes I got it wrong. But he was hospitalised then, too. Quite a while."

"And then?"

"And then, Roy. And *then*." And her face lit up.

Leo said, "And I was a bloody alcoholic, Roy. I'm not now. Oh I like my dram. A glass of wine. But the shit stuff all went. I'd had nothing in my life. D'you know what he said to me, Sej? *Life plays with us. So we don't play that game. We play our own game. Harder.* That's what it is, Roy. It's *play*.

Like kids do. Cruel sometimes. Funny sometimes. But it breaks the mould. Then *we* can get out."

"Out of what?"

"Ourselves. Ourselves."

Cart said, "My nickname is Carton, when spoke in full. I own three tobacconists, now also general grocers and off-licence. *Bits and Booze* they are called. So, not Carton for the hero in Mr Dickens's work of the French Revolution, but Carton for the cartons of cigarettes. My wife died of cancer - oh, not of cigarettes, not she nor I smokes. But my son got into drugs and my beautiful daughter ran away with a man unworthy to lie under her foot. I tried to survive the lack of revenue for cigarettes, as everyone is told they must give up, and branched out into the groceries and alcohol. I paid my tax and my VAT. At night I go up to empty flat over shop and watch TV. One morning Sej comes into my shop. What you want? I ask him. You, he said. *You interest me.* Of course, I am going to call the pigs. They forget to arrive. But he arrives. Over and over he arrives. My cousin then was in a business, the sort you think I am in, Mr Roy. Only I am not, that is the playing. I hired for real these men to warn off Sej. They beat him up. As we have pretended to. He is a very strong customer, Sej. Only one week in hospital. He makes me strip and get in bath and then - he washed me. He does this without aggress, no nasty sex, like a kind mother when you are only four. That for me was my breaking. More gentle than with Marga. Or you, I think. To me, he is my mother. I call him this sometimes. I call him up and say, Mumma, how are you?"

The one they called Sid (Obsidian) spoke from another chair, a palmful of nuts ready in his hand to eat. "He breaks you. He breaks you and then you remake yourself, Roy. Get it innit? Like you're badly made, but then you go to pieces and when you're repaired, *better* than new. Now you *work*."

The other man, who had been silent in his suit and shoes, said, "My name's Jeremy. Only I'm not that here. I gave myself a new name, which is Biro. Marga's name isn't the original, nor Leo's."

His voice had the twang of the stockbroker belt. But he spoke quietly, modestly. I thought, *this is AA. Hello, I am Biro...*

"I am very, very rich," said Biro, "And I, along with Marga, or should I say Marga's husband unbeknownst to him, bankroll this group. None of us, however, are in this for profit or gain. We are in it, as Leo said, to *play back at life.* I first tried to top myself at fifteen. I've done that seven times in my life. Never made it. Cry for help? Cry for cry. I didn't kill Sej either. It was a bit like you. I clubbed him with a cricket bat. Tough skull. Maybe now it's just been thumped once too often." There was a pause.

Now I knew him. I thought, He was with Sej the first time, in the pub in the Strand. That whole thing they did - Biro quiet, Sej volatile - attracting attention - an act to snare one more possible target. And it worked.

Leo, since deciding he would be the volunteer to relieve the girl Liss at the hospital, had left his second glass of champagne untouched.

"Are there more of you?" I asked. Sometimes one asks these things, whether believing they may be facts or not.

"A few," said the man who called himself Biro. "You'll get to meet them. Probably meet Liss tonight. Second time you meet her, of course. She works for a very prestigious company, likes her job. You're our first writer."

I said nothing. I wasn't theirs.

Sid said, "All this is just sketches like, man. Just an overview."

And then Leo got up. "OK, folks. I'll go and relieve Liss. She must be worn out. See you later. Keep some dinner for me will you, Margie? I'm going to be famished."

"Yes, darling. Lots of dinner. And I'll roast your potatoes freshly." To me she added "I love to cook. Husband never let me."

"Blessings upon ye," said Leo.

I found I too got up. "Wait."

"OK," said Leo.

"I'm going with you," I said. "To this fictional hospital."

"OK. "

Marga said, "That is a very good idea. Roy, a suggestion. Why not pretend to be a relative of Sej's. You'll get more access."

"Why not," said Leo. "You don't reckon this is for real. You'll get to see it is, maybe."

I said, "Unless you kill me on the way."

"Ah come on," said Leo, smiling. It was Sej's smile. They all had it - or one of them. I - had it. "We don't kill people. Life does that. It can maim you, kill you. We just take risks. The same kind life *makes* us take, whether we want or not."

We were at the opening in the green plasterboard, the blue door ahead, and Marga called after us, "Sej once said to me, he was like Jesus Christ. He said *I teach you how to live. Then you crucify me.* I'm quite religious, in a laid-back sort of way. I'd have been offended. Only he was in the hospital bed then, getting over my carving knife."

"He isn't Christ," I said. "Whatever Christ was or wasn't."

"No, he didn't mean that, Roy. He doesn't think he's Christ. But he does teach, he does it with a scourge and a sword, and with - parables. And then we crucify him. And one day, one day, the cross and nails and lance will work. Perhaps it already has. And he won't rise on the third day."

Bitterly I said, "I wouldn't put it past him."

And they laughed. My God they laughed, with a kind of

happiness in the concept, and in me for proposing it. And Sid and Biro raised their glasses, clinked them, and drank.

Then Leo went out and I followed him, down to the car. It was a Skoda, mid-eighties model, and it had taken a few knocks. But it was red, the colour of my mother's glass dog.

In the car, as we rumbled off among the jolting back streets, I sat quiet for a while. I was in the front with him. The back seat was full of a medley of magazines and old books, and a cardboard box with what looked like tools in it. My bags had gone in the back, too.

I had done up my seat-belt. He hadn't, only draped it over his shoulder.

But then, they took risks, didn't they?

Finally he said, "You OK there? This is the quickest way, but it's going to take about half an hour even at this time of night. The hospital, I mean."

"I'm all right."

"Don't you want to ask me some more things? I'm fine to talk while I drive. Believe me, when ye've scannied the craggy glens o' the Heelands, London hails nae chinny." Or so I thought he said.

"Tell me about the other people in the flats," I said. "Are they all part of your, what shall I call it? Fraternity?

"Not them, Roy old love." He'd reverted to the London accent. "Sej owns the house, No 66, Saracen. So he gets some rent, but not much. I can pay, because I'm on an early retirement deal with a pension. But most of them are crazy, with drink or drugs higher on the must-do list than the monthly retail - I know that one. Been there, done that. Thank God didn't buy the T-shirt. He lets them off, poor bloody cretins. Unless they cause dangerous bother. In that case C steps in. It's like my music. I can play two million decibels, but if Sej asks me to turn it down, or off, I do."

"He gives the orders."

"If you like. But I love the guy."

"And if you don't C steps in."

Eyes on the road, he was smiling. "I was part of the show that brought C in. You'll hear his story sometime. No, it isn't a threat with us. Just - mutual courtesy."

"But," I said deadly, "you love him. Sej."

"Yes. "

"Because he broke you free of yourself."

"That's the one."

"I remember Mr C thumping the man from flat 2."

"Oh *him*. The guy in flat 2 is a cunt," said Leo indifferently. "He likes to get off his skull and hurt things, cause damage for no reason. Sej lets him stay but only if he leaves Tina alone, when she's there."

"So there is a Tina."

"Yes, there's a Tina. She's in rehab at the moment. Sold everything she had for a blast of crack and then it's an ambulance and one more programme, poor cow."

"Why doesn't he rescue *them*?" I asked. I sounded older than normally I do. "Free them from their moulds."

"You can't, Roy, can you, some people. Most people. Sej looks out for the ones who seem like they might have potential for change, for growth. We're a bit thin on the ground. He's always prepared to try. Some of them freak out and run away and don't come back anywhere he, or any of us, can find them. Some of them cling on to him but still don't change. Some he'll give up on after one meeting."

"His life's work."

"Right again."

"And you are all what? Disciples?"

"Still swimming with that stick Marga threw to you? No, we're not disciples. We have our own lives, but he calls us up sometimes. *Militia*, Roy. How's that? *Reservists*."

"In which war?"

"The war against terrifying real life."

We swerved around a corner and a cat darted over the narrow road. Leo slowed the car like a sensitive knife in butter. He drove well, but not exactly as they tell one to. Well. Of course not.

"Then," I said, "did he meet you when you moved into the flat?"

"No, the flat was after. He offered me the flat. The last guy had it was dead."

"What from?"

"Old age. He was ninety-one. He climbed those flamin' stairs at least twice every day. One day, he left a note that said he'd had enough climbing. Took some tablets. Ninety-one. Tablets. No more climbs. Bit classy that."

"Was he one of you?"

"No. He just let us use the door now and then."

"Tell me what you know about Sej."

We had come out on to a tree-lined road. We were by now in that place all taxi drivers fear to go late at night. South of the River.

"I don't know much. Honest injun. None of us do. He was brought up in a children's home. Then someone he didn't know left him some dosh and the flats. That's it."

"What's his mother's name?"

"Oh *that*." Leo laughed. In his laugh I heard again the laughter of Sej. "He calls her Cinderella. Or Ashabelle. Always something like that. It's a joke. He never knew her. Let alone any daddy figure."

"Why Cinderella?"

"She went after a ball, lost her shoe... the shoe is a sexual symbol here and there."

"I know."

"Speed humpies," he said, as the things once known as

sleeping policemen rose up before us along the road. "We are getting near."

I thought, *He's taking me somewhere, but to a hospital? Sej isn't in any hospital. This will be one more set-up, one more round in the game.*

And then we drove into a square and through another street and the grey depressing bulk of a building that could be nothing *but* a hospital stood shining in its cold clear light.

A memory of my dying mother came unwanted into my mind. She'd always been afraid of hospitals. Over the door, for her, would hang that warning from Dante's Gate to Hell: *Abandon Hope all Ye that here Enter.*

At the car park he paid the toll and we got out. I couldn't carry the bags anymore, less weight than distraction, and left them on the seat. I felt old, I felt beaten.

I stopped Leo some yards from the building's glass entrance.

"Did Sej ever punch you, slap you, anything?"

"Once. That's when I threw him down the stairs. That's what it's all for, Roy. We said. To get you to break and mend yourself and *react* and come back different. Ach, laddie," he tenderly said, not to me.

An oldish man had emerged from the hospital entrance. He stopped on the forecourt and put a handkerchief to his face and wept, his shadow falling black in front of him.

In the other shadow beyond the blinding light, Leo and I stood and watched him.

Softly Leo murmured, "That is what life does. That's what we get. However stupid or clever or rich or poor or good we are. So take it by the seat of its pants. Rebellion. We move first. And if we get hurt? If it be now, 'tis not to come; if it be not to come, it will be now; if it be *not* now, yet it *will* come."

"*Hamlet*," I said.

"*Hamlet*. Shakespeare. *There's* a feller knew a thing or two. And look where it got *him*. In the ground. Y'know, some teacher once said to me that the only flaw in *Hamlet*, both the play and the character, is their predictability. But Roy, *Hamlet* isn't predictable, even though you know how it, and he, is going to end."

The man had put his handkerchief back in the pocket of his coat. It had been linen, I suppose. Not Kleenex. He walked past us into the car park, not seeing us. He would be driving away alone. As we all do, in the end.

He was in a glass-walled room set apart.

I gazed through the glass. It was him.

I could see that, even with the network of wires and tubes, the machines that clicked and whirred, the strange specific pillows.

It was Joseph. Sej.

And a doctor came out and spoke to me.

"Mr Phillips? You're his uncle, I gather."

"Yes."

"Right. Well I can tell you what we know so far."

When we had got up to the correct floor, the young woman called Liss was standing in the bright light among the piles of magazines you look at in hospital waiting areas, trying to take in articles and pictures of super models and rabbits, with your heart in your mouth.

Liss had a plastic cup of coffee she wasn't drinking. Like Marga she could doubtless cry to order, but now she came up to Leo and he held her and she howled. Her jumper was a deep purple-blue.

C was there too in a navy shirt. He raised his hand to me.

"Hi, Roy. She's upset."

"I've seen her upset," I said.

"Sure. But that wasn't for real. How are you, OK? Hang

on," he added. "I'd better give you these while I think of it."
He handed me a set of keys. They were mine, the originals,
the ones I'd posted back through the front door of the house.
Meaninglessly I shoved them in my pocket. Props... keys,
cars... the toy white dog, by now dry-cleaned of the ketchup
poured over it to represent its running over – yes, Marga
had flourished that too, to show me no animals had been
harmed in their production...

Did Alice ever feel, in her sinister Wonderlands, as if she
were losing her mind?

Leo had already got hold of someone and informed them
I was Sej's uncle. "Be a relative. The only way you'll be able
to get near him. What name do you want to use?"

Oddly I'd thought at once that changing my name would
be a sensible move. *William* crossed my mind, my father's
name. But then there was my mother. She'd been called
Denise. Quite a daring French name in the late twenties.
"Denis," I said, "Denis Phillips."

"They have Sej as Joseph Traskul. Phillips - Traskul?"

"Then I must be his mother's brother, mustn't I?"

"I understand," said the doctor now, "your nephew
collapsed due to a mixture of pain-killers and alcohol, and
hit his head on the corner of a table. This was what his
friends thought. The injury is consistent with that. Perhaps
they'll have told you Joseph was attacked a short while
before - some blows to the ribs. Not too serious. And there's
an old injury - a titanium pin in the right leg. But he was
depressed?"

"I didn't know."

"No, of course not. This must be a shock. You've come
down from Manchester, they said."

"His skull's fractured?"

"That's the better news. It isn't. To be honest, Mr
Smithson – that's the surgeon - took a look at him and had a

definite feeling there was a hairline fracture. But there isn't. But it's a major concussion. The brain is bruised. In these cases, I'm afraid, we can only hope for the best. Sometimes there is damage to nerves, and so on. It can affect..."

Just then something happened in the room, a flare of green lights and a terrible beeping screeching sound.

The doctor forgot me, sweeping me aside.

From nowhere nurses of both genders came rushing.

Leo ran up, grabbed me and pulled me away.

I was standing by a blue wall, (or do I only imagine it was blue?) and there was pandemonium in the glass-walled room, a white flurrying like snowfall on a windy night. And then out came the bed very fast, with his body on it, and all the wires snaking out of him, and machines wheeled along with him, his head turned away, his closed eyes stained darkly, and one hand lying deadly. His pianist's hand.

And the woman called Liss put her arm round me. She was sodden with tears and her nose ran. She said gently, "Roy, it's all right. We've all done this in the past. He's been hurt so often. He makes us. Don't be sad. He'd never blame you."

The four of us, C and Liss and Leo and I, stood by the blue wall and watched as they hurried him away and were gone with him, while overhead the lights burned white.

I always dreamed I met him where there was water. Fluidity, what was mutable, in alchemic terms. His danger was apparent in the dreams, also the psychosis of threat, and his omnipresence. Even unseen, he would be immanent. Less God or demon than spirit.

The name Denis, of course, comes from the name of the Greek wine god Dionysos. As well as inventing wine and so allowing men and women to become drunk, thereby sloughing all convention and restraint, he was called the Breaker of Chains. No god of the ancient world could be more terrible. Or, in other circumstances, more seductively gentle.

But that's a diversion. A swift psychoanalysis of that single choice of naming, which anyway sprang from the memory of my mother.

Neither I, nor Sej, have anything to do with the gods.

There was a single graffito in the lift. *SHITE* , it read.

Someone had obviously tried to clean it off, but then the perpetrator, or some other linguistic artist, had spray-painted it back on in whitest white, and two feet high.

At the top floor, the fourth, I got out. The lift had lurched like a hippo on the way up and even bracing myself for the landing hadn't quite been enough.

I crossed the space and looked at the smartly painted indigo door.

It stood ajar.

This was in Camden Town, and the month by now was August.

Something horrible and extreme, subconsciously

expected yet prayed into impossibility, had become possible and occurred in London this last July. The perfection of its date - 7/7 - stayed in my mind. It was as if it had been planned for that day and month in order not only to maim and kill, but to enable Londoners not to have to worry about the opposing reversal of day and month of the USA and England. So it would be simple for us to equate 7/7 with 9/11. They even rhymed. Just supposing the bombs had been detonated on the *8th* July - what then? 8/7 or 7/8?

You could still feel and see the afterimage of the attack in the city. On the tube no one spoke about bombs. If the train stuck for two minutes between stations the fume of fear rose with an already everyday accustomedness. "Ain't got no choice but be cannon-fodder, has we?" some man asked me in a pub. "It's not the bleeding wartime spirit. Wasn't in bleeding *wartime* neither. You gotta get on. Or you lose yer work, yer income. Get on - what else you s'posed ter do."

Beyond the indigo door the hallway stretched off to the right. It was clean and unexceptional. A lavatory and then a bathroom opened to the left as I walked through, then a biggish kitchen. These rooms and their furnishings were universally white, and with the same beige carpet as in the hall. The kitchen though had brown lino tiles. At the end of the hall was a large lounge. This too was white and beige, but had a couple of armchairs upholstered in a deep blue which seemed fresh and recent. A wide sash window in the left hand wall looked out, as the others had in the lavatory, bathroom and kitchen, to where tall green trees were in heavy leaf, and through them, just visible, ran an overland railway line.

He was sitting in one of the armchairs. No colour match. He wore light blue jeans and a faded cream shirt.

As I went in he smiled, but didn't get up. "Hello, Denis."

He'd altered - *been* altered. He looked ill even now, pale

and haggard. And he looked young as only the very old do. How old was he really? In his early forties perhaps? It couldn't be more than that.

His left eyelid had a slight droop to it, and his mouth that side, only very slightly. This wasn't anything you could fake, not so close, not some cunning injection or theatrical subterfuge. I'd heard he limped a little too. Even the pin in his right leg hadn't caused that. But the brain, of course... Of course.

And when he spoke, even the two words, *Hello Denis*, there was an almost undetectable slur. That certainly was as if his mouth had not quite recovered from dental work. Or a blow. Or a minor stroke.

Marga had 'prepared' me over the phone.

"They said it may all go. Or - it may not. But it doesn't spoil his looks. You can *see* it's still Sej."

Leo had also called to reassure me. "He's OK."

I hadn't bothered to replace the TV. But I'd got my landline phone sorted out in late June, about the time I got the cooker fixed and the new carpet and coverings for the front room. It hadn't been too difficult. A routine check on my bank balance had shown me someone had paid in anything I might have spent during my tussles with Sej - the cost of staying at the Belmont, new bolts and locks, the alarm. (I hadn't had to pay for the kitchen repairs. C had come over unasked and done it, gratis. He'd also cleaned the white paint off the lavatory window. "No charge," he'd said to my silence. "If you're going to be one of the family.") And of course Cart's Bits and Booze had never taken any money off the credit card. He had called and explained that carefully. The way they all seemed to take such pleasure in explaining their cleverness, their *plays*. When I told him I had thought someone in the publishing world I knew had put his hit-team on to me, he rejoiced down the line at the often helpful nature of coincidence. I had been meant to think someone corrupt in the police service had done me this kindness. He reminded me there had been something like that in one of my short stories. Cart also pointed out to award me a handy assassin was in fact to prevent my doing something like that off my own bat - as Cart himself once did. Personal attack against Sej must, it seemed, be acted only, unless it were to come from Sej's chosen victim. Which, Cart added, in the end generally it did.

To that I said nothing. Nothing at all.

"Sit down," said Sej from the blue chair. "You look tired. I'll make some tea."

I sat down in the second armchair. Yes, just the feel of the material showed it was brand new. This was Sid's place. Presumably he didn't mind our meeting here, or the new colour scheme, if someone else - Marga? Biro? - forked out for it. Sitting, I looked round at Sid's TV and various radios and stereos and the antique record-player for playing vinyl, his plants in the window. He had some Escher prints and the print of one of Picasso's blue girls, and a photo of a man and a woman circa 1980, perhaps his parents. A guitar and a piano were over against the far wall, where another closed door perhaps gave on the bedroom.

Once out of his chair and moving, Sej did limp. He could have acted this. But perhaps not. I didn't think he did, not now. The impression given was all that, with me, was done with. We'd reached the breaking point and travelled through, and on. Now... But I didn't know about Now.

"Go and see him, Denis," had said Marga, scrupulous as they all were over my newly-picked name. "The last time you saw him was when he stopped breathing."

And that *had* been the last time. There in the hospital. When they wheeled his bed away in the snow-storm of white nurses and wires.

When I'd stood there like the other three, C and Liss and Leo.

I had stood and stood, and then someone came and told me, as his only valid relative, that Sej was on a ventilator, and these things could happen, not to give up hope. I felt nothing, nothing at all. But I must have looked as if I did, I thought.

They took me to see him after about two more hours. I saw him.

The Sci-Fi aspect of his care was quite extraordinary. Such a huge, alien machine.

After a while I went out and into the lavatory. And as I stood there pissing in the urinal, I recalled how I'd done this when my mother lay dying.

In the mirror I looked to myself like an old man of eighty-five or more. A bald old man with a moustache. Nobody I knew.

When I came out I didn't go back to the others. I rode the lift down to the entrance and called a cab, and I went home to my house, leaving my clothes, my documents, everything, even the files and the novel *Untitled* there in Leo's skoda.

The door keys they had returned to me were in my pocket. I let myself in.

I walked about the house most of what was left of that night-morning, but it was already getting light. About six I fell asleep, sitting on the paint-splashed couch in the front room, facing the smashed TV.

A day later Leo came over and dropped off my bags.

"He's off the ventilator, Denis. And conscious - off and on. He knows who he is. And us, he knows us. Thought you'd like to know. You should've stayed, come back to the flat. Marga's roast lamb - you missed a treat."

I didn't ask him in, nor had he attempted to enter.

I have tried to estimate how long I holed up there in the house. I've never been quite sure. Some days, weeks.

When I went into the back garden one morning, and stood on the paving, head and face unshaven, George had come out too and glared at me over the lowest part of the fence.

"Well I have to say," he had to say, "you know some funny types, Roy. I'm quite put out, you know, by that last upheaval. That young man. Those other ne'er-do-wells. An awful scare for Vita."

I turned and looked at him and heard myself say quietly, "Fuck off, you fucking old freak."

And he went crimson then grey and did as I had suggested. He didn't even bang their kitchen door.

"This is good tea," said Sej. "Sid's a fan of tea, like me. An Assam blend, with ginger. And look, ginger and chocolate biscuits. Have one." I had one.

"And how are you?" he asked me.

"All right. How are *you*?"

He smiled, then the smile opened out into a laugh. "I am entirely fine, Denis. Look, you were worth it, like the advert says."

"Why do you do this?"

"I thought they filled you in? Thought *I* had, really. Because life does it. Disease, bombs, so-called natural disasters. We should get in first. Teach the lesson life is supposed to and seldom does. You know the old saw, *Not Care was made to care*?"

"Yes. "

"Well, I know you don't like to be ungrammatical, Denis, but: *Care was made to NOT care*."

"And that's what you do? Risk one of us murdering you, in order to get rid of our misguided carefulness."

315

"Oh, Denis. *No*, Denis. You *know* No. We have to learn to let go of the blind safety that isn't even real. We all die. Do you prefer to be inadequately secure and entirely bored and dead-alive, or to learn and grow?"

"That's your aim, not mine."

"No. Not *my* aim. *My* achievement."

The calm certainty with which he said this convinced me, if nothing else ever had, of his totally certifiable madness. But his dignity made me look away. Where my eyes fell was on the piano.

I thought, *I have succumbed to the unsubtle flattery of his pursuit of me, as have the others, his intense coercion and concentration on me. No one else - no one, not parents, never friend, not even she, my Maureen - no one ever gave me so much -* **attention.**

Still looking fixedly at the piano I said, "That evening, as per your instructions, I assume, everyone wore dark blue. And the door there, and here, and these chairs, are dark blue."

"Indigo, Denis. Homage to your book. When the flame hits the sixth chakra and turns to indigo, and the self is realised and *used*. I never met anyone, old sport, who put it more clearly, more - exquisitely. Indigo. The Indigo Instant when everything superficial burns off - hope, fear, denial - and only self-dominion remains, and after that, you can rule the world."

"That was Vilmos," I said.

"Yes, Denis. Or should I say, Roy. And Roy, *Vilmos* was always *you*."

I swallowed noisily.

Outside, as if to cover my swallow and then silence, a train zoomed by, flashing away along the track towards home or hell.

"Can you still play?" I asked. I heard what I'd said. I

amended, "I mean, a piano."

"Ah, that."

He looked down and I found I watched him.

Then he got up and he went to the piano by the far wall, and I could see how he strained to make the left leg move, and at the same time strained not to show it. It was the way an old man, a proud old man, would go on. It wasn't an act.

As he sat down at the piano on the stool there I wanted to shout out. I wanted to grab hold of him. The last time he had sat at a piano, his back to me - But even now the train was gone, I still kept my silence.

Sej sat there a long while.

Then he put his hands on the keys.

As once before, a rill of notes came, flawed. They stumbled and fell over each other. A little phrase of music leaked between, all disjointed, like a stammer that can't catch itself and so can never be put right.

I too had got up.

I bawled at him. I stood there bellowing at him, roaring. I can't remember what I said. It was about his loss of something so true - his wicked wilful throwing away loss of it - and, I believe, about my unwilling part in this.

In the end I stopped and sat down again. I put my head in my hands.

When I glanced up once more he was looking at me, over his left shoulder from his impaired left eye, a laughing look, a loving look. That of a father or a mother. Or a son.

"*Gotcha,*" he softly said.

And then his hands sprang back on to the keys.

He played me Liszt's Hungarian Rhapsody, which is the concert showman's piece, melodic, episodic, pyrotechnic, *impossible*. He played it perhaps as Liszt may have done, the golden notes firing off like showers of bullets, striking the ceiling, the windows, the earth and the sky.

When he'd finished he sat on there with his back to me. I sat staring out of the window. And another train, having it seemed waited for him to conclude, rattled along the track.

When ultimately I rose he said, "So long, Denis. Take care."

The lift felt like a hippo going down too. The sun had come out. My eyes were full of golden bullets.

Near Camden Lock I saw a man selling violins on the pavement. I remember that. I'm not convinced he was real.

He called me this morning about ten, via the landline. The number remains the same as it was.

"Outside the V and A at 4 p.m.," he said, without any preamble. "Smart casual dress. Leo will be there. You go up to him and start to shout at him. You're angry, a bit out of control. He's taken something of yours - doesn't matter what - a lover, a rare book, a CD - something important. He'll improvise on what you do, he's had more experience. Trust him. Keep this up a bit, then I'll be there. There'll be a woman around. She shows promise, but it's early days. Not like you. I knew with you from the first. Anyhow, you ignore her. And I, to you, will be a stranger. I'll calm you and Leo down. Make it difficult for me, but after a while, give in grudgingly but completely."

I didn't speak nor did he require me to.

He added, "Then just walk off, any direction you like. It's straightforward, if not undemanding. But then it's your first real go at this sort of thing. There'll be a meeting later, Marga, Leo, me if I can make it. Marga will call you, tell you where. She'll call you at home, unless you want to let her know your mobile number. If you decide you don't want to be involved in any of this, just don't turn up this afternoon. That's understood. We'll manage, though we could use you. In the case of your absence, I won't bother you again.

Though of course, you do know where I live, so to speak. Cheers, Dad. *Au revoir.*"

The dialling tone came.

That was it.

His voice had been as I recalled from the beginning, only occasionally, on certain words - *lover, straightforward, cheers* - had I noted there still remained a slight slurring?

For a while I walked about the house. I thought of them, and their 'meetings', a roasting joint in the oven, the lamps all on. "The family" C had said. Family.

Now I'm sitting in the front room, looking at the clock with the little red drip of paint still on it. The red glass dog, once I'd mended it, had stood there, but today, about an hour ago, I moved it back to the top of the piano.

The clock, as does my watch, tells me it's not yet twelve-thirty. I haven't made a move. Why would I? Hypothetically of course I've got plenty of time to get ready and travel up to the V and A. If I were going. If I were. Only I'm not going, am I. I'm not going. Am I. Am I?

About the Author

Tanith Lee was born in North London (UK) in 1947. Because her parents were professional dancers (ballroom, Latin American) and had to live where the work was, she attended a number of truly terrible schools, and didn't learn to read – she is also dyslectic – until almost age 8. And then only because her father taught her. This opened the world of books to Lee, and by 9 she was writing. After much better education at a grammar school, Lee went on to work in a library. This was followed by various other jobs – shop assistant, waitress, clerk – plus a year at art college when she was 25-26. In 1974 this mosaic ended when DAW Books of America, under the leadership of Donald A Wollheim, bought and published Lee's *The Birthgrave*, and thereafter 26 of her novels and collections.

Since then Lee has written around 90 books, and approaching 300 short stories. 4 of her radio plays have been broadcast by the BBC; she also wrote 2 episodes (*Sarcophagus* and *Sand*) for the TV series *Blake's 7*. Some of her stories regularly get read on Radio 7.

Lee writes in many styles in and across many genres, including Horror, SF and Fantasy, Historical, Detective, Contemporary-Psychological, Children and Young Adult. Her preoccupation, though, is always people.

In 1992 she married the writer-artist-photographer John Kaiine, her companion since 1987. They live on the Sussex Weald, near the sea, in a house full of books and plants, with two black and white overlords called cats.